THE BETRAYAL

A Dylan Kane Thriller

Also by J. Robert Kennedy

James Acton Thrillers

The Protocol
Saint Peter's Soldiers
The Fourth Bible
Brass Monkey
The Thirteenth Legion
Embassy of the Empire
Broken Dove
Raging Sun
Armageddon
The Templar's Relic
Wages of Sin
No Good Deed
Flags of Sin
Wrath of the Gods
The Last Soviet
The Arab Fall
The Templar's Revenge
Lake of Bones
The Circle of Eight
The Nazi's Engineer
Fatal Reunion
The Venice Code
Atlantis Lost
The Resurrection Tablet
Pompeii's Ghosts
The Cylon Curse
The Antarctica Incident
Amazon Burning
The Viking Deception
The Ghosts of Paris
The Riddle
Keepers of the Lost Ark
No More Secrets
Blood Relics
The Tomb of Genghis Khan
The Curse of Imhotep
Sins of the Titanic
The Manila Deception
The Heretics Bible

Dylan Kane Thrillers

Rogue Operator
The Agenda
The Messenger
Containment Failure
Retribution
The Defector
Cold Warriors
State Sanctioned
The Mole
Death to America
Extraordinary Rendition
The Arsenal
Black Widow
Red Eagle
The Betrayal

Just Jack Thrillers

You Don't Know Jack
Jack Be Nimble

Templar Detective Thrillers

The Templar Detective
The Unholy Exorcist
The Black Scourge
The Parisian Adulteress
The Code Breaker
The Lost Children
The Sergeant's Secret
The Satanic Whisper

Kriminalinspektor Wolfgang Vogel Mysteries

The Colonel's Wife
Sins of the Child

Delta Force Unleashed Thrillers

Payback
Forgotten
Inside the Wire
Infidels
The Cuban Incident
Charlie Foxtrot
The Lazarus Moment
Rampage
A Price Too High
Kill Chain
Righteous Hell

Detective Shakespeare Mysteries

Depraved Difference
Tick Tock
The Redeemer

Zander Varga, Vampire Detective

The Turned

THE BETRAYAL

A Dylan Kane Thriller

J. ROBERT KENNEDY

UNDERMILL
PRESS

This is a work of fiction. Names, characters, places, and incidents are products of the author's imagination. Any resemblance to actual persons, living or dead, is entirely coincidental.

ISBN: 9781998005918

First Edition

For Mahsa Amini, a 22-year-old Kurd, beaten to death by the Guidance Patrol, the religious morality police of the Iranian regime, for the crime of showing her hair in public.

THE BETRAYAL

A Dylan Kane Thriller

"In any authoritarian society, the possessor of power dictates, and if you try and step outside, he will come after you. This is equally true of Sovietism, of China and of Iran, and in our time it has happened a lot in Islam. The point is that it's worse when the authoritarianism is supported by something supernatural."

Salman Rushdie

"You can chain me, you can torture me, you can even destroy this body, but you will never imprison my mind."

Mahatma Gandhi

PREFACE

Iran has a long history of human rights violations, often surrounding their treatment of women, but also in their refusal to live by the rules civilized countries have generally agreed upon. Search the Internet for stories about child abduction back to Iran, and you will be overwhelmed.

Perhaps one of the most famous was given the Hollywood treatment. The movie *Not Without My Daughter*, starring Sally Field, chronicled the 1984 events surrounding an American woman and her Iranian-born husband who visited Iran with their daughter. The family convinced him to stay with his daughter, and, unwilling to leave her behind, his wife was forced to remain, beginning a horrifying experience.

The disturbing thing is that this is happening all the time. Iran is not a signatory to the Hague Convention, and therefore it is almost impossible to settle domestic disputes such as it is in most countries. Iran also doesn't recognize the citizenships of anyone originally born there that chose to leave. If an American citizen, born in Iran, returns, they are treated as Iranian citizens, with all the rights and freedoms citizens of that country enjoy.

Almost none.

But what would happen if an innocent family were detained because of their Iranian born father and the job he held? What if that job was for the CIA? What would America do to save his family from a lifetime of abuse?

Nothing?

Or everything?

And would it be because it was the right thing to do, or because of the secrets this leverage risked exposing?

Arlington, Virginia

CIA Security Officer Chuck Hogan cursed as he jerked back from the doorframe, another heavy burst of AK-47 gunfire spraying his position. He flipped around the camera he had been holding out into the hallway so Control could see his face. "Did you get that?"

"Affirmative, Zero-Five. We got what we needed. Take cover."

"No shit," muttered Hogan as he fell back deeper into their target's apartment, now secured by others on his team.

Echo Team, a CIA special ops unit seconded to Homeland Security so it could operate on American soil, had been deployed minutes ago on a mole hunt. Instead, they had found a den of vipers, and this was quickly turning into a Charlie Foxtrot. To hell with that, it already was one. How the hell could a terrorist cell this size be operating fifteen minutes from Langley, where what was supposed to be the most sophisticated intelligence operation in the world, the envy of our allies, the bane of our enemies, was headquartered? Some fans were certainly getting hit by shit when this was all over.

Somebody wasn't doing their job.

Control continued updating the stairwell teams. "Echo Team, Control Actual, you have four targets to the left of the apartment door, all armed with assault rifles, all directing fire toward the door. You have three hostiles in the clear to the right of the door, all with assault rifles. Stairwell teams, it appears they are not aware you're there. Take them out."

The team lead, Brooklyn Tanner, shouted something over the comms but he couldn't make it out as the terrorist gunfire continued. Hogan took another step back as heavy gunfire erupted from both ends of the hallway, the AKs falling silent to the expert marksman manning both stairwells.

A crash deeper in the apartment sounded like a window shattering as the all-clear was announced by the stairwell teams. Another team member, Mike Lyons, shouted from inside. "Everybody out!!"

Hogan's eyes bulged as he realized what was going on. They were using the window as a means of escape. It meant this was serious. He glanced up and spotted wires running along the ceiling, small packages duct taped overhead every five feet, spelling his doom.

"Get the hell out of here!" he shouted as he sprinted for the hallway, the order coming through from Control to immediately evac. He dodged the bodies left behind by the stairwell teams as he pumped toward the door so far away. He tossed his weapon aside, leaning into it when crackling behind him sent shivers up and down his spine. He didn't bother looking back.

There was no point.

A massive explosion erupted behind him, the floor shuddering under his feet as he continued to sprint. The door was just ahead, a fire door that might provide him with some blast protection if he could reach it.

Another explosion, then another, each closer, somebody having set off what could only be described as a self-destruct sequence designed to take out the entire floor of this large apartment building. The motivation, whether it was to destroy any evidence or to kill as many as possible, didn't matter.

He was caught.

And there was no way he was reaching that door.

The apartment immediately to his left erupted, the door shredded from the force of it, debris, flame, and hatred erupting and slamming him against the wall as the opposite apartment belched evil in his direction, flinging him yet again.

As he smashed against the hard concrete wall, shattering most of the bones in his body, he slid to the floor, his life fading fast, and he pictured his wife and son, saying a final prayer as the ceiling above came down on top of him.

I don't care where you send me, God, just watch over them.

Virginia

Two Weeks Earlier

"Your father wants to see you."

Cyrus Farzan sighed heavily, his chest tight, his stomach in knots. It was the call he had always known would come someday. It was inevitable. Yet even though you were expecting it, it was always a shock when it finally occurred. "I'm sorry, Mom, but you know I can't come."

"He wants to see you one last time before he dies."

"And I want to see him, but you know I can't. And you know why I can't."

"What nonsense! You would choose your job over your father?" The anger in her voice stung, but she didn't understand. She couldn't understand. It wasn't just the job. In fact, he could quit the job tomorrow and it still wouldn't change anything.

"You know I can't travel home, Mother. You know why."

"Even your own son is coming to pay his respects!"

His eyes widened slightly. "Ray is going? I don't understand. How do you know?"

"Your cousin, Kaveh, has been speaking with him and told him what's going on. He's already said he's coming."

Farzan grunted. "Well, that would be a neat trick, considering he has no money. Does he plan on walking there?"

"You'll pay for his ticket."

It was a demand, one he could give in to and perhaps placate her, if only a little bit. Yet he hesitated. He couldn't travel to his former homeland because of his job. The question was, could his son safely travel there? He had already had security look into it several months ago when there was talk of the family, except for him, of course, returning home for a visit—this phone call wasn't a surprise, his father in decline for many months. The trip was approved, the assessment assuring the likelihood of anything happening to them was minimal.

Minimal.

In the type of work he did, it was a common word, usually meaning the risk was acceptable. There was minimal risk the system could fail. Minimal risk the hack might be discovered. Minimal risk the operative might die.

Minimal risk your family could be jailed and used as leverage against you.

When that minimal risk involved a code name on a file, it was easy to say, "Yes, go ahead." But when it was your son, your daughter, your wife, it changed the math. They had algorithms. As long as the math worked out to be less than 0.05, you went ahead. 0.05 still meant five times out of 100 something could go wrong. Of course, that worst-case scenario of your operative dying was even less than the 0.05. But when that word "operative" was replaced with "son," "daughter," "wife," "family," the only acceptable number was zero.

"I'll talk to him, but I'm concerned for his safety."

"Nonsense. He'll be perfectly safe here, despite the fact his father's a traitor."

He bristled. "I am *not* a traitor. You know why I had to leave. In fact, you're the one who told me I had to."

"Only because you were a traitor."

Her words hurt, but they also angered him. To call him a traitor was to call herself a traitor. She had believed as he did back then, but now she sounded fully indoctrinated. He paused as a thought occurred to him. This call was definitely being monitored. Could everything she was saying be with that in mind? He closed his eyes in relief. That had to be it, and he was a fool for not having realized it until now.

He had to play along.

"Listen, Mother. I know you don't agree with a lot of the decisions I made, but they've been made. You support the regime, so does Dad, so does the family. And that's fine, I understand that. Obviously, I don't support them, but I also don't work against them. It's still my home. America is where I live, but the streets of Tehran are where I played as a child. The schools are what taught me the skills I needed to get through life. My family and my faith have always guided me. Iran will always be my home. But because of the work I do, despite it having nothing to do with Iran, my home, your home, our family's home, I simply can't come back. But you're right, it should be perfectly safe. If Ray wants to go, I'll let him. I'll talk to Kiana and Tara, and if they want to go, they can as well. I'll record a video message for Dad. I'm afraid that's the best I can do."

A heavy sigh came through the earpiece. "I suppose that's the best we can hope for. Your father will be extremely disappointed, but finally meeting his grandchildren will ease the disappointment somewhat."

He squeezed his eyes shut, the burn intense. He should never have taken this job, yet when offered to him, he had leaped at it. He loved his homeland, and did indeed consider Iran his home, though not under the current regime. It had to be brought down, and hopefully, in time, it would be, by people like him, by people under his command, by the missions he authorized.

There was a knock at his door and it opened, his deputy chief leaning in. Farzan held up a finger. "I have to go, Mother. I'll call you as soon as I can. I love you."

"I love you too."

"And tell Father I love him as well, and that my heart breaks that we'll never see each other again."

"You will, my son. You will see him once more when you meet again in Jannah."

He wiped a tear away that threatened to roll down his cheek. "Goodbye, Mother. I'll talk to you soon." He hung up the phone and leaned back with a heavy sigh.

"Problem?" asked Kyle Baxter.

"My father's dying."

Baxter stepped inside. "Oh, I'm sorry to hear that. Has he been sick long?"

"About six months ago he fell ill. Never really recovered. Healthcare isn't that great over there, as you know. And unfortunately, I can't send them money."

Baxter tapped on the title on the door. "If you wanna get your security clearance revoked, then this guy can't be sending money to Iran."

Farzan frowned as he rose. "Let's get to our one o'clock. I can keep *you* waiting, but not the president."

"This is true. I am but a peon in the almighty Central Intelligence Agency."

Farzan chuckled as he stuffed his laptop into his attaché case and headed out the door, closing it behind him, staring briefly at the sliding nameplate with his name engraved on it, a constant reminder of how replaceable he was, and under it the title of the position he hoped would help secure his homeland's future.

Chief of Iranian Affairs.

Farzan Residence

Great Falls, Virginia

"How long have you been talking to your cousin?"

Raymond shrugged. "I dunno."

Cyrus Farzan resisted the urge to roll his eyes at yet another useless answer from his teenage son. The boy seemed determined simply to drift through life. He was a constant disappointment. "A week? A month? A year?"

Another shrug. "About a year, I guess."

"Why didn't you say anything?"

His son glared at him. "Why would I? It's not like you care about anything that happens in my life."

Farzan sat on the corner of the bed, staring at his son, sitting up against the headboard, his phone in his lap, his thumbs flying the entire time they had been speaking. "Why would you say that? Of course I care."

"Whatever."

A pit of anger flared for a moment in Farzan's stomach. He hated that word. "Whatever." What a bullshit word. If he could go back in time and throat-punch the lazy piece of shit that invented it, he would. Repeatedly. "Listen, I love you. No matter what you might think, you, your sister, your mother, you mean everything to me."

"What a crock. Your job is all that you care about."

"So, that's what this is about. Listen, you know I have an important job, and we discussed this before I took the promotion, and we all agreed that it was important despite the fact it would mean longer hours."

His son scoffed at him. "Fine, you're right. It's my fault. I guess I should have said 'no.'"

"You had that option."

"Like you would've listened to me anyway."

"Of course I would've listened. But ultimately, it is an adult choice, and you were only thirteen at the time, your sister eleven. The decision had to be made by your mother and I, but your input would've been considered. Just because when you're asked your opinion and the decision doesn't ultimately go in your favor, doesn't mean your opinion wasn't taken into account. That's just life. We don't always get what we want. Contrary to what our ridiculous education system would have you think, in life, there are winners and losers. In life, score is kept. Life is full of disappointments. There are reasons for all those cliches. 'Win some, lose some,' 'Take the win,' 'Hate the game, not the player.'

"Do you think I get my way all the time at work? Of course not. There are times where I've been working on a plan for weeks, sometimes even months. I think it's great, I think it's gonna work, I think it'll do a lot of good. And then it gets shot down by somebody higher on the food chain than me. Do I bitch and moan and cry about it? No, because that's life. Win some, lose some. But you're getting mad at me for a decision you agreed with. I love you with all my heart. I would do anything for you, I would die for you. And that goes the same for your sister and your mother. You're all that matter to me. But the job I do is important. It pays the bills around here, it keeps this roof over your head, keeps you fed, pays for that cellphone that you never look up from. And if you want, it pays for your ticket to Tehran so you can meet your grandfather."

Ray's eyes shot wide as his chin finally lifted from his chest, and he made eye contact. "Really?"

"Yes, but there are rules."

His son eyed him skeptically. "What?"

"You don't talk about my job. You don't brag about the life we have here. You obey the authorities. It's not like here. They *will* arrest you. They *will* beat you. They *will* shoot you. It's not America."

Ray smirked. "So, what you're saying is, we're all Black over there?"

Farzan chuckled. "I'm not sure if that's racist, but I'm quite certain someone would think it is. But yes, crudely put, the authorities over there are not like here. It doesn't matter if what you were doing was right or wrong. If they take an interest in you for any reason, eye contact, a smile, a smirk, a misconstrued laugh or snort, they could lay a beating on you just for fun. They could toss you in a prison cell for ten years and continually torture you. So, you do what they say. You listen to your relatives. They live there. They know the rules. They know what to do and what not to do. And you better bone up on your Koran because you will be going to prayers every day. They take this stuff extremely seriously there."

Ray jerked his chin toward his nightstand, and Farzan was surprised to see a Koran sitting there. "I read it every day."

Farzan wasn't sure how to feel about that. "How long has this been going on?"

"About a year."

"So, about the same time you started talking with your cousin?"

Yet another shrug. "I suppose."

Alarms went off, and Farzan tensed. "What's he been saying to you?"

"Nothing."

"Nothing, huh? What's he been saying about Islam?"

"Nothing much. Just how much he loves it, how great it is, how it has all the answers."

Farzan inhaled deeply. While he considered himself a Muslim, he wasn't a practicing one. He believed in Allah, believed in the Prophet, and believed the Koran was a guide, though a product of its time. He chose his words carefully. "Islam doesn't have all the answers, though it can guide you to them. Believe in Allah, believe in the Prophet, believe that they guide you, but be careful it is they that guide you, rather than those who would speak in their name. Too many in our faith have been led astray by the charismatic teachings of those who only quote the Koran without understanding the words.

"While you're there, you're going to see and hear a lot. Just remember yourself. Remember who you are. It's far too easy, especially at your age, to fall into the snake pit of fundamentalism, which, trust me, is not Islam. It's a fanatic cult of people that twist the words of the Prophet for their own gains. Most are nothing more than criminals, thugs. Here we would call them a gang boss, a cartel leader, and we would try to arrest them and throw them in prison. But these people cloak themselves in a bastardized version of our religion, claiming religious persecution should we make any attempt to stop them. If you're going to go, you have to promise me that if you ever feel uncomfortable, you contact me or tell your mother, and we'll bring you home right away. And if your sister's going with you, it'll be your job to help protect her. Because over there, your mother has no power. That world is run by men and men alone. Understood?"

"Yes."

"Look at me."

Ray looked up from his phone.

"Do you understand me?"

"Yes."

"Good. Now, I'm gonna talk to your mother." Farzan smirked. "In *this* house, she runs things."

Zhangbei County, China

"Oh my God, that's her!"

CIA Operations Officer Dylan Kane peered through his CIA-issued sunglasses, the image transmitted via satellite to his off-the-books operations center so the love of his life, former Chinese Special Forces Major Lee Fang, now living in exile after being forced to betray her country, could see what he did. "So, that's your mother?"

Fang sniffed, her voice cracking. "Yes."

His heart ached for her. An unofficial agreement between Washington and Beijing basically stated she would be left alone as long as she stayed out of China and didn't meddle in its affairs. It meant never seeing or talking to her family again. She couldn't risk it. They had been fed a horribly biased story, and if they were to have any phone calls, emails, or social media contact with her, they could be red-flagged and potentially imprisoned.

Fang had made no contact in all the years since she had left, but young Tommy Granger, a tech wizard Kane used from time to time, had set up a routine for her that scraped the social media feeds of her family and friends so she could keep up with what was going on. And two weeks ago, the first post had gone up that her father was ill and not expected to make it.

It had crushed her.

"We were so close. He was so proud of me, of everything I had accomplished. 'My daughter, the hero.' That's what he called me. 'The hero.'" She sniffed. "I have to see him. I have to talk to him. I have to tell him the truth. I can't have him dying thinking I was a traitor."

But seeing him was impossible. Kane might sneak her in, but what if she were caught? She would be tortured and imprisoned, perhaps with her family alongside her. It simply wasn't an option. They had brainstormed a solution. It was still risky, but it protected her, which was all he cared about.

Fang's mother, Jing, picked through some vegetables at the local market, and he smiled slightly as she exhibited mannerisms he saw in Fang, and he wondered if this tiny little woman was how Fang would be in twenty years. She still had her figure, though it was a hard life here, and she appeared at least ten years older than she should. He cursed the situation. He could help these people. He could help her family if it weren't for the politics, if it weren't for the regime and its distrust of the world.

"Any sign she's being followed?"

Kane scanned the area from the driver's seat of the Geely Xingyue L SUV he was driving. He was using his CIA-developed cover as an insurance investigator for Shaws of London while here. He was legitimately in the region on business, all his IDs and paperwork in order, his rental appropriate to his position.

He took a bite of his *maocai.* If any of the police in the area took an interest in him, he had an excuse as to why he was sitting here alone in a car, a white man standing out like a sore thumb in this region of China. He moaned as he savored every chew.

"How is it?"

"It's unbelievable, babe."

"I told you. Wu's is the only place to get that. He's been there since before I was born. Best maocai you're going to find anywhere."

"You're right. If I could, I'd bring you some back."

"It wouldn't keep."

"No, probably not, but that wouldn't be the problem."

"Oh?"

"I don't trust that I wouldn't eat the damn thing myself."

She giggled as he finished his scan of the marketplace.

"I don't see anybody following her." He checked his phone, a custom app from Langley indicating the immediate area was free of drones, the satellite overhead not picking up anything. This hadn't originally been a CIA op, but when he approached his boss, Deputy Director of CIA for Operations Leif Morrison, and told him he needed a week off, the Chief had insisted on knowing why.

"There's no damn way I'm letting you go to China without an explanation."

"R&R."

"Bullshit. You and I both know all your R&R is spent with Fang. This has something to do with her, doesn't it?" Morrison had leaned forward from behind his desk. "Don't forget I used to do what you do. I know when I'm being bullshitted."

"Fine. Fang's father might be dying. I'm going in to facilitate a conversation between the two."

"No damn way."

"Sir, this is happening with or without your blessing."

Morrison sighed. "Fine. But if you're caught, you're disavowed."

Kane shrugged. "What else is new?"

Morrison rolled his eyes. "Fine. Use your Shaws cover. I'll authorize the op."

"What am I there to do?"

"Where's her father?"

"A few hours outside of Beijing."

"Anything of interest there?"

"Funny you should ask that." Kane grinned as Morrison rolled his eyes again.

"Why do I think I was just played?"

"Your suspicious nature?"

Morrison urged him on with a twirl of his hand. "Out with it."

"We've had reports they might be testing their own hypersonic missile at a range in Inner Mongolia. It might be useful to get a peek while I'm there."

Morrison leaned back. "Actually, that might be useful." He pursed his lips before answering. "Fine. Try not to get yourself killed."

"You know me, sir. I always *try*."

"Uh-huh. Get the hell out of my office."

"Yes, sir." He had minimal support for this phase of the operation since this part wasn't official business, but he did have comms capability with Langley in case he needed assistance.

He took another bite, continuing to scan the crowd, the glasses pulling faces and transmitting them to Langley where they were run through facial recognition. Most were coming up with no ID, but the occasional face did match, their identities projected onto the lenses. Mostly city officials, no one of importance.

"I'm not seeing anyone. And so far, Langley hasn't recognized anyone of concern."

"When are you going to make contact?"

"Not in public. I'll do it at the family home like we planned."

"Just make sure my brother Wei isn't there. He's too loyal to the party. He'll turn you in, and he might even turn in my parents."

"Don't worry about him. Langley's already confirmed he's fifty klicks from here. We should have plenty of warning."

"I hope so. Just remember, no matter what, my brother's not to be trusted."

"Don't worry, babe. I've got this." He spotted two policemen walking toward his position. "I better go. I might have attracted attention. Talk to you later. Love you. Bye."

"Bye. Love you too. Be careful."

He ended the call and took the final bite of his maocai then threw open his door. He made a show of disposing of the bowl that had contained his delicious meal, and wiped his mouth with the back of his hand. He waved at Mr. Wu who waved back, smiling.

"How was it?"

"Unbelievable! I think I'm going to have to have another bowl," he said in perfect Chinese. He closed his car door and smiled pleasantly at the two officers as he strode back toward the happy street vendor. "I'm definitely telling my colleagues about this place. We don't get out here often, but I tell you, the next time my company has business here, I'm volunteering."

The police continued past, a reasonable explanation now provided for why he had sat there for so long. He was full already, but he wasn't sure when he would get to eat again. And he wasn't lying. This was some of the best damn food he had ever eaten, despite Fang's warning to him.

"Don't ask what the meat is."

Imam Khomeini International Airport

Tehran, Iran

To say Kiana Farzan was uncomfortable would be an understatement. And she was certain, despite her best efforts, that discomfort was on full display. She wiped beads of sweat from her forehead once again. It wasn't just the nerves, it was the chador. She hadn't worn one in so long, she had forgotten how uncomfortable it was, especially in the heat. If there was air conditioning at the airport in Tehran, it certainly wasn't working.

The flight here had been uneventful. She didn't want to come. This was her father-in-law. She barely knew him and hadn't seen him in over twenty years. Unlike her husband, who still believed this was his home, that there was hope for this country, she had long put it behind her. She had no interest in Iran, in Tehran, in any of the relatives that she still had here. Her parents had died long ago. She had no brothers or sisters. Yes, she had aunts and uncles and cousins, but she didn't care. They were part of a past she had escaped, a past she had no interest in reliving. Iran was bad two decades ago when she had left.

It was even worse now.

But she had no choice. There was no way in hell she was letting her children come here unaccompanied. Yes, her son was eighteen, but he was eighteen going on twelve. Children today were ridiculous. People made fun of Millennials. My God, Gen Z was a joke, and she could just imagine how bad Generation Alpha would be. If something were to happen, her son, and especially her daughter, would have absolutely no clue what to do. They would probably pull out their phones and go on TikTok to find a video, "How To Stop The Iranian Revolutionary Guard From Beating You To Death. All You Need To Know In Eight Seconds Or Less."

Ridiculous.

Her daughter had already cleared customs and was standing a few paces away. Her son was at the window now, and she suppressed a sigh of relief as his passport was handed back. The official said something, and her son smiled. "Thank you very much, I will," he said in perfect Farsi. It shocked her. They had taught the children Farsi when they were young, but English was spoken at the home almost exclusively. She couldn't recall the last time her son had spoken a word of it.

How much time has he been spending talking to his cousin?

Her husband hadn't noticed it, probably because he was at work too much, but their son had taken an interest in Islam over the past year. A Koran had appeared on his nightstand table. First it had been hidden inside the drawer, but over the past few months, he had stopped hiding what she already knew. She had also heard him praying, his prayer mat rolled up and hidden behind his guitar case in the closet. It had her more than concerned.

She stepped up to the counter and handed over her American passport. A frown creased the official's face, despite the fact he had just dealt with two, though they belonged to an 18-year-old and a 16-year-old. She was a 40-year-old woman, and the passport listed Iran as her birthplace. Her husband had assured her that the visa was valid and would get her in with no problem, and once she was there, simply dressing local and staying inside as much as possible would be all that was needed for a safe visit.

A two-week-long visit.

Two weeks. God, give me strength.

The official picked up his phone, something that hadn't happened with her children. Something was murmured. She couldn't pick up the words. The phone was hung up, and the man pointed to their left. "Get in that line."

Her heart raced. "Is there a problem?"

"Get in that line."

"What about my children?"

"They're free to leave, but you have to get in that line."

"Can they come with me?"

The man stared at her. "You don't want them in that line."

Her full bladder almost let go.

He pointed again. "Now." The tone was firm, the voice slightly raised. There was no room for protest. Negotiation wasn't possible.

She held out her hand. "My passport?"

"You'll get it back once you've cleared. Now go." He leaned over and beckoned the next in line.

She had no choice. She pulled her luggage toward her children. "They want me to go into this line over here. You're not allowed to come with me."

Her daughter's eyes filled with tears. "Are you in trouble? What are they gonna do to you?"

Kiana forced a reassuring smile. "I'm sure everything's fine. It's just a random check, but I don't know how long it'll take." She gestured toward the exit. "If you go through those doors, your grandmother and a whole bunch of the family are waiting for us. They already texted me that they're there. They know what you both look like, and you've seen their pictures. Just go through those doors, and they'll be there waiting for you. Tell them what happened, and that I don't know how long I'll be. Understand?"

Tara's lip quivered. "Yes."

Kiana turned to her son, apparently unaffected by the news. "Understood?"

"Yeah."

She gave them both a hug. "Now go."

They headed for the exit, her son eagerly, her daughter staring back at her the entire time until she disappeared through the doors. A raucous chorus of cheers erupted, relief sweeping through her with the knowledge her children were in the hands of her family. She joined the line as instructed and counted the solemn faces ahead of her.

Ten.

How long was this going to take? Half an hour? An hour? A day? She reached for her phone then thought better of it. Her husband had instructed her to use it as little as possible and had even bought them all new flip phones. They could make or take calls, send and receive texts. That was it. There were no apps, no social media, nothing.

"You don't want them searching your phone. You don't want them connecting to your Facebook or email. If they ask you, you just say you bought it for the trip because you didn't think your iPhone would work here. They probably won't believe you, but there's nothing they can do about it. They might ask you about my job, and you just tell them. Be completely honest."

"Why would they ask about your job?"

"Remember, it's a male-dominated society. Whatever you do in life is unimportant. It's trivial. To them, anything important in your life has to do with me."

"Fine. I'm sure they'll be titillated to know that I'm married to a project manager at a utility company."

He had laughed. "It might sound boring, but you know it's important and they might think so too. You always hear about it on the news where they're messing with the utilities."

She had grinned and thought nothing of it. Her husband's job was boring, which was just the way they liked it—a nice, normal, peaceful existence in their new home without worrying about corrupt authorities hammering on their door and taking them away.

Yet here she was, standing in a lineup, wondering what the next few minutes, perhaps hours, had in store for her.

This wasn't her life anymore. She had escaped all this. She was used to living in a free society where you didn't worry about what the police would do to you, where you didn't worry about that knock on the door and what it could mean for you or your family.

She sighed.

Why the hell did I agree to this? I should have said no. I should have put my foot down. It's that damn Kaveh.

She had no idea he had been communicating with her son for over a year. What had he polluted Ray's mind with? She recognized that zeal, that religious fervor. There was a hint in her son's eyes, but that hint had grown since the moment the plane had touched down, and it scared her more than what the authorities might be about to do to her. She couldn't lose her son, not to fanaticism, not to fundamentalism. But they were now in the heartland, in the beast's belly that funded most terrorism around the world, that didn't tolerate any dissension, that enforced the rules without mercy.

The line shuffled forward, another soul disappearing through the door ahead. Her heart skipped a beat. No one had come out. Was there another exit? And where did it lead? Was there a door past this one that led into the arrivals area where her family would be waiting for her, or was there only one other way out of that room that led to imprisonment and torture?

She tensed. She never should have come. They were attempting to appease their son, and as her husband had pointed out, he was eighteen.

He could make his own decisions, yet they could have said no and not bought the plane ticket. And with his complete lack of ambition, he never would have got a job to fund it.

The door opened again, and a guard with a scowl beckoned the next person, and the entire line lumbered forward toward what she was certain none of them knew, though with each step, her fear grew, and she could see it on the faces of the others. Nobody wanted to be in this line, yet there was nowhere to go. You couldn't change your mind and walk back and get on the plane. She was in Iran. Even though she was in the international arrivals area, it meant nothing here. She was subject to Iranian laws despite her passport saying she was American. They didn't care about technicalities like that. All they cared about was that she was born here.

Please, God, don't let them know anything about my husband. Let this just be routine because I'm an American adult with an American passport. Breathe!

She inhaled deeply, holding it for a moment before exhaling heavily as the line edged forward again and again. She wasn't certain if the fact it was moving reasonably quickly was a good sign. She still hadn't seen a single person come back out. Surely, everyone in this line couldn't have been found guilty of something. Surely, somebody here was innocent and allowed to continue on. There had to be another door, another door that led to freedom. Though was there really any freedom here under the Ayatollah who led with an iron grip?

Finally, she was next in line. Her heart hammered now. She struggled to remain calm, to hide her fear, to bury the panic that threatened to overwhelm her, but it was no use. She was terrified. She couldn't remember being so scared. The door opened, the man with the scowl beckoning her as she willed herself forward, her legs carrying her toward the room, as she prayed it had at least two other exits.

She stepped through and the door closed behind her. A man sat behind a desk, her passport in his hand. He said nothing as he stared at a computer screen, his eyes darting back and forth between the passport and the display. Was it merely the routine records that the airlines provided, or did they have a file on her?

He finally looked up and pointed at a chair. "Sit."

She sat, finally noticing there were indeed two doors.

"You are Kiana Farzan?"

She nodded.

He eyed her. "Do you not speak Farsi anymore, or are you afraid to talk?"

Her hands gripped the armrests of her chair, her knuckles turning white. "Yes, sir. I speak Farsi. And yes, sir, I'm scared." She figured honesty was the best way to go.

"Why are you scared? Are you hiding something?"

She vehemently shook her head. "No, sir. Not at all. It's just, well, you know how things are."

He leaned back and regarded her. "How things are? What do you mean?" He was toying with her. He knew exactly what she was talking about, but he wanted her to say it.

"Things between America and Iran haven't been good in a long time."

"No, I suppose they haven't. Yet here we sit. You, a sister who was born not five kilometers from here, holding an American passport, your country's sworn enemy. How do you explain that?"

How did she explain she was sick and tired of living under a brutal regime that oppressed its women, where every day was a terror, where every night you went to bed not knowing what horrors the next day might bring?

But she couldn't tell him that. She couldn't tell him the truth. "To be honest, sir, I left more because of my family than anything else."

His eyes narrowed. "'To be honest?' You know, whenever I hear those words, I know I'm being lied to."

"I assure you, sir, I'm not lying."

"I think you are. I think you left because you disagreed with those who would guide our country to ultimate victory. I think you betrayed your country and moved to its greatest enemy to assist them in defeating us."

Her heart raced, her pulse pounding in her ears. He was baiting her. There was no way he could possibly think any of this was true. "That's not true, sir. My mother and I, we never got along, and I felt it was best to start my life elsewhere, away from her."

"And yet you chose America."

"It seemed like the right decision at the time, and it's where the man I loved wanted to go."

He tossed the passport on his desk and leaned forward, staring at his computer screen once again. "Yes, your husband, Cyrus Farzan, isn't it?"

"Yes, sir."

"How long have you been married?"

"Almost twenty years."

"And it says here, you have two children?"

"Yes, sir. They're traveling with me. They're outside waiting for me now."

"What does your husband do?"

"He's a project manager at our local power utility."

"Interesting." He leaned back again, folding his arms as he stared at her. "Are you lying to me, Mrs. Farzan, or is your husband lying to you?"

It was her turn for her eyes to narrow. "I…I don't know what you mean. I'm not lying. Trust me, I know better than that. I have nothing to hide."

"I'm not so sure about that. But then again, people like your husband are experts at lying. Is it possible that he didn't tell you the truth, that he's been lying to you for all these years?"

Her pulse pounded in her ears like a bass drum. She could barely hear him. "I don't know what you're talking about."

"Your husband doesn't work for the power company, Mrs. Farzan."

"Of course he does. He's worked there for years."

"No. And if you truly do believe that, then your husband has been lying to you." He leaned forward. "Your husband is a traitor."

"He most certainly is not! He would never betray his country!"

"And just what country are we talking about, Mrs. Farzan? His new homeland, or his old?"

She caught herself, and she looked away. "He wouldn't betray either."

"Oh, I believe he wouldn't betray his new country. But your husband is a traitor to his homeland."

"I'm sure you're wrong."

He leaned forward again, his elbows on the desktop, his chin resting on his interlaced fingers. "I think you're telling me the truth, Mrs. Farzan. I think you really don't know what your husband does."

"I told you, he's a project manager at our local utility."

Her interrogator's smile spread. "No, Mrs. Farzan. Your husband is the Chief of Iranian Affairs at the Central Intelligence Agency."

Lee Residence

Zhangbei County, China

Kane sat parked in front of the Lee residence. He had easily reacquired Fang's mother after she left the market and followed her home. He had spotted at least ten people so far in the family home his love had grown up in, and it broke his heart. He had had no idea how poor they were, yet there was a quiet dignity. The property was tidy. Nothing appeared dirty. It was simply run-down, cobbled together over decades, a mix of cinder block, wood, and corrugated metal. A good storm might knock it down.

Mrs. Lee had arrived home from the market to be met by a gaggle of children of various ages. He was assuming grandchildren, perhaps cousins, nieces, nephews, a handful of whom might not have even been born before Fang's exile. He checked his tracker app to confirm her brother was still making a delivery in the next city, then stepped out.

"I'm going in now. Are you ready?"

"Yes. Please be careful, not only for your sake but theirs."

"I will. Don't worry."

He walked up the pathway to the home that stood in front of a subsistence farm that stretched out in a long, narrow plot behind it, the fields freshly harvested. If her father was dying, the rest of the family was certainly picking up the slack.

"How do things look?" asked Fang in his ear.

"I don't know what to say, babe. It looks pretty run-down, but everything seems to be tidy. The walkway is swept. The fields have been harvested."

"I'm so sorry." She was crying.

"What for?"

"That you have to see how I grew up, how poor we were."

"That's nothing to be ashamed of. You should be proud of where you came from. There's no neglect here. There's no lack of pride, only lack of money. Like I said, everything is neat and tidy." He directed his gaze, the image still transmitting. "Look at those flowerbeds in front of the house. They're immaculate." He shifted his gaze again. "The windows are clean. The porch is swept. And look at the steps. They've been repaired only recently. There's pride here, respect. There's absolutely nothing here to be ashamed of. And if anything, it makes me love you even more."

"Thank you." Her voice was barely a murmur, and he found himself emotional, picturing her all alone in his ops center in the middle of nowhere, no one to comfort her, no one to hold on to.

"Okay, baby, I'm at the front door now." He smiled at a little girl peering through the open door. He wiggled his fingers at her and she spun. "Grandma, some foreigner is coming!"

He chuckled. "My cover is blown. One of your nieces just ratted me out."

"I think that was Chun. I've never met her. She was born just after I had to leave."

"All right. Stand by."

Mrs. Lee approached warily, standing in the doorway. "Can I help you?"

He smiled at her then bowed deeply, showing his deference to the matriarch of the family. "Mrs. Lee," he said in perfect Mandarin. "My name is Dylan Kane, and I'm here to talk to you about your daughter, Fang."

CIA Headquarters

Langley, Virginia

Farzan stepped off the elevator, frowning as he stared at his phone. He had messages. A ridiculous amount. That was the job. But he didn't care about any of them. He only cared about the one he was waiting for.

The one from his wife.

She had landed three hours ago and there was nothing, no word. He wanted to reach out to his children on their cellphones, but there was no point. If they had made it out of the airport, then at least one of them would have reached out to let him know, and he didn't want to attract any undue attention to them while they were under the overly watchful eye of the oppressive regime he worked day in and day out to contain and, hopefully, eventually overthrow.

He never should have let her go. It had been stupid, but he was placating his mother, honoring his father, and getting his son to like him.

Foolish. You know better.

The regime couldn't be trusted, and if they had any idea what he did for a living, not the cover that he told his wife, but the truth, they could be in danger. Yet they shouldn't know.

He sighed. They shouldn't, but traitors were everywhere. It was a definite possibility they could know. Yet the security division had assured him the risk was minimal.

Minimal.

There was that word again. No amount of risk, no matter how small, should be tolerated when it came to your family. This wasn't saying yes or no to your daughter going on a ski trip because you feared she might break her leg. This was life and death, a regime so brutal it beat women to within an inch of their lives and sometimes past that, all for showing hair in public.

"What's wrong?"

He flinched as his deputy chief, Kyle Baxter, walked up. "Nothing."

"Bullshit. I can see it on your face. You haven't heard from your family yet, have you?"

"No."

"How overdue are they?"

Farzan sighed. "It's been three hours since they landed."

"So, if it was JFK, I'd say they're a couple of hours late. But this is Tehran. Everything is slower there. There are any number of reasons to have not heard from them."

Farzan headed for his office, Baxter beside him.

"I can make inquiries."

Farzan dismissed the idea. "Definitely not. Anything that draws attention to them puts them in danger. I'm just going to have to wait."

"Can you call your family?"

"If I don't hear from them in the next two hours, then yes. But again, I have to worry about the call being monitored, so I don't want to start calling too soon." His phone pinged and he glanced at it then froze. It was a text message from his brother. He tapped it and read his worst fears.

They have your wife.

He felt dizzy, and Baxter grabbed him by the arm, providing him the support he needed.

"What is it?"

Tears threatened to overwhelm him, and he instead handed the phone over to a man he considered not only a colleague, but a friend.

"Son of a bitch! What are you going to do?"

Farzan sighed. "I don't know. Give me a second."

"To hell with that! Seconds could count. Let's go see Leif. He'll know what to do."

Farzan acquiesced. "You're right. He'll know." He took back the phone, finally thinking straight, and typed a quick reply.

Where are my children?

Lee Residence

Zhangbei County, China

The mention of Fang's name had resulted in a dropped jaw, tears, then a rapid beckoning for him to come inside, followed by a head poked out the door looking in all directions, as if Fang's mother was concerned with prying eyes. The open door closed then the children were shooed into the backyard, though many faces were pressed against the windows. "You know my Fang?"

"Yes, ma'am."

"Is she all right?"

Kane smiled. "She is, and she misses you and her father and her entire family terribly."

"But we were told…" The woman's voice drifted off.

"No doubt what you were told didn't sound good."

"No, it didn't. They said she was a traitor, that she murdered an important man, that she betrayed her country."

"None of that's true. Your daughter did kill a man, a general, but he attempted to rape her, so she defended herself."

The mention of the word "rape" had Mrs. Lee gasping, tears flowing anew.

"Your daughter was forced to flee the country, and yes, she provided information to my government in exchange for asylum. But that information wasn't betraying your government or your country. The man she killed was one of four conspiring against my country without the knowledge of yours. Your daughter did the right thing and stopped a war before it got started. Your daughter's actions probably saved millions of lives, and were honorable and loyal."

"But why would they lie?"

"A man did die, an important man, like they told you, though now you know why. They couldn't exactly admit to that, so instead, they came up with a story that blamed her for everything. Otherwise, they'd have to admit that senior members of the party and the military had betrayed their country. Do you believe me?"

"How do you know all this?"

"Because I was the man sent in to get your daughter to safety."

She eyed him. "Are you an American spy?"

Kane chuckled. "I think it's best you don't know what I do for a living."

She frowned. "I suppose not. But you know my Fang?"

"Ma'am, I love your daughter deeply, and she loves me, and we intend to spend the rest of our lives together."

Her face brightened. "Are you married?"

Kane smiled. "Not yet. I couldn't exactly marry her without asking for her father's permission, now, could I?"

"Oh, Dylan," wept Fang in his ear, and his own chest ached as he struggled to control his emotions.

Mrs. Lee stood. "Then you must meet him at once. He's not well. I'll explain everything you said so I can tell him that I believe you, that I believe every word. I always knew our daughter couldn't have done the things they said. She could never betray her country." She reached out and squeezed his forearm. "Thank you for restoring an old woman's faith in her daughter." She stared up into his eyes. "Future son-in-law." She darted out of the room and he turned away from the prying eyes of the children, wiping his own dry with a handkerchief.

"Thank you, hon."

He inhaled deeply before replying. "I think that went rather well."

"It did. My father might be a harder one to convince, however."

"Oh, I don't know about that. Fathers have a way of forgiving their daughters. But I think that's probably why your mother wanted to talk to him first." His phone pinged. He held it up and cursed.

"What is it?"

"Your brother's on the move. He's heading back."

"How long do you have?"

"It looks like he's hauling ass. If he's coming here, twenty minutes, though there's a chance he could be going off on another delivery."

"Don't risk it. If it looks like he's coming home, which he quite often does for dinner, you have to be out of there and long gone. My parents might not say anything to him, but there's no way those children won't.

He'll absolutely report you to the authorities, and then the entire country will be looking for you."

"Don't worry, babe. I've been in worse positions."

Mrs. Lee reappeared. "He'll see you now."

Leroux/White Residence, Fairfax Towers

Falls Church, Virginia

CIA Analyst Supervisor Chris Leroux froze, drawing back from his girlfriend, CIA Operations Officer Sherrie White, her lithe naked form lying beside him in bed. "What's wrong? Did I hurt you?"

She stared at him, puzzled. "No."

"But you said, 'Ow.'"

"I didn't mean to."

"Are you sure? I don't want to hurt you."

"Suck it, baby!"

He stared at her then burst out laughing, shocked at the demand but excited, nonetheless. "Your wish is my command." He moved back in and returned to work, his girlfriend groaning and moaning as he did everything he could to make her as happy as she made him. He loved this woman more than words could say. He didn't care about any other relationship out there. All he knew was that in his mind, he was the luckiest man in the world and she was the most perfect woman he could ever imagine.

He came up for air and stared into her eyes. "I love you."

She took his head in both her hands, staring back, and she didn't need to say the words. He could see it in her eyes. She loved him. He had no doubt. "I love you," she said needlessly, and he smiled, a wave of pure bliss washing through him. This was the woman he intended to spend the rest of his life with.

If she didn't get herself killed.

Being madly in love with a spy had its rewards, though it also came with substantial risk. But he wasn't letting that stop him.

She pushed his head back down. "You've got work to do, mister."

He grinned. "I think the twin is getting jealous."

His phone rang as he switched breasts, and they both groaned.

"Don't answer it."

"You know I'm on call. I have to."

"Shit!" Sherrie rolled over and grabbed his phone off the nightstand, checking the call display. "It's Sonya."

He took the phone. Sonya Tong was one of his senior analysts and second-in-command of his team. She was exceptional at her job, and she also carried a torch for him. Fortunately, Sherrie wasn't the jealous type. If she were, Tong would be long dead.

Though Tong was probably the last person she wanted calling during their lovemaking.

He swiped his thumb. "Hey, Sonya, what's up?"

"Sorry to interrupt. I know Sherrie just got back from a mission."

He could almost hear the smirk and perhaps a tinge of heartbreak. Everyone on the team knew Sherrie was insatiable after she returned from an op, and he usually booked a couple of days off to satisfy her. "That's okay. What's going on?"

"Priority from the Chief. He wants us to assemble the team."

"Why? What's happened?"

"You know Cyrus Farzan?"

"Yeah. Chief of Iranian Affairs, isn't he?"

"Yeah, that's the one. Looks like they have his wife."

"Who's 'they?'"

"The Iranians."

Leroux's eyebrows shot up, and he let go of the nipple he had been teasing, signaling to Sherrie that this was serious. She rolled out of bed quickly, gathering his things. "How the hell did they get her?"

"She traveled to Tehran with their son and daughter."

"Are you kidding me? Why in the hell would they do that? They have to know he's a priority target."

"Apparently, security cleared it. They said his cover was intact, no signs of it having been broken, and they said it was safe for them to go."

"They might've said it was safe, but why the hell did he let it happen?"

"I don't know, Chris, but they want us to look into it."

"Okay, I'll be leaving in five. Call in the team. Where are you?"

"Five minutes out."

"Okay. When you get there, start gathering all the intel you can on all the family, not just the family here but the family back in Tehran. I want to know who they are, who they work for, if they're in any of our databases, have we red-flagged anyone. I especially want to know if anyone works for the Revolutionary Guard. Put feelers out to see if somehow his cover has been blown. I want to know why the hell they decided to take her. Do they even know who they have, or do they just think they've got another American wife that they can toy with in front of the media?"

"I'm on it."

"Good. See you soon." He ended the call and swung out of bed, Sherrie dangling his underwear from her teeth.

"Did you say you were leaving in five minutes?"

"Yes."

She leaped at him, knocking him back onto the bed. She reached down and grabbed him and squeezed. "Make it ten."

Lee Residence

Zhangbei County, China

Kane stepped through the door to find a frail man sitting propped up in his bed, surrounded by family photos and mementos, many handmade by children, along with countless religious icons he noted from multiple faiths. Lee Chen appeared to be in his sixties, perhaps even seventies, but Kane knew for a fact the man was only 52.

"Husband, this is the man I told you of who brought the truth about our daughter."

Kane bowed deeply. "Mr. Lee, my name is Dylan Kane, and it is an honor to meet you. Your daughter has told me so much about the two of you, that I feel I know you already."

The man pushed up on his elbows slightly, shuffling into a more seated position, his wife rushing forward to adjust his pillows. "So, you are the one who claims my daughter is not the traitor Beijing would have us believe?"

"Yes, sir. And I can assure you she is not a traitor."

"Yet my wife seems to think you're an American spy."

Kane smiled at the woman. "And as I said to your wife, the less you know about me, the better."

"So, you are a spy, and an American one at that."

"Yes, I am American. But as I explained to Mrs. Lee, the general your daughter killed not only tried to rape her, but was a traitor to his own country, along with several others. Unbeknownst to Beijing, these four conspired with traitors from my country to take over the United States. That, if successful, would have then triggered wars of territorial expansion by your government. Your daughter bravely defended herself, then made contact with civilian friends in America. I was sent in to retrieve her and bring her to safety. The conspiracy was stopped with the help of your daughter, and potentially millions of lives were saved, thanks to her actions. You should be very proud of her, and not believe anything that you were told."

The old man's eyes glistened, the hint of a smile visible. "How I wish I could believe you, but you're an American spy. Anything you say can't be trusted."

Kane stepped closer. "Sir, please look beyond what you think my job is, and listen to my words, spoken by the man who loves your daughter and would do anything for her. I would die for her."

Mr. Lee regarded him for a moment. "What are you saying?"

"I'm saying Fang and I have been together since shortly after she was exiled. We love each other dearly, and we share our lives in every way. We intend to spend the rest of our lives together."

"How am I supposed to believe you? What proof do you have of this?"

"Ask me anything only she would know."

The man pursed his lips as if searching for a suitable question. Mrs. Lee beat him to it. "She has a birthmark. Where is it?"

Her husband dismissed the question with a bat of his hand. "This man could have killed her then searched her body and found it." He smiled. "But she has a scar on her left knee. How did she get it?"

Kane didn't need Fang in his ear to know the answer to this one. He had asked her about it early in their relationship, during his exploration of every square inch of her gorgeous form. "She was six years old, and you were working in the fields. She had come home from school and was excited to show you a drawing she had done in class. As she was running toward you, she tripped and her knee hit a rock, cutting it open. You and your brother rushed over and you picked her up, taking her inside the house where you cleaned her wound then gave it a kiss. Do you remember what you said to her?"

The man's eyes were pools of tears. "I do, but this is your test, not mine."

"You said, 'When your mother gets home, have her kiss it too, because my lips only take the pain away. Your mother's will heal what causes the pain.'"

Fang wept in his ear as Mrs. Lee dabbed her eyes dry with the corners of her apron, and her husband, battling his emotions the entire time, was finally forced to wipe his own eyes dry with the back of his hand. "You *do* know my daughter."

"I do, sir. And I hope one day to marry her. Assuming, of course, I have your blessing."

The ailing man squared himself away. He regarded his daughter's suitor, his emotions checked, once again the proud man Kane had been told of. "You seem a fine young man, and for my daughter to have told you that story means she must care about you as well. I fear your profession or your presumed profession could, however, put her in danger. Yet I assume she's fully aware of what you do."

"She is."

"And I also assume it's very dangerous for you to be here right now."

"It is."

"That suggests to me you were telling the truth when you said you would die for her."

"I wouldn't hesitate."

"Then you have my blessing."

Fang gasped out a cry in his ear, and Mrs. Lee embraced him, her tears flowing freely. Kane returned the hug then once again bowed deeply to Mr. Lee before stepping forward and shaking the man's hand. "You've just made me the happiest man in the world, sir. Now I have a surprise for the both of you that you must keep secret."

"What's that?"

Kane reached into his satchel and pulled out a tablet. He entered his password then turned it around for the Lees to see.

"Hello, Mother. Hello, Father."

Wails filled the room.

And his own tears flowed.

Meeting Room 3C, CIA Headquarters

Langley, Virginia

"Why in the hell would you let your family go to Iran of all places? That's idiocy!"

Deputy Director Leif Morrison held up a hand, cutting off the inappropriate though accurate observation from the Chief of Internal Security, Tim Alzate. "Listen, we're not here to play the blame game. We're here to find out what happened." He turned to Farzan, his distress evident. "Cyrus, why don't you tell us everything you know?"

Farzan drew a deep breath before exhaling loudly. "My mother called me a couple of weeks ago—"

Alzate interrupted. "A couple of weeks ago? We need specifics here if we're gonna do any good."

Morrison held up a hand again. Sometimes Alzate had no tact, though he was correct most of the time. "He's right, Cyrus. We need specifics, as accurate as you can get."

"You're right." Farzan picked up his phone and tapped away at the display. "I got a text message from my mother on the twelfth, 10:03 AM our time."

"What would that be local?"

"18:03," said Leroux, sitting beside Morrison.

"She said it was urgent I call her, so I did, right away."

"What phone did you use?"

Farzan flicked his cellphone. "This one. I never make personal calls to Iran on anything but this or my home phone. I don't want them tracing anything here."

Alzate rolled his eyes. "With the proper access, they can figure out what cellphone tower was used to make your call."

Leroux dismissed the comment. "No. All senior level staffers have all their calls automatically redirected to cellphone towers near their residences or external covers. There's no chance of someone tracing the call to here."

Alzate sat back in his chair with a scowl, evidently displeased at being shown up by the much younger Leroux.

Morrison urged Farzan to continue with a twirl of his hand. "What was said in the conversation?"

"She said my father's dying and wanted to see me before it was too late."

"And what did you tell her?"

"I told her I couldn't because of my job."

"And what did she say to that?"

"She was none too pleased."

"And then what happened?"

"She said that my son had already said he wanted to come and see his grandfather before he died."

Leroux cocked an eyebrow. "Wait a minute. She talked to your son before she talked to you?"

"No. Apparently my cousin, Kaveh, has been talking to him and told him what was going on, and my mother found out through him."

Leroux tapped away on his tablet. "This cousin have a last name?"

"Yes. Jafari. He's my mother's nephew. Her side of the family."

"What do we know about him?"

"Not much. He was a child when I left."

"How old is he?"

"Twenty-five-ish, I think."

"Who initiated contact?"

"I have no idea. All I know, which I found out only later talking to my son, was that they've been in contact for about a year."

"You weren't aware of this?"

"Not at all."

Morrison regarded the man. "And if you had been aware of it, would you have put a stop to it?"

Farzan chewed his cheek for a moment. "I don't know. To be honest, I don't really know much about him. I'm not close with my family anymore. They were never happy that I left, though when I did, they understood why. But the way my mother spoke on the phone, it sounded like she had been completely indoctrinated by the regime."

Leroux pinched his chin. "Perhaps she was afraid someone was listening in."

Farzan stabbed a finger at him. "That's exactly what I was thinking, so I played along just in case."

Alzate threw out a hand, clearly frustrated. "None of this explains why the hell you let your family go to Iran. You're the Chief of Iranian Affairs, for crying out loud!"

"I sent them so that my son and daughter could meet their grandfather at least once before he died."

Morrison could understand on an emotional level why Farzan would want his children to meet their grandfather. If Farzan were a civilian, there likely wouldn't be any issues. But in his position, it wasn't just that he worked at the CIA, he was the damn Chief of Iranian Affairs. Not only should he have known better, but there was no way it should have been permitted. "Listen, Cyrus, I know this is emotional. I know this is getting a little heated, but we're asking these questions for a reason, because we need to know everything if we're going to help your family. Why didn't you follow protocol and check with security about sending them?"

"I did check! A couple of months ago, and they cleared it."

Morrison's eyebrows rose. "Wait a minute, they cleared it?"

"Yes. They said I couldn't go, of course, but they said the risk to my family going would be minimal."

Morrison focused on one word. "Minimal?"

Alzate stared at Farzan. "'Minimal' was acceptable to you?"

Farzan glared at him. "No, it wasn't, which is why we never made any plans to go. I wasn't willing to put my family at risk."

"So then, why the hell did you do it now?"

"Because my father was dying, my mother was saying horrible things to me, and my son was demanding to go. He's eighteen years old, so he can do whatever the hell he wants. He was going whether I wanted him to or not."

"Why didn't you just take his damn passport?"

Morrison held up his hand yet again. "You know as well as I do that that's illegal. He's eighteen. He's an adult. That's his passport. If he wants to go, he's going."

"So, your son is the reason they're there?"

Farzan's shoulders slumped. "Yes. And, he apparently talked to his sister, then she wanted to go as well. She's only sixteen, but I figured if one was going, then they both should go so they could support each other. And then, of course, my wife insisted on going with them despite the fact she hates her former homeland for more than just political reasons."

Morrison pursed his lips. "Fine. That explains why they're there, so let's move on from that point. You received a text from your family saying that the authorities had your wife?"

"Yes."

"Have we confirmed that? What about your children?"

"The children are safe. They're with my family in Tehran. They're back at my parents' place now."

"Any sign they've been followed? Any interference from the authorities?"

"Not that was mentioned, but they know those are the type of things you don't say on the phone. You never talk about the regime, the government, anything like that."

"Other than your family saying your wife's been taken, do we have any other confirmation? Anything to corroborate that?"

Farzan eyed him. "You don't think they're lying, do you?"

Morrison dismissed the question. "No, not at all. But they could be mistaken. There could have been a medical emergency. She might have been kept longer for some reason and she's sitting at the airport right now with no way to communicate because her cellphone's been confiscated. There are any number of innocent to not-so-innocent reasons why you haven't been able to make contact with her."

Leroux, staring at his tablet, cleared his throat. "I reached out to some contacts in Mossad, and they just sent me this footage." He sent it to the main display at the front of the meeting room, and everyone watched what appeared to be security camera footage from an airport.

"What are we looking at?"

"Security footage from Imam Khomeini International Airport for the time in question. This is from the moment they landed. We've got about eight hours here, but based upon the photo of your wife from your security file, my team managed to find this." He tapped and the footage leaped ahead almost thirty minutes.

Farzan shot forward in his seat, pointing. "That's Kiana! And those are the kids with her!"

Leroux used his thumbs to zoom in then track Farzan's family. Kiana Farzan was in traditional Iranian garb despite being a very Western woman. Morrison had met her once. A chance encounter on the street. He would never have guessed she was Iranian let alone Muslim by the way she dressed and acted, but here, she was clearly smartly playing a part. It was best not to antagonize the Iranians, as had been proven with the beatings and killings of young women who merely wanted to show their hair in public.

The daughter was dressed similarly, and even the son wore respectable clothes—no jeans, no loud shirt with a slogan or branding that screamed America. They were doing everything right. The daughter cleared customs then the son. It was Kiana's turn, the children standing off to the side waiting for her. She joined them for a moment, then watched as they headed through a set of doors and out of sight of the camera. As soon as the doors closed, she stepped to the rear of another line, and Farzan leaned back, his mouth agape.

"I can't believe she let them go. Why would she do that?"

"She likely had no choice," said Leroux. "According to Mossad, this is a secondary screening line."

Alzate pursed his lips. "Could it be a random selection?"

"I doubt it. The Iranians don't need to do random screenings to have enough people they want to look at. My guess is, she was flagged either by the customs officer for simply having an American passport, or they had flagged her before she even landed. Remember, the Iranians issued them the visas, which means they were already checked out."

"But why didn't they flag my children?"

"Probably because they're children. They wouldn't know anything, and besides, they were both born in America. The Iranian government considers anyone born in Iran to still be Iranian despite citizenship, but they can't make the same argument with your kids. My guess is, they want to talk to your wife about you. They figure the kids know nothing, and they're not going anywhere anyway. They'll be with your family if they need to be picked up. Remember, they have the address from the forms that would have been filled in, indicating where they're staying."

"Is this all we have?" asked Morrison, jerking his chin toward the video.

"That's all we were able to obtain, though Mossad's working on it."

"Anything else on the rest of it?"

"No."

They watched as she disappeared through a door. "Does she ever come out of here?"

"No. Nobody ever does."

"Do we know where that door leads?"

"According to Mossad, it's a secondary screening room. They interrogate passengers one at a time, and then if they're cleared, there's a door that leads into the arrivals area. If they're not, there's another door where they're taken for further interrogation, and that's where things can get rough."

Farzan flinched at the word, and Leroux immediately leaned forward. "I'm sorry, I shouldn't have said that."

Farzan dismissed the apology. "No, you should. I don't want anything held back. I need to know all the possibilities." He turned to Morrison. "What can we do?"

"That depends. What does your wife know?"

"The cover."

Morrison stared at him. "Forget security clearances. Forget everything. The truth."

"I swear to you, Leif, she thinks I'm a project manager at the power company."

"And what did you tell her about not being able to go to Iran?"

"I said I needed a security clearance for the job, and I would lose it if I went to Iran because of the tensions between the two countries."

"And she believed you?"

"Absolutely. I'm her husband. I'm not going to lie to her." Farzan grunted. "Well, you know what I mean."

"I do."

Alzate folded his arms. "Why did you go with the cover and not the truth? Spouses are permitted to know."

Farzan sighed. "My wife grew up in Iran like I did, but her family had it particularly hard, getting on the wrong side of some important people for petty reasons. She's terrified of all that nonsense. Security, politics, espionage. If I told her I was working for the CIA, she'd be constantly worried, constantly stressed. So, I decided it was best she think I was just a boring manager at a boring job."

Morrison regarded the man. "Well, that decision, as difficult as it may have been, might be the thing that saves your wife's life."

Alzate grunted. "Or costs her it."

Lee Residence

Zhangbei County, China

Kane checked his phone once again as the tearful reunion continued between Fang and her parents. Her brother Wei was only five minutes away, though he had stopped several minutes ago, the satellite image suggesting he was at a street vendor. If they were lucky, he was buying food for one with the intention of eating it before coming here. If they were unlucky, he was picking up food for everyone. The way his luck ran sometimes, Kane was expecting the latter, though there were so many children here, takeout for everyone could be expensive, and this appeared to be a family that enjoyed few luxuries and didn't spend a single Yuan unless it was absolutely necessary.

Either way, the moment Wei moved in this direction, this was over. The first several minutes of the reunion had been apologies back and forth, then it had turned to family news, confirmation of her relationship with him, and now finally they were on her father's condition. What Tommy's social media scraping had discovered was confirmed. He was dying and had little time left. More tears and apologies followed the confirmation, and Kane had a hard time controlling his own emotions. It broke his heart every time Fang cried.

And it was why he was here risking his life, hoping to right a wrong, to give her closure with her family before her father passed.

"I'm so happy I got to speak to you, Father."

"As am I, my child. And I'm even happier to have learned the truth. I was heartbroken when they told me those lies, and I'm ashamed that I believed them. But deep down, I always questioned it. What they said didn't sound like the daughter I raised, the woman who set out to take on the world. Can you ever forgive me?"

"Of course, Father. There's nothing to forgive."

Kane glanced at his phone and cursed. Wei was underway, and heading in this direction. He stepped forward. "I'm afraid we have to end this now. Wei is four minutes away."

"I wish we had more time," said Fang. "But you know how he is. It's essential you don't tell him anything about our conversation, about Dylan being there."

"But the children have seen him."

Kane stepped closer. "Tell them you dropped your wallet in the market, and I found it and returned it. You thanked me and insisted I meet your husband. We had a pleasant conversation about the weather, about the farm, and his condition, then I left because I had business that I couldn't be late for. Now, say goodbye. I have to leave in sixty seconds."

The final goodbyes were tearful, a mixture of joy and sadness. Kane took the tablet and turned it toward him. "Sorry, babe, no more time."

"I understand."

He turned off the device and placed it back in his satchel before bowing deeply to them. "I regret I have to leave so quickly. We may never meet again, but rest assured your daughter has a good life, has friends, and is loved. You can rest easy that the job of protecting her, of caring for her, is now mine. Now I have to go."

He bowed deeply then headed for the front door. The moment he cleared the threshold, the sound of children bursting through the rear erupted. He jogged down the lane to the road where he was parked and climbed into his SUV, starting it and putting it in gear before hammering on the gas and pulling away. He checked his rearview mirror to see a ZTO Express delivery vehicle approaching, its signal light on. Kane eased off the gas, not wanting to attract any attention.

"Looks like I got away just in time, babe."

Fang sniffed in his ear. "That's good."

"Are you gonna be all right?"

She sighed heavily. "I will be. I just wish you were here."

"So do I, babe, so do I. Why don't you give Sherrie a call? She's in town."

Another sniff. "That's a good idea. I'll do that."

"Okay, babe, I'm gonna let you go. I have to change my super boyfriend cape for my super spy cape."

"All right, be careful."

"Don't worry about me, babe. I'm more worried about you."

"I'll be all right. I'm going to call Sherrie like you suggested. Don't be surprised if the next time we talk, I'm either drunk or hung over."

He snickered. "That's definitely one way to take your mind off things. Love you, babe."

"Love you too."

He disconnected his comms, eyeballing the turn up ahead that would take him back toward Mr. Wu's food cart. Would it draw too much attention? No self-respecting spy would ever go to the same place three times in one day, yet a self-indulgent insurance investigator just might. He grinned, his decision made. The chances of him ever being back this way were slim to none.

What the hell? You only live once.

Farzan Residence

Tehran, Iran

"What are they saying?"

Tara Farzan was desperate. She had been taught Farsi when she was a child, but hadn't spoken it in years. And the Farsi she had learned had always been spoken calmly and at a relaxed speed. This rapid fire, angry style, had her struggling to keep up. Surprisingly, her brother followed the conversation, even participating.

"Please, Ray, tell me what's going on!"

He shushed her. "Is there somebody we can speak to?" he asked, and their grandmother shook her head.

"No, it's best not to do anything. We'll just have to wait and see what happens."

The statement horrified her. They weren't going to do anything? They were just going to let them keep her mother? "But she's an American!" she cried out, and the entire room turned to stare at her, her cousin Kaveh glaring at her.

"She was born Iranian! She'll always be Iranian!"

"But she's an American citizen!"

Kaveh dismissed the fact with a bat of his hand. "Irrelevant. Once an Iranian, always an Iranian." He wrapped an arm around her brother. "Don't you agree?"

To her horror, her brother's head bobbed, though she sensed some hesitancy. Despite that, she stared at him, her mouth agape. "How can you agree with that? She's our mother! She didn't do anything wrong! God knows what they're doing to her!" She had switched to English, but her brother replied in Farsi.

"If she's innocent, then they'll let her go."

A doorway filled with beads rippled and an old man entered the room, everyone falling silent in deference to who must be her grandfather. "Can't an old man die in peace?" He spotted her and a smile spread. "Is this our little Tara?"

She nodded.

"I'm your grandfather." He held out his arms, and she rushed forward, hugging him as she sobbed. She didn't know the man. She had only spoken to him on the phone over the years, and that was only a couple of times a year, if that. But so far, her grandmother had proven cold, though that could be due to the events currently underway.

"Oh, Grandfather! You have to help my mother!"

He gently pushed her away then sat at the kitchen table. He appeared exhausted. "Tell me what's going on."

Kaveh began loudly, and her grandfather cut him off with a raised hand. "Someone else. Calmly."

A man she believed was her uncle stepped closer. "The plane arrived on schedule. The children cleared customs with no problem, but their mother was taken for further questioning, and we haven't heard from her since."

The old man frowned. "It wouldn't be the first time, especially since she's traveling on that American passport of hers. What does my son have to say about it?"

Her uncle shrugged. "Not much. He said to wait and see."

"I think that's a wise suggestion. We all know antagonizing the authorities is never a wise move."

"But my mother, they could be torturing her." Tara sniffed, tears streaming. "They could be beating her. They could be raping her." She squeezed her eyes shut as her shoulders slumped, her chin pressed against her chest. "They could kill her."

Her grandmother came over and wrapped her arms around her. "It's all right, dear. I'm sure none of that's happening. They just want to ask her questions because she was born here then left. They just want to make sure she's not a spy." Her voice was gentle, kind, and comforting. It was what she needed. Perhaps the woman wasn't as cold as she had feared.

"What can we do?"

"Like your father said, we'll just wait. But for now, let's get you two settled in and fed. Hopefully, we'll hear something by morning."

Tara sniffed hard and nodded, the prospect of food improving her mood slightly. She was starving, and the best thing she could do right now was to get something in her stomach then go to bed. When she woke up in the morning, everything might be all right. She just prayed her mother was safe and unharmed.

Kaveh, his arm still around her brother's shoulders, grinned. "Yes, let's eat. Then in the morning we'll take you to prayers and you can see how it truly is to be a Muslim."

Her brother smiled broadly at him. "I look forward to it, cousin."

Kaveh turned and grabbed Ray by both shoulders, staring into his eyes. "Now that you are here, we are no longer cousins. We are brothers!"

Her stomach churned at her brother's eyes, wide with a zeal behind them she had never seen outside of the movies or news reports, and for the first time, she noticed her brother's beard. It wasn't very long, nothing compared to their cousin's, but it was there, nonetheless. He had been clean-shaven until about six months ago, and she had thought nothing of it. But now, in this new context, she had to wonder, was he being radicalized like so many others she had read about? Was that why he wanted to come here? Did it even have anything to do with their dying grandfather who still sat in the chair, who he hadn't even approached yet? She caught her grandfather staring at her brother, and she was certain it was with concern. Did he see what she did? Did he recognize what might be happening here?

And if he did, could he help stop it before it was too late?

Imam Khomeini International Airport

Tehran, Iran

Kiana cried out, the sting of the slap intense. Nobody had punched her yet with a fist, but she had lost count of how many times she had been slapped open handed, her face now afire. Another question asked, another answered, always to their dissatisfaction, resulting in yet another slap.

"Please stop!" she pleaded. "I don't know what you want me to tell you."

The man interrogating her for the past several hours stared down at her. "I want the truth, Mrs. Farzan."

"I'm telling you the truth!" She had been the entire time, yet they didn't seem to care.

The man began pacing in front of her as he did between each slap, the clop of his boots on the concrete floor echoing off the cinderblock walls. "You say you're telling me the truth, but I cannot believe that you don't know what your husband's job actually is. You know his cover and that's what you're telling me. Well, there's no way a husband works for the CIA for that long without telling his wife the truth."

"You have me mixed up with someone else. You have to. I swear he works for the power company. Is that what this is about? Are you trying to hack the power company?"

He stopped and stared at her. "What would make you say that?"

She wasn't sure if she should answer. This was the first thing she had said that appeared to pique his interest. "I heard it on the news. Iran has been conducting cyber warfare against my country for years now, including trying to hack power plants."

He folded his arms and stared down at her. "Lies. Propaganda. Your country is always falsely accusing us. All we want to do is live in peace. But 'your country,' as you call it, wants nothing but war, wants to destroy us, wants to destroy Islam." He resumed his pacing, his eyes always on her. "It breaks my heart that a sister would not only leave her country, but become the citizen of its greatest enemy and then call it 'my country.' I want to weep with the tragedy of it all. Is it your husband who told you this, who told you that we might try to hack where he works?"

She recognized the trap being set for her and shook her head, perhaps a little too vigorously. "No, it's just from the news."

"So, these lies didn't come from your husband?"

"Of course not. He's a good man."

"Yet he betrayed his country."

This time, she did vehemently shake her head. "He has done no such thing! He loves America and he loves Iran. He holds no ill will."

"So you say, yet he works for the CIA."

Her shoulders slumped, and she closed her eyes. "So *you* say." She gasped in shock at the unexpected sting as he smacked her again. She whimpered, her tears flowing anew. The door opened and she turned to see an unfamiliar face.

"That's enough," said the new arrival, and her interrogator stepped back.

"Yes, sir."

Her shoulders shook with relief. It was over. They were finally done with her. She wiped her eyes dry and looked up at the man standing in the doorway. "Can I see my children now?"

The man laughed and her interrogator joined in, stepping closer to her and leaning forward, his mouth pressed against her ear. "My dear, if you thought I was hard on you, as you Americans say, you ain't seen nothing yet."

Operations Center 3, CIA Headquarters

Langley, Virginia

Marc Therrien interrupted a conversation Leroux was having with Tong. "I might have something."

Leroux turned toward his senior analyst. "What have you got?"

"We've got satellite coverage of the airport. I've been reviewing it, and watch this." Therrien tapped at his keyboard then jerked his chin toward the main display arcing across the front of the state-of-the-art operations center.

"What am I looking at?"

"Overhead shot of the Tehran Airport." Therrien worked his station and a portion of the image zoomed in. "Watch this rear exit."

A black SUV pulled up, no markings, and all four doors opened. The exit, tucked away where it couldn't be seen by prying eyes at ground level, opened. Two men appeared, then a moment later, a woman, her head covered with a hood, was led out by two others and shoved into the back of the SUV. One man followed her in, the rest returning inside. Those who had come with the SUV climbed back in before it pulled away.

"Any biometrics to suggest it's her?"

"No biometrics, but I do have this." Some more tapping and an image, pulled from Tara Farzan's Instagram feed, showing the family at their home the day of their flight, confirmed the woman they had just seen was wearing the same clothes as the missing Kiana Farzan. "That can't be a coincidence."

"What time is this?"

"It happened exactly twenty-three minutes ago."

"Track that vehicle. We need to know where they took her." Leroux headed for the door. "I need to brief the Chief. There's no doubt now that Mrs. Farzan's detention has gone beyond routine. See if you can get any other angles on her. Keep trying to get footage from inside. And analyze her gait. I wanna know how she was walking. Was she in pain? Is there any indication of torture?"

"We're on it," said Tong.

Leroux cleared the double security doors and fired a text to Morrison's assistant, informing her he was on his way with an important update. She replied a few moments later, confirming the Chief's availability. He had flashbacks of when Sherrie had been tortured during the attempted coup, and prayed Mrs. Farzan wasn't being subjected to something similar. But he feared she was. This was Iran. Not only did they care nothing about women's rights, they cared nothing about the laws that governed civilized nations. If they thought she knew something they wanted, they could beat her mercilessly, but right now, what had happened to her and what would happen to her was pure conjecture. There was a chance they hadn't laid a finger on her yet and perhaps wouldn't, though he was certain that was wishful thinking.

He rode up the elevator in silence. The doors opened on the executive suites floor, and he headed toward Morrison's office, clearing security before entering his boss' anteroom.

The Chief's assistant smiled at him, gesturing toward the door. "Go right in. He's expecting you."

"Thanks." Leroux rapped twice then opened the door, surprised to find Morrison wasn't behind his desk.

"Over here."

Leroux turned to see Morrison sitting in a comfortable chair with Farzan in his own, Baxter on one end of a couch that formed a casual meeting area. Leroux sat on the other end of the couch, acknowledging the others.

"You have an update?" said Morrison.

"Yes, sir." He faced Farzan. "This is going to be difficult to hear, sir. However, we just found footage showing who we believe to be your wife being placed in a vehicle that then left the airport about half an hour ago. We're trying to trace the vehicle now to see where she was taken."

All color drained from Farzan's face as his hands gripped the arms of his chair.

Morrison spoke first. "Are you sure it's her?"

"No. Whoever it was had a hood over their head. However, they were wearing the same clothes that Mrs. Farzan wore when she left for her flight. We confirmed it from an Instagram posting made by your daughter before they left."

Farzan grasped at the straws that statement offered. "Maybe they just dressed someone else in her clothes."

Leroux conceded the desperate hope. "It's a possibility. But even if that were the case, it means they were actively attempting to trick us, so this has gone far beyond a routine check. They've definitely taken a significant interest in her, and right now, I'm inclined to believe that the woman we saw was indeed your wife."

The man's eyes were wide, and he turned to Morrison. "What are we going to do?"

"We do nothing. We're the CIA. We're going to continue to gather intel as we normally would, but we can't do anything that would tip them off as to whom they have."

"They have to know, don't they? Like, why else would they do this?"

Baxter pursed his lips. "Any number of reasons. Just to piss us off, to punish her for being an Iranian who dared to become an American. There are any number of reasons for these guys to do something like this. Worst case scenario, of course, is that they know exactly who they have and unfortunately, that's a distinct possibility."

"If they do know, what will they do to her?"

Baxter sighed heavily, compassion finally having found the man. "I don't think you want to know the possibilities."

"Could they torture her?"

"Absolutely."

"Kill her?"

"Absolutely."

"We have to do something. We have to save her."

Morrison dismissed the idea. "No. All we can do is utilize diplomatic channels. And since we have no diplomatic relations with Iran, we'll have to do that through intermediaries. I'll talk to State, have them reach out to the Swiss, see if they can make contact." He turned to Leroux. "Meanwhile, have your team find out where they took her. See if there's any way to confirm that it actually was her, and start working on an extraction plan that gets the rest of the family out. Who do we have in the area?"

"Take your pick, sir. A lot of our officers are already in the region, including Kane."

Morrison rejected the suggestion. "No. Kane's on personal business."

"Not anymore. He just finished it and is moving into position for his op. If all goes well, he's available in the next couple of hours."

"Good. Then that might just work out. Let him know."

"I will."

"Overtime is authorized. Pull any resources you need, and you better put a tactical team on alert just in case."

Leroux paused. "Do you really think the president would authorize an insertion?"

"He might, though I doubt it. I just want them in the area in case Kane does make it out, but has somebody on his ass. As soon as they cross that twelve-mile limit, we can blow the shit out of them with impunity."

Leroux smiled. "Sounds good to me."

Morrison rose, ending the meeting. "I have a teleconference in ten, gentlemen. Chris, I'll want you in on that. The rest of you, let's meet later to discuss any updates."

The others left and Leroux turned to Morrison. "Do you realize how many ops could be compromised because he was an idiot?"

Morrison held up a finger. "Don't forget, he followed proper procedure, though he forgot an important part."

"What's that?"

"Procedure said he gets the trip vetted by security, but just because security says it's all right doesn't mean you still go ahead with the trip. He should have known better."

Leroux scratched his chin. "Have we checked into that vetting?"

"What do you mean?"

"I mean, should that trip have been cleared? Was there legitimately little risk to allowing them to go, or did somebody screw up? Or…" Leroux hesitated.

"What's that gut telling you?"

"Was he set up? Do we have another mole or someone on the take?"

Morrison's jaw loosened slightly. "My God, Chris, if there's one time I want your gut to be wrong, this is it. If we have a leak in Security, we could have a far bigger problem than we thought."

People's Liberation Army Rocket Force Testing Range

Outside Jilantai, China

Kane lay prone in the grass, a Chinese People's Liberation Army testing grounds ahead. Security was tight around the perimeter, but he had used his ghillie suit to approach undetected. At first, there was nothing to see, the Chinese aware of when many of their adversaries' satellites passed overhead. In some locations, the US kept 24/7 coverage, but others, like here, they either intentionally left a gap, or occasionally arranged one.

Like today.

One of the primary satellites the Chinese were well aware of had been temporarily re-tasked to provide coverage over the Red Sea. The Chinese would pick up on that fact and might just take advantage of the opportunity.

"Fly Guy, Control, the satellite is below the horizon, over."

"Copy that, Control. And I thought I told you it was 'Pretty Fly for a White guy,' not 'Fly Guy.'"

Tong snickered. "Negative, Fly Guy. Your original callsign request was rejected as being too long. Just be thankful I shortened it to 'Fly Guy' and not something else."

Kane thought for a moment. "'Pretty Guy?'"

"That was on the list of choices. I suggested Vanilla Ice, but someone here wasn't sure you'd actually respond."

"Fine, 'Fly Guy' it is." A claxon sounded, and Kane adjusted his angle. "Stand by, Control. We've got some activity here." A large portion of the ground ahead slid away, revealing a massive dark opening. Vehicles and personnel began emerging up what must be a ramp he didn't have a line of sight on. "Control, are you getting this?"

"Affirmative."

His feed from his binoculars was being relayed back to Langley for later analysis, but he didn't need the eggheads back home to confirm what had just emerged. Two DF-27 hypersonic missiles on launchers. "Bingo. I think we found what we're looking for."

Tong agreed. "It looks that way."

Kane adjusted his angle slightly. "Looks like they're going to do a launch."

"Let's hope so. We've never actually seen one of these things in action."

"Well, if they're hypersonic, we're only gonna see a couple of seconds of them in action."

An alarm sounded, and the personnel scurried away from the launchers.

"This is it." He steadied his breathing in an effort to provide the most stable image possible. The first missile's engines ignited, a sight that usually meant death and destruction always exciting to see. But it wasn't to be. A massive explosion erupted, black and orange flame, followed by billowing smoke, surged outward, engulfing the entire area, revealing why the Chinese didn't want its enemies seeing the launch of their new super weapon.

It didn't work yet.

He smiled broadly at the failure when his comms squawked, and his best friend's voice cut in. "Fly Guy, Control Actual. We need you to use the distraction to extract yourself. Let us know as soon as you're clear. You have a new urgent assignment."

Kane lowered his binoculars and stuffed them inside his ghillie suit. "Roger that, Control. Where have you got me heading now?"

"Tehran."

He grunted. "Out of the frying pan and into the fire."

There was a shout behind him and he cursed.

Maybe the fire was here.

Fayetteville, North Carolina

Sergeant Carl "Niner" Sung leaned over in the passenger seat and cocked a cheek, releasing a brown cloud before taking another drag of his strawberry shake.

Sergeant Leon "Atlas" James stared at him in disgust. "You're a pig, you know that?"

Niner eyed him. "This is news to you?"

"Do you do that around Angela?"

Niner shrugged at the reference to his girlfriend. "We only recently reached the fart-in-front-of-each-other phase of our relationship."

"Really? I think Vanessa and I got there within a week."

"Who broke the seal first?"

Atlas grinned. "That'd be me."

"That must have terrified the shit out of her. Was it a rumbler or a squeaker?"

"It started as a squeaker, but when she began laughing, I would call it a stuttered rumble."

Niner snorted. "I can almost picture that."

Atlas swatted him with a meaty hand. "I told you to stop picturing me like that."

"Who said anything about you being naked?" Niner's jaw dropped. "No way! Your first duck call was when you were naked together?"

If Atlas' brown cheeks could turn red, they would be crimson right now. "It was an accident."

Niner eyed his best friend. "Let me guess, Taco Tuesday?"

"You know me way too well."

Niner leaned over to deliver another back blast.

"At least put a window down, man."

Niner pressed the button, lowering the window as he steam-pressed his Calvin's.

"Dude, you know you're lactose intolerant. Why the hell do you keep eating dairy?"

"I like the taste. And once you get past the stomach cramping, the farting is really fun."

"I think you stopped maturing at twelve."

Niner sat back in his seat. "Might have had an accident on that one."

"If you shit your pants in my car, I'm tossing you out right here right now."

"Don't worry, I'll pay for the cleaning."

"Where are your pills? I thought you had some pills you could take when you're eating dairy."

"I do, but I forgot them."

"You knew we were going for burgers and shakes and you forgot your damn pills?"

Niner shrugged. "Angela distracted me." His eyebrows bobbed suggestively.

Atlas held up a hand. "Please, please, for the love of God, don't give me details."

"Well, see, we were in the kitchen, and I had my finger—"

Atlas swatted him again. "Don't you dare finish that sentence."

"—stuck in the peanut butter jar. What the hell kind of disgusting mind do you have? Angela is a lady."

"Mm-hmm. You do know her and Vanessa talk?"

Niner grinned. "So then, you've heard the reviews?" He shoved two thumbs into the air. "I'm assuming they were raves." His eyes narrowed. "Wait a minute. Do you mean that Angela talks to Vanessa, then Vanessa tells you what Angela says?"

Atlas dismissed the concern. "No. I'm in the other room. But have you ever heard those two together on their second bottle of wine? It doesn't matter how thick the walls are. There's no way you're not hearing them. My God, can those women talk. And like, I mean, there's no subject they won't discuss in graphic detail. You think we're bad? Sometimes I have to put my noise-canceling headphones on. Otherwise, I don't know if I could look at her in the morning without blushing."

"Really? Next time Angela comes over, I'm going to sneak in. You and I can cuddle up in bed and listen."

Atlas swatted him yet again. "Boundaries."

Niner twisted in his seat and batted his eyes at him. "Some lines are meant to be crossed, mister."

Atlas' phone rang through the car's speakers, the call display appearing on the dash showing it was their team lead, Command Sergeant Major Burt "Big Dog" Dawson. Atlas frowned. "This can't be good." He tapped to take the call, but before he could say hello, Niner intervened.

"Hello, you've reached Atlas' voicemail. He can't come to the phone right now because he's too busy treating his best friend like a chew toy."

Another swat, this one a little harder.

Niner gave him a look. "They say you only hurt the ones you love."

A fist was clenched. "Let me show you how much I love you."

Niner squealed.

Dawson chuckled. "Are you two about done?"

Atlas' impossibly deep voice rumbled. "If we aren't, we're about to be. Permission to pummel the sergeant?"

"What you two do on your own time is no concern of mine. Don't ask, don't tell might no longer be policy, but it's just a good way to live your life if you're on the don't ask side of things."

Niner snorted at Atlas' shocked expression. "I think our big friend is at a loss for words," he said. "What's up, BD?"

"We're being called up. Leave is canceled."

"Where are we headed?"

"Somewhere warm."

Niner's eyebrows shot up. "You mean like Nevada? Please tell me we're going to Vegas. I'm feeling really lucky right now."

"No, not Vegas. Let's just put it this way. If any of those showgirls were to show up on the streets of this place, they'd be beaten to death."

Niner frowned. "Ah, not Nevada—"

Atlas cut him off from what he was sure his friend was about to say. "Don't you dare say Utah."

"Then I won't. When are we deploying?"

"Wheel's up in three hours. Briefing in one."

Niner floated another loud air biscuit.

Dawson groaned. "Let me guess. Hamburgers and shakes?"

"You know it, baby."

"And you forgot your pills again, didn't you?"

"Shit happens."

"By the sounds of what I just heard, I don't doubt it. See you guys at the Unit. And Niner?"

"Yeah?"

"Get some Beano or something into you. If I hear one thunderclap during the briefing, I'm shoving a flashbang so far up your ass, you're going to be able to pull the pin with your teeth."

Niner stared at the display in the center of the dash. "Sweetheart, don't make promises you're not willing to keep."

People's Liberation Army Rocket Force Testing Range

Outside Jilantai, China

"Control, what the hell's going on?"

"It looks like you might have been spotted."

Kane didn't bother checking behind him. Instead, he kept slowly moving forward toward his ride hidden just ahead. Gunfire erupted, out of range, but the shouts grew. "Talk to me, Control. Any sign they actually see me, or are they shooting at shadows?"

"They're definitely firing in your direction, Fly Guy."

"But no signs of pursuit yet?"

"You appear out of range."

"Watch for drones."

"Roger that. The sky is showing clear."

"Keep watching. If they get a bead on me, I'm done." He continued his slow, methodical movement forward. It was highly unlikely they had a clear view of him. His ghillie suit was custom-tailored for this environment—he matched the foliage perfectly. The fact they weren't pursuing him on foot and the gunfire was sporadic at best, suggested they weren't certain as to what was seen by probably a single soldier. But drones could be deployed rapidly, and if they had infrared sensors, they would pick him up in a heartbeat.

The ridge that would put him out of their line of sight was just ahead. Ten paces. Yet he had to continue moving slowly, despite every fiber of his being demanding he make a run for it.

"Control, report."

"Still no drones. Still no signs of pursuit…stand by."

He could sense the change in tone from Leroux.

"Two vehicles emerging from underground. They're heading toward one of the secondary gates we've designated Charlie."

Kane pictured the map he had memorized. That gate was hundreds of yards away from the underground entrance. They had to head all the way there then cover uneven terrain all the way back. They weren't the immediate threat. "Copy that, Control. Let me know when they reach the gate. Keep monitoring for drones."

"Roger that, Fly Guy."

Kane inched over the embankment, his dirt bike lying in the grass not ten feet away. He stripped out of his ghillie suit then rolled it up, stuffing it into a nearby culvert before quickly squeezing a pressure point on the suit three times, triggering a chemical process that would melt the suit into a puddle of goo in the next fifteen minutes that would either be washed away by the next rain, or blown away as it dried up in the sun.

"Fly Guy, Control. We have two drones about to be deployed."

He cursed as he grabbed the bike and straddled it. He shoved the helmet over his head then started the silent electric motor and gunned it. He raced across the grass and toward a civilian road ahead. "Give me a traffic report."

"Light traffic in both directions. Be advised, the two pursuit vehicles have reached Charlie gate."

"Acknowledged." He spotted the road ahead, the traffic indeed light. He would have preferred heavy.

"One drone has deployed. ETA your position sixty seconds."

He had to change that position. He gunned it, reaching the road, and headed right, toward Yinchuan where he had stashed another vehicle. He cranked the throttle, sending him surging ahead. "Control, update."

"Second drone deployed. The two pursuing vehicles are approaching your original position. We no longer believe them to be a threat. The first drone is already at the ridgeline. The second is approaching."

"Any indication anything has eyes on me?"

"Negative indication. However, our confidence isn't high that there isn't surveillance on the road since it's so close to the base."

"We always knew that was a possibility." He raced ahead silently, the electric bike designed to not draw any attention. The weaving in and out of traffic, however, did draw the scorn of those he was impolitely sharing the road with. But they weren't his problem. If he could reach his exchange point, his chances improved dramatically, though he would likely have to enter the Underground Railroad since he had been spotted, and security would be tightened across the entire region.

The unlikeliness of him being spotted had him wondering if he actually had been, or had a nervous guard spotted movement caused by some random bit of wildlife, some oddly shaped bush shaking in the wind. He would never know, but whatever had happened had made his next 24 hours much more difficult than he had planned, and it made him thankful he had taken care of his personal business first, otherwise, Fang would have never had her virtual reunion with her parents.

The town was just ahead, less than two minutes. "Status on those drones?"

"It looks like they've spotted your ghillie suit. The two pursuit vehicles are heading toward its position. One of the drones has just left, heading toward the road."

"Let me know which way they go."

"Stand by, Fly Guy."

The more Kane heard his abbreviated callsign, the more he hated it.

Vanilla Ice would have been better.

He smirked.

Or Ice Cube.

He eased off the throttle as he reached the outskirts.

"Fly Guy, second drone has now deployed toward the road. First drone is heading in your direction. Second appears to be heading in the opposite, both traveling at high speed."

"Copy that, Control. ETA on first drone reaching my current position?"

"Less than sixty seconds."

"Copy that." He turned left then made a quick right, gunning it silently down a side lane then into an alleyway. A nondescript white Volkswagen Lavida sat parked in front of a large garbage bin. He activated the self-destruct on the bike, all the electronics instantly frying, leaving nothing to reverse-engineer. He dismounted then hoisted the bike up, tossing it into the bin and closing the lid before rapidly climbing into his ride. He cautiously rolled out of the alleyway then headed for the far end of town, keeping a wary eye out for any locals taking notice of him while he obeyed all the traffic laws, not wanting to draw any attention.

"Fly Guy, Control. The first drone has made it to the outskirts. No indication as of yet that they have any idea where to go next."

"They'll figure it out once they review the footage."

It didn't take long before he reached the outskirts of town. The road would lead him to the next town, but also to the highway.

"Fly Guy, Control, the drone is on the move again. Looks like it's heading toward your exchange point."

Kane cursed. "Copy that, Control. Requesting activation of the Railroad."

"Stand by, Fly Guy."

Kane continued out of town. He had little time before China's extensive surveillance network identified the car that had left the alleyway where he had stashed the bike, then found him.

"Fly Guy, Control. Request for railroad access granted. Directions being relayed to your phone now."

His phone vibrated in his pocket and he fished it out, bringing up the routing app. He was five minutes away from the nearest access point to the railroad. "Control, Fly Guy, I've got it. ETA five minutes. Will the engineer be there?"

"Affirmative. Engineer is already on the way. Challenge is Hammerhead. Response is White Lion."

"Hammerhead, White Lion, got it." He pressed his foot a little harder on the accelerator.

"Primary drone has left the alleyway and is headed in your direction. Pursuit vehicles have also reached the edge of town. Looks like they might know where you're headed."

Kane pressed the gas even more. This was where seconds could count, though he still couldn't draw attention to himself. He was driving one of the most popular cars sold in China with the most popular color. He had already seen two others that looked exactly like him. It was chosen for just that reason.

Kane checked the GPS. "Two minutes. Control, where's that drone?"

"Just leaving the town now, following the highway you're on."

"How long before it intercepts me?"

"We estimate sixty seconds tops, unless they get distracted by something."

"Shit. If they see the rendezvous vehicle, this whole thing is pointless." He floored it, but he was in a race he couldn't win. He had to change tactics. "Tell me I'm getting lucky."

"It doesn't look like it's gonna happen."

He cursed again. "Time for a Hail Mary." He pulled to the side of the road and hammered on his brakes, a symphony of horns the response. He stepped out and drew his Type 77B handgun. "Control, talk to me."

"The drone is coming up your side of the road. It appears to be directly over the left lane, two hundred meters out, ten meters off the ground."

"Got it." He adjusted his aim and waited for it to come within range.

"Five seconds."

He inhaled, holding his breath for a moment, then exhaled slowly as he squeezed the trigger twice. The drone jerked, both his shots finding their mark. He fired twice more and again the drone shook, this time collapsing to the ground as cars around him slammed on their brakes, terrified looks from the drivers and passengers directed at the man with a gun firing in the air.

He jumped back in his ride and floored it, leaving the traffic chaos behind, along with the prying eyes. "Talk to me, Control."

"You're clear for the moment. We're not showing any drone or aircraft activity over your position, and no known Chinese spy satellites are in range. The only thing you have to worry about at the moment are traffic cameras."

"And my station?"

"Your railroad station is a blind spot."

He turned off the highway, spotting a large overpass ahead, a white box van parked under it on the side of the road. He pulled in behind it and quickly exited, but not before popping a small canister he had been carrying in his pocket. He slammed the door shut and gas started billowing from the canister as he rushed to the box van's passenger side, the released chemical mixture designed to break down any biologics, destroying any DNA evidence or fingerprints he might have left behind. He couldn't be linked to any other mission where something might have been accidentally left.

"Hammerhead."

A tenor responded. "White Lion."

He opened the door and climbed inside, surprised to find a woman behind the wheel. She picked up on it.

"You don't think a woman can do this job?"

He chuckled. "I know women who can do it better than me. In fact, one of my previous contacts here was quite capable, and she was probably thirty years your senior."

They pulled away, merging back into traffic. "Twenty-eight years, actually."

Kane eyed the woman and his jaw dropped. "Oh my God! You're related to the Chans!"

The woman flashed him a grin. "I'm her niece, daughter of her sister-in-law."

A flood of emotions threatened to overwhelm him. "I was there when your aunt and uncle died. If you have any questions…"

The woman firmly shook her head. "No. I read the CIA's report. Your report. It told me everything I needed."

"They died heroes."

"I know."

"Did they know you were working for us?"

"No. I never told them."

"Then how did you get involved?"

"I was recruited just like they were." She pointed ahead. "Next station. There'll be several more quick swaps to break the chain."

Kane smiled at her. "It was a pleasure to meet you. I hope we work together again."

"You can count on it." She handed him a burner phone. "I'm speed dial number nine. I'm my uncle's replacement." She brought them to a stop and pointed at an SUV ahead. "You didn't think this was just coincidence, did you?"

"I suppose not."

"Good. Then you're smarter than I thought. I'll be talking to you soon if you make it out of this alive."

"I look forward to it." He stepped out and headed to the next stage of his escape, still struggling to suppress the memories.

God, I miss those two.

Chief of Iranian Affairs Office, CIA Headquarters

Langley, Virginia

Farzan sat at his desk, gripping the photo of his family that had sat there since the day he started the job. It was an older photo. His wife looked pretty much the same, but the children had grown so much they were barely recognizable, especially his daughter. She was sixteen now, so much different than the eleven-year-old delivering a toothy grin for the camera. His son had matured as well, though the difference wasn't as dramatic. He had started puberty early, and at thirteen, already appeared fifteen or sixteen.

He ran a thumb over his wife's face, tears welling, and prayed to a god he wasn't sure he believed in, his religion co-opted by the crazies, his entire country going mad and destroying his faith.

Please, God, take care of them. Protect them like I couldn't.

His cellphone vibrated, his desk amplifying the sound. He glanced at the call display. Unknown caller. Very few people had this number, which likely meant it was some scam robo-call, though due to the nature of his job, he took every call just in case.

He swiped his thumb, pressing the phone to his ear. "Hello?"

"Mr. Cyrus Farzan?"

His heart hammered, his stomach flipping as he recognized a slight accent from his former homeland. "Yes."

"It is important you listen to me very carefully. As I'm sure you're aware, we have your wife."

He caught himself before answering. He didn't know what they knew. If they were torturing her because of his cover job, there was no way he could know they had her. He stuck to the cover. "What are you talking about? Who is this?"

"Who I am is of no importance, other than the fact that I am the man who controls the fate of your wife and children."

Farzan didn't have to act, the emotions real. "Why are you doing this? Why are you holding my wife? She's done nothing!"

"That's not entirely true now, is it? She's a traitor to her country."

"She's no such thing! Just because someone moves to another country doesn't make them a traitor. They're only a traitor if they work against their old country. And even then, that's not necessarily true."

"Interesting that you should say that. Perhaps you're attempting to assuage your own guilt at being a traitor."

"I am not a traitor."

"And yet you sit in your office at CIA Headquarters, issuing orders day in and day out in an attempt to weaken the country that gave you your start."

His heart drummed rapidly. How could they possibly know who he was and what he did? At most, his wife would have given the man the cover job and this phone number, his private cell. There was a leak somewhere. Which wasn't surprising. With so many immigrants coming in from all over the world, some were bound to be plants. The CIA was actively working on the theory there was a massive fifth column of Chinese living in America, waiting to be activated for when war came, something that appeared more inevitable with each passing day.

"I don't know what you're talking about. I'm a manager at a power utility."

"No, Mr. Farzan, you're the Chief of Iranian Affairs at the Central Intelligence Agency. Don't try to deny it. Lie to me again, and I won't just have your wife beaten, I'll let some of our young men spend some quality time with her."

Bile filled his mouth at the thought of his wife being defiled. "Please don't."

"Cooperate, and that won't become necessary. Lie to me, don't follow my instructions, and not only will I send you video of what we do to your wife, but we'll do the same to your daughter."

He stifled a sob, biting down hard on his index finger. "What is it you want?"

"For now, you'll await our instructions, and you'll cease any efforts to recover your wife or family. Understood?"

He closed his eyes, the burn intense. "Yes."

"You'll be hearing from me soon."

The call ended and his shoulders slumped. He inhaled deeply, steadying his heavy heart before reaching for his desk phone. His assistant answered.

"Yes, sir?"

He hesitated. The right thing to do was to report the call. Morrison had to be informed. Yet this was his wife, his children. What they had threatened them with was horrifying, repugnant, barbaric. Yet that was what he expected from those who ran his former home. It wasn't an empty threat. They would do what they said. And that wasn't an option he was willing to risk. Especially with his sweet, innocent Tara.

"Sir?"

"Sorry, Alex. Brain fart."

He hung up the phone and stared at the photo. He could play along. But if he did, he would end up betraying his new country, the country that had done so much for him, the country he loved, the country he called home, where his children had been born.

The country he had vowed to protect.

And then there was the fact the Iranian regime couldn't be trusted. They could milk him for information for years, holding his wife and family hostage. His best hope of saving them was an extraction. And that meant taking advantage of his position and the assets already being provided by his employer.

He gripped his forehead, squeezing his eyes shut. He didn't have a choice. He had to play both sides. He would have to betray his new country to save his family from the old. The fact it made him sick to his stomach gave him some comfort.

His moral compass hadn't yet failed him.

Zhangbei County, China

Kane chowed down one last time on Mr. Wu's delectable delicacies. The railroad had worked. He had made it out of the area, and there was no evidence anyone had caught his face on camera, not that it would matter—it had been a mask. With the face any camera might have caught not his own, and instead that of a party official who might have some explaining to do, he was free to return to his cover. It would be too suspicious for Dylan Kane, insurance investigator for Shaws of London, to merely disappear and show up somewhere else in the world.

It wasn't plausible.

China was too well secured. He had to leave on time, on schedule. And it also meant sticking to habits that might have been observed. Showing up here, in the same place he had been twice before just yesterday, would be exactly what a Western businessman would do who had nothing to hide. Spies varied their routines, but right now, he wasn't a spy, so routine gave him credibility.

He finished his last morsel of maocai, savoring every chew, for this was it. He was heading back to his hotel, then to the airport. He swallowed, a satisfied sigh escaping when a hard rap on his window harshed his mellow. His training and experience had him not reaching for his weapon. People who wanted to kill you didn't knock on your window.

They just shot you through the glass.

He turned to see Fang's brother Wei glaring at him. Kane suppressed a curse. The man must have recognized the car. He lowered the window. "Yes?" he asked in Chinese, his cover speaking it fluently.

"Why were you at my parents' house yesterday?"

Kane regarded the man, the hot-headedness Fang had warned him about on full display. "I'm sorry, you'll have to be more specific. I visited a lot of homes yesterday."

This appeared to catch him off guard. "My parents. Lee Chen and Jing."

Kane shook his head with an apologetic smile. "I'm sorry. The names don't ring a bell, though I have no doubt I met with them, if you say so. There are a lot of Lees in this area, as you know."

"You're American."

"Yes, I am." He extended a hand through the window. "Dylan Kane, pleased to meet you."

The hand was taken hesitantly, weakly. There was a lot of bluster here. Nothing more.

Kane reached into his shirt pocket and produced a business card made with paper treated by a chemical that, when exposed to sunlight, would erase the lettering within half an hour. "Here's my card. I'm with Shaws of London. We're an insurance company. One of our clients has had a lawsuit filed against them for a problem with one of their fertilizers. I'm just interviewing local farmers to see who uses it, and if anyone's experienced any problems."

Wei stared at the card printed in English on one side, Chinese on the other. "My parents don't use fertilizer. They can't afford it." Wei flicked the card at him. "You're lying. You're a spy."

"Why would you say that?"

"Because my parents said nothing about this. My mother said you were there because of a lost wallet."

Kane feigned a surprised dawn of recognition. "Oh, yes! Now I remember them. No, I didn't visit them for business at all. I found your mother's wallet lying on the street. I asked a vendor if they knew where I might find her so I could return it, and they gave me directions. Your mother is a lovely woman. I'm so sorry about what's happening with your father."

"Why were you there so long?"

Kane shrugged. "I was only there a few minutes. Not long at all."

"That's not true. I spoke to my nieces and nephews. They said you were there for at least twenty minutes."

Kane chuckled. "If you're referring to the children I saw there, don't forget their age. They have no concept of time. Especially when they're seeing something fascinating."

Wei squinted at him. "Fascinating?"

Kane waved his hand in front of his own face. "When's the last time a White man came to their house?" Wei frowned and Kane started the engine. "Listen, I have to get back to my hotel then catch my flight. It's been a pleasure meeting you. And give my best to your mother and father. They're both in my prayers."

He shifted the car into gear and Wei stepped back, clearly baffled. Kane slowly pulled away with a wave and a smile then pressed the button to roll up the window. He was pretty sure he had confused the man enough for him to no longer be a problem, and despite the unexpected encounter, one good thing had come of it.

He had met his future brother-in-law.

Operations Center 3, CIA Headquarters

Langley, Virginia

Leroux stood at the heart of the operations center, his head shaking with a slight smile at the security feed showing Kane in Beijing, about to board his flight, chatting up two blondes.

Child spun in his seat. "He has to be the luckiest son of a bitch in the world."

Tong turned, no doubt to have some fun at the young man's expense. "Why's that?"

Child killed his spin. "Look at him. Everywhere he goes he has women clinging to him."

"Maybe if you weren't so fugly, women would be clinging to you too," said Therrien from the back of the room, eliciting laughter from the team.

Child's cheeks flushed, and he was about to deliver double birds when Danny Packman, openly gay and happily married, leaned over then delivered the punchline with a lisp that would have made a seventies Hollywood casting director proud.

"Oh, I don't know. I don't think he's all that bad."

Child's cheeks turned a brighter shade of red. "Umm, thanks?"

More snickers at the poor kid's expense. Leroux decided to rescue him. A message had just arrived from the Chief approving his special project. "Okay, okay. We've had our fun. And for taking it so well, Randy, I've got a special project for you from the Chief. You too, Danny." He tapped at his keyboard, sending the details of the assignment to both of them. "Check your inboxes. Get yourself a secure flex space. Report only to me or the Chief."

Packman's eyes bulged as he read the executive summary, Child's a moment later. "Holy shit! Is this serious?" asked the wunderkind.

Packman swatted him on the shoulder. "What part of 'classified' don't you understand?"

Child flinched. "Sorry."

Leroux chuckled. "This is priority one. Get yourself a flex space. Lock yourselves in it. The file indicates all the resources you have available to you. If you need anything else, let me know. And if you find something, contact me immediately. I'll come to you."

Packman rose, grabbing his personal items, then leaned closer to Leroux and lowered his voice. "Do we wanna find something?"

It was a good question, to which Leroux wasn't sure how he felt. "Look at it this way. If there is something to find, we want to find it."

Farzan Residence

Tehran, Iran

Tara woke with a start, panicking for a moment before she remembered where she was. She was in Tehran, in the heart of Iran, a country she already hated. She hadn't thought much of it one way or the other until she arrived here. It was where her parents were from. It wasn't where she was from. Anything she heard in passing about the country was always negative, especially from her mother or the news.

Everything was so unfamiliar here. The way they dressed, the way they spoke, even the smells and sounds were alien. This was a world she was entirely unfamiliar with, though she was thankful her parents had insisted she learn Farsi. If they hadn't, she would be completely lost.

There was a rap at the door, answering the question as to what had woken her.

"Time to get up! Hurry! You don't want to be late!" It was her grandmother.

She didn't know what to make of the woman. Was she mean? Was she nice but just had a curtness about her? All she knew was that, at the moment, she didn't like the woman. She didn't like any of them. She was terrified. This country had taken her mother.

"Did you hear me?"

"Yes! I'm coming!"

She scrambled out of bed, though to call it a bed would be an insult to beds. It was a bedroll, and nothing more. How could people live like this? She quickly dressed, noticing the other two beds were already empty. She walked down the hallway toward the bustle of noise and entered the main living area. All the girls were gathered at one end of the room, the men at another, including her brother, food handed about.

She headed for her brother and the room fell silent, shocked utterances and loud admonishments freezing her in place. Her brother stabbed a finger toward the women.

"Sit over there with the other women."

It was an order, and her eyes bulged, her jaw dropping at the vehemence. This wasn't her brother. Then again, the Ray she had been living with for the past year wasn't her brother. Tears flowed down her face and she scurried away. Her grandmother reached up and pulled her down beside her.

"You must always sit with the women." She reached up and pushed several tresses of hair up under her headscarf. "And you must learn to dress properly. You're no longer among the infidels. You must learn to be a good Muslim girl. Learn the Koran, learn what's expected of you so you can make your future husband happy."

Husband? What the hell was she talking about? She was sixteen and had already decided she didn't want to get married, at least not anytime soon. She wanted to finish high school, go to college, and become a doctor. A general practitioner. She wanted to take care of people over the course of their lifetime, not just during the worst day of it. It meant at least ten years of education and residency. There was no time for a husband, certainly no time for children.

It sounded as if they wanted to prepare her to be a slave to some man.

"What are you talking about?" she finally said.

"A good woman knows her place."

"Her place?"

"She is there to provide for her man, to support him. She shouldn't do anything to bring shame or embarrassment to her husband or family."

Immediately, something her mother had said popped into her head, and unfortunately, spat from her mouth. "What kind of twelfth century nonsense is that?"

Gasps erupted across the room, followed by angry shouts from not only the women, but the men as well, her own brother joining in. The verbal assault was terrifying, the anger, the hate, the insults hurled at her for being American, insulting her mother, insulting her father, some of the men threatening to beat her.

Her cousin Kaveh glared at her, delivering the worst of it. "You deserve to die like the infidel you are."

She bolted to her feet and rushed back to her room, slamming the door and dropping onto the bedroll, hugging her pillow. Her body, racked with sobs, shook as the anger down the hall continued. Why had she ever agreed to come to such a horrible place? And why was her brother not defending her?

Mom, where are you?

Sepah Command Center

Tehran, Iran

Kiana sat on an unforgiving metal seat. She had no idea where she was. They had forced a hood over her head at the airport then led her outside and shoved her into a car. She wasn't sure how far they had driven, though it wasn't too long before she was hauled out and escorted into a building where she was shoved into this seat where she had sat since.

A metal door had clanged loudly, suggesting she was in a prison cell. Sobs and wails echoed off the walls around her. She wasn't alone here. Others were suffering, the sounds of torture a constant reminder of what she had already been through and what she suspected was to come.

But why? It was obviously a mix-up. She had heard of people with the same names as others on the No Fly List having difficulties. Could this be something similar? Could another man named Cyrus Farzan work for the CIA? What had her interrogator said? That he was the Chief of Iranian Affairs? Her husband worked for the power utility. It was an important job, and he had said the Iranians might be interested in it because of their constant hacking attacks on utilities.

Yet that wasn't what was going on here. They claimed he didn't work for the power utility at all, but instead worked for the Central Intelligence Agency. It was laughable. Her husband, a spy? But no matter how many times she insisted they were wrong, they refused to believe her, refused to listen. They were convinced he was CIA and, because she was his wife, she somehow knew state secrets.

She sighed heavily. She desperately had to go to the bathroom. Add to that the fact she was starving, and oh so thirsty. Her tongue stuck to the roof of her mouth, and she forced herself to produce some saliva, something she was still thankfully capable of.

Self-pity threatened to overwhelm her. Didn't she have rights as an American? She squeezed her eyes shut. Of course she didn't have rights. Iran didn't believe in human rights, despite the fact the UN allowed them to chair a Human Rights Council meeting. It just showed how much of a joke the UN was—dictatorships, theocracies, autocracies, all telling democracies how they should live. An absolutely ridiculous cabal. While the world needed a forum in which to air grievances, unless you were a democracy in the truest of senses, you shouldn't get a vote. It was such a corrupt organization, filled with staffers from third-world countries desperate for a paycheck far larger than anything they could get back home, and the connections to collect bribes on an unprecedented scale.

A farce, as her husband had said one night after a news report on UN corruption.

In a civilized world, she would have rights, but that wasn't where she was. She was in Iran, one of the most horrific countries in the world, fueled by hatred of everything her new home represented. They had taken Islam and twisted it into something it was never meant to be.

A woman screamed for mercy, her pleas abruptly cut off, and Kiana's shoulders shook as the tears took over. What could she do? They refused to listen to her. They absolutely believed her husband was CIA. She sniffed hard. This wasn't helping. She had to be strong. Her children were out there somewhere. Her husband was stuck back home. She had to be brave for all of them, strong for all of them. She couldn't give in to self-pity. Even if the pain proved unbearable, she would have to tolerate it, to push past it.

She had to think her way through this. The Iranians were convinced there was a man with the same name as her husband who worked for the CIA. How could she convince them it was a case of mistaken identity? She didn't have her phone to show family photos.

She paused. There were family photos in her wallet. Her husband was in some of them. Did the Iranians know what her husband looked like? She frowned. If they did, surely they would have shown her a photo to prove she was lying. Then again, if they were certain of who she was, in their mind there would be no need.

What if she gave in? What if she told them what they wanted to hear, even if it was made up, even if it was a lie? Could that help?

She dismissed the foolish idea. No. The moment she admitted her husband was CIA when he wasn't, her entire family was doomed. Her eyes narrowed. She thought back on the questions she had been asked.

They were all surrounding her husband's job. Did she know he was CIA? Where did he work? What days of the week? What hours did he keep? Did he go on business trips? If he did, where and when? What car did he drive? What was the license plate? She had answered the questions she could, but it wasn't enough to satisfy her captors.

What did they expect the wife to know? Even if her husband was CIA and had told her, he wouldn't be discussing his work with her. It would all be classified. She couldn't possibly know anything important.

A thought dawned on her, and her jaw slackened. They weren't sure. That had to be it. They only suspected her husband was CIA. It would explain the questions. If she had simply admitted it at the beginning, before the torture had begun, they would have their answer, but because she continually denied it, they had to press her for details they might check. If that were the case, then perhaps there was a way to get out of this. If they weren't sure, and they were simply attempting to prove their case, perhaps if she provided them with enough information, she might prove hers.

She struggled to remember the names of some of his coworkers, but she came up blank. They mostly socialized with people they had known for years. Neighbors, friends they had made, many from her job, some from his previous jobs. She chewed her cheek. She couldn't think of anyone from his new job that she had met.

No. That wasn't true. She had met a couple in passing. At stores, sometimes someone would approach her husband. Pleasantries would be exchanged, introductions made, nothing beyond the weather ever discussed. If someone waved and she asked who it was, it was just someone from work. She never gave it a second thought.

They had enough good friends. They didn't need more. And from what he told her, his job was tremendously boring. Two men talking about power distribution over dinner while she attempted to make small talk with a woman she didn't know, or worse, a man, held no appeal. There had never been any work gatherings, no picnics, no barbecues, no Christmas parties. She had asked him about it once and he had said since it's a public utility, no one could have fun anymore because it might offend someone. She had never wondered again because he was right. Today's society was a joke where people reveled in looking for an excuse to have their feelings hurt.

She cursed. She couldn't name a single person at the utility that could vouch for her husband. But surely, if they simply called the main switchboard, they could be directed to someone who worked with him. But that wouldn't work either. She had watched enough spy movies to know that those numbers could be rerouted to trained operators at the CIA, and the Iranians would know that as well.

She inhaled sharply. If that were all true, could her husband be CIA? How would she know? He left in the morning in his own car. She assumed he was heading to the utility, but he could just as easily be heading to Langley. He usually took her calls, though sometimes he was in a meeting. And she normally dialed his cellphone or his direct office line, never calling the utility itself. She had never seen his office, never met any of his coworkers for more than two or three minutes, and those could easily be people he worked with at the CIA.

She tensed. Could the Iranians be right? Could her husband have been lying to her all these years? And if so, why? Was he ordered to, or was he doing it to protect them? An ember of anger flared in her gut.

If he was CIA, why would he ever agree to let them come here if he knew how dangerous it could be?

Morrison's Office, CIA Headquarters

Langley, Virginia

"The director is thinking of benching you for now," said Morrison.

"I don't think that's necessary," replied Farzan, a little too rapidly.

"We think you're distracted. Kyle can take over until we get this situation resolved."

Baxter agreed. "That's no problem. Cyrus, you've got your family to worry about. Let me take this load off your shoulders so you can focus on that."

Farzan protested. "You both know it's not as simple as that. With all due respect to Kyle, while he might be read-in, it's only partially in some cases, and he's not privy to all the nuances and the background wheeling and dealing that go into these ops that never make it into the file."

"If I have any questions, I'll just ask. It's not like you'll be going incommunicado."

Farzan vehemently shook his head, and Morrison resisted the urge to cock an eyebrow. "No!" snapped the man. Farzan held up a hand, bowing his head slightly. "I'm sorry. I'm just stressed. Listen, Leif, I know you're concerned, but trust me, I can do my job. It'll help distract me from what's going on."

Morrison regarded the man. "Fine. You can stay on the job for now, but I'm trusting you to tell me if you're having problems."

"Of course, Leif. I would never jeopardize any of our missions for personal reasons."

"I know you wouldn't." Morrison leaned forward. "But if I suspect there's a problem, I'm benching you. No questions asked. Agreed?"

"Agreed."

Morrison turned to Leroux, sitting quietly the entire time, working his phone. "What have you got for us?"

"Not much, I'm afraid, though we are quite certain that it was your wife that was caught on camera leaving the airport. The biometrics we've been able to gather, height, weight, and body measurement estimates, all match her file and what you provided. Her gait suggests she was in pain, though there's nothing to indicate severe torture. That's not something they would do at the airport. It'd be more psychological, a little bit of slapping and punching. They would want people to walk out under their own power. The really rough stuff happens elsewhere."

"Were you able to track them?"

"Yes. And it's as we feared. They took her to the Sepah Command Center. It's the headquarters for the Revolutionary Guard Intelligence Organization."

The start of a whimper from Farzan was cut off with a sharp inhalation. Morrison sympathized. If it were his wife, he would be feeling the same.

"We have video of them arriving then pulling into an underground garage. We've yet to see that same vehicle emerge, though others are coming and going regularly, and she could have been transferred to any one of them. Frankly, there's no way to know if she's still there, though it is highly likely. And if she's in there, then there's no way we're getting her out. A direct assault on the building is out of the question."

"And the children?" asked Morrison.

"No sign of them, but we have an asset sitting on the house. There's no evidence the authorities are involved there yet."

Farzan pinched the bridge of his nose, closing his eyes. "This keeps getting worse and worse."

"Yes, but so far, there's nothing unexpected. This is what we thought would happen once we discovered your wife had been detained."

"What are we going to do?"

Morrison replied. "We stick to the plan. We get Kane into position, and if diplomatic efforts fail, he extracts your son and daughter, then we negotiate for your wife." He gestured toward the door. "Now, if you'll excuse me, gentlemen, I have a meeting in ten minutes that I can't be late for."

Everyone rose and Morrison noted Leroux hesitating.

"Chris, hang around for a minute. I have a question to ask you."

"Yes, sir."

Farzan and Baxter left, closing the door behind them, and Morrison regarded his protégé. "I get the distinct impression you have something you're dying to say."

"Yes, sir. We may have a problem."

"What's that?"

"I found Farzan's request to remain on the job a little too desperate."

"So did I. What does that famous gut of yours tell you?"

Leroux wagged his phone. "I had Sonya run his phone. Just before he came in here, he had a six-minute conversation on his private cellphone. The call was bounced around the world several times, but we managed to trace it."

Morrison sighed. "Let me guess, Tehran?"

"Yes, sir."

Morrison cursed. "And the fact he didn't tell us…"

Leroux finished his thought. "Means he might not be playing for our side anymore."

Secure Flex Space 6C, CIA Headquarters

Langley, Virginia

Leroux entered the secure flex space, having been messaged only minutes ago by an excited Danny Packman.

We've got something.

He closed the door, the indicator by the frame confirming it was secure. He turned to Packman and Child. "What have you got?"

Packman gestured toward a screen mounted on the far wall, a personnel record displayed. "We think this is your mole."

Leroux stepped closer, reading the file, little there beyond the tombstone data and a standard employment history including a final entry, that one Ali Hassan had left the agency months before. "Why do we think he's the guy?"

"He's the one who did the vetting on the travel review request. He recommended approval."

"Any red flags?"

"Nothing. All of his personnel reports, reviews, everything, it was all perfect. His supervisors never complained, praised his work."

"There was one unusual thing," said Child. "He refused a promotion. And then, of course, there's the fact he left immediately after approving Farzan's travel review."

Leroux sat, scratching at two days' worth of growth on his chin. "Do we know where he went?"

"Not an employer, no. Wherever he went isn't government. We have a home address on his personnel file, but that's it." Child tapped at his keyboard, Google Maps appearing. He switched to Street View. "This is where he apparently lived the entire time he worked here. Definitely seems a little too coincidental. Less than six months at the Agency, refuses a promotion, which suggests he wanted to be in that particular job, and then he leaves within a week of approving what by all accounts was a travel review that never should have been."

Packman leaned back, folding his arms. "That's one hell of a long game."

"Yeah, it is. But we're assuming this is the only thing he did. He could have been doing someone else's bidding since he was hired. Let's run down his history. Give priority to anything Iranian that he dealt with, then widen the search to anything Middle Eastern, anything dealing with the traditional hotspots, and find out everywhere he's been in this damn building and order security sweeps. He could have planted listening devices, data taps, anything." Leroux rose. "Excellent work. Keep digging. And send me and the Chief that file. I think it's time Echo Team conducted a post-employment follow-up interview."

Child grinned. "Sweet!"

Approaching Hassan Residence

Tysons, Virginia

CIA Security Officer Brooklyn Tanner sat in the passenger seat of their SUV, her laptop open as she read the file on their target and examined the official plans on file with the city for the building he was last known to reside in. She was the leader of Echo Team, a CIA rapid response unit seconded to Homeland Security. Their IDs were Homeland, their vehicle was Homeland, their equipment was Homeland, but they were under the command of Langley, specifically Morrison.

They didn't get deployed often. It was a rare occasion when the FBI wasn't simply informed of a problem and they dealt with it. It could be a boring job with long stretches between the action, most of it filled with training and security assignments. But today would hopefully prove to be fun.

Mike Lyons, her second-in-command, was driving at the head of their three-vehicle convoy. "What are the chances I'm firing my gun today?"

"Zero to low. Nothing in this guy's file suggests he's dangerous. They don't even know yet if he actually did anything wrong. They just suspect he might be a mole or have been under the influence of someone. Perhaps the Iranians. But we're going to go by the book. Assume the worst, then hopefully we go home with our man in custody. No shots fired." She pointed ahead at the large apartment complex. "There it is."

"Man, that looks like a shithole," commented Chuck Hogan from the back.

Tanner twisted in her seat and scolded him mockingly. "Now, now, you know we're not allowed to call places shitholes anymore, even if they are. It upsets delicate people."

"Never had much time for snowflakes."

"What the hell is a snowflake, anyway?" asked Lyons. "Like, I know what it means today. But where did that come from?"

Tanner shrugged. "Probably because they turn into puddles of tears at the slightest hint of friction."

Lyons grinned. "I like that." He gestured out the windshield. "We're here," he announced as he pulled up in front of the building.

Tanner glanced in the side mirror to see the second vehicle with them, the third having proceeded to the rear. Her heart started pumping a little faster as she stepped out of the ride. She took in the situation from behind her ballistic sunglasses, assessing each of the score of layabouts mingling around the front entrance. Several were packing. Local gangsters. They shouldn't be an issue, not for eight heavily armed team members in special ops gear. She had no doubt they appeared as intimidating as hell.

"Echo Team Charlie, this is Echo Leader, report your status, over."

"Echo Leader, this is Echo Team Charlie Lead. We're in position, covering the rear, over."

"All teams, this is Echo Leader. Alpha Team is now entering." She and three others headed for the entrance, Baker Team covering. She addressed one of those packing with the most eyeball. "Don't worry, boys, we're not here for one of yours. Just stay out of our way."

The stereotype opened his mouth to say something that would no doubt be rap song worthy, but she cut him off with a raised finger.

"We're not who you think we are. They'll never find the body."

The punk's eyes flared with fear before he managed a response. "I ain't got no beef with you, lady."

"Good."

They entered the building as Baker Team covered the lobby. Lyons cursed, gesturing toward the bank of elevators, signs on all of them indicating they were out of service.

"Son of a bitch. Those signs look old." He looked around. "Is this where Sheldon and Leonard live?"

Carlos Lopez grinned. "Then that means Penny does too." He growled suggestively.

Tanner headed for the stairwell. "I'd tap that, though her ex-boyfriend, what's his name? All muscles, no brains? Now that's a weekend in Vegas I'd be willing to regret."

Lyons opened the door. "Yeah, I'd switch for that." He flashed a toothy smile. "Just for a weekend in Vegas. No long-term commitment to the other team."

She snorted as they hurried up to the fourth floor. She paused on the third, graffiti on the wall ahead not fitting the normal gang patterns. She adjusted her camera to make sure the artwork was visible. It appeared to be Arabic writing, a language she had no interest in learning. "Control, Echo Leader. Are you seeing this, over?"

"Affirmative, Echo Leader. Translating now."

Another voice cut in. "The first line says, 'America is Satan.' The second line, 'Death to America.'"

Leroux, Control Actual on the mission, joined the conversation. "Echo Leader, Control Actual. Advise caution. For that to be openly written suggests possible radical control of more than just an apartment unit."

"I was thinking the same thing. Put backup on standby and get a bird in the air." She approached the door. "Baker Team, Charlie Team, eyes wide. This may not be the cakewalk we were expecting. Redeploy two each to the fourth-floor stairwell, east and west."

Both team leads acknowledged, then she peered through the wire mesh reinforcing the glass of the third-floor entrance. She found it clear, then indicated for the others to proceed up to the fourth floor. She followed then looked through the window of their target floor, finding it too clear. She ignored footfalls rushing up the stairs below—it was just the redeployed team members.

Her comms squawked. "Echo Seven and Eight in position at the west entrance of the fourth-floor stairwell."

"Acknowledged." She glanced over her shoulder to see two members from Charlie Team arriving. "You two, cover our sixes. Take out anything with a weapon."

Lyons gestured at the wall. "We've got more writing here." He adjusted his camera. "Control, what does that say?"

The same voice from earlier replied, "Infidel-free zone."

Tanner frowned. "Lovely. Better roll that backup."

Leroux cut in. "Already rolling. ETA, six minutes by chopper. Additional units rolling by ground, fifteen minutes ETA."

"Echo Leader, Baker Leader. We just had someone bolt. Middle Eastern male, Ayatollah beard."

"Were you able to apprehend?"

"Negative. Looks like he was tipped off by our homeboys outside."

Tanner cursed. "Control, Echo Leader. We may have been made. We're proceeding with the mission, over."

"Acknowledged. Helo ETA, five minutes."

"Acknowledged." Tanner opened the door and surged down the hallway toward their target's last known address. She took up position on one side of the door, Lyons on the opposite, Hogan covering their six, Lopez manning the battering ram. "Three, two, one, breach, breach, breach," she whispered.

Lopez swung the battering ram and grunted as the door splintered but didn't give. He cursed. "It's reinforced." He swung again, but there were shouts now on the other side as the door continued to hold.

"C4!" ordered Tanner.

Lyons grabbed a small package off his utility belt and slapped it on the lock, shoving a detonator into the malleable explosive. "Fire in the hole!"

Everyone stepped back and turned away. The explosion tore apart the door, the sound deafening in the confined space of the hallway, and Tanner turned to see Lyons' handiwork. "Homeland Security, executing a search warrant!" she shouted as she stepped inside.

A man lay in the entranceway, badly bloodied, his head probably pressed against the door when the charge detonated. He reached for an AK-47 lying beside him and she put two rounds in his chest after confirming he wasn't who they were after. They needed their target alive for interrogation, though she suspected that wouldn't be his first choice. She moved in deeper, her MP5 raised, Lyons beside her.

Something moved ahead through the dust and debris and the dim lighting. It appeared all the windows were covered with blackout curtains, the only light from several lamps. The silhouette ahead swung a weapon toward them and she took the target out. He dropped and she advanced as Lyons and Lopez cleared the bathroom to the left. No shots fired. They continued forward, Hogan covering the door behind them.

Gunshots from an AK rang out from their left and Lyons grunted, dropping to the ground. Tanner spun, putting half a dozen rounds in the man who had stepped out of a bedroom. She advanced, pointing at Lyons. "Check him!"

Lopez dropped beside the downed Lyons. "You okay, dude?"

Lyons winced. "Caught one in the vest. I'll live. Cover her."

Lopez followed Tanner toward the door to the lone bedroom in the apartment. It was slightly ajar, but she could hear voices inside. "Come out with your hands up and you live! Otherwise, you're going to discover what the opposite of Jannah is in the next sixty seconds."

Instead of surrender, she received the standard nutbar greeting, shouts of Allahu Akbar giving them their answer.

"You take left, I'll take right," she said to Lopez as Lyons pushed to his feet. Tanner tossed a flashbang into the room and closed her eyes, her Sonic Defender earbuds protecting her from the din of the detonation. Cries rang out inside and she rushed in, Lopez slightly behind her. Two men were gripping their ears on the far wall. She recognized the one on the right. "Target on the right." She fired twice, eliminating the man on the left, then stepped forward and tore the AK-47 out of their target's hand before sweeping his legs out from under him. He hit the ground with a groan, and she aimed the muzzle of her submachine gun against the man's skull. "Twitch, and I'm adding holes to that empty skull of yours."

Lopez zip-tied the man's hands and feet. She stepped back, sucking in a deep breath, her heart pounding from the effort and excitement as she activated her comms. "Control, Echo Leader, we have the target secured and alive, over."

"Copy that, Echo Leader. Good work. Helo is landing at your location in sixty."

Hogan shouted from the doorway. "We've got a problem!"

Gunfire erupted and Tanner cursed. "Control, get that backup up here now!"

Operations Center 3, CIA Headquarters

Langley, Virginia

Leroux cursed as helmet cam footage from Echo Team's op showed doors opening in the hallway, armed hostiles emerging, opening fire at one of the team members. He turned to Tong. "Notify the locals of the situation. We're going to need a perimeter set up. Tell them we have an active terrorist incident in that building on the fourth floor. Unknown number of hostiles. Shots fired. Have them activate their emergency plan for this eventuality. Contact Homeland, tell them what's going on. We need response teams now."

"On it," replied Tong as Leroux sent a message to Morrison, notifying him of the Charlie Foxtrot. He cursed again as Hogan's camera feed showed them nothing but a blown-apart door as he took cover. The live audio continued to play overhead on the ops center speakers, heavy gunfire, none of it MP5s, revealing the situation as dire.

"If they have explosives…" muttered Therrien.

"This is Foxtrot Team Lead. Approaching fourth floor now from the east and west stairwells."

"Acknowledged, over," replied Tanner.

Two members of Tanner's team covering the stairwells responded between bursts of gunfire.

"Echo Zero-Five, Control Actual, can you give us a visual on the hallway, over?"

"Stand by, Control." A hand momentarily covered the helmet camera's lens, and the angle changed before the image went haywire as the device was removed and attached to an extendible rod. "This is Echo Zero-Five. Let's hope this doesn't get shot out of my hand." A shattered door filled the screen then was replaced with a shot of the hallway, revealing four hostiles. The camera jerked back and the angle changed to the opposite direction, revealing three more.

"Did you get that?"

"Affirmative, Zero-Five. We got what we needed. Take cover."

"No shit," was the muttered reply, causing a few exchanged smiles.

"Echo Team, Control Actual, you have four targets to the left of the apartment door, all armed with assault rifles, all directing fire toward the door. You have three hostiles in the clear to the right of the door, all with assault rifles. Stairwell teams, it appears they are not aware you're there. Take them out."

"Acknowledged, Control," came two replies, and they all watched with bated breath, one of his team switching the display to show the stairwell teams' helmet cams.

Echo Team's fate was about to be decided.

Hassan Residence

Tysons, Virginia

Tanner hauled their target to his feet and noticed in addition to the maniacal eyes, he also had a shit-eating grin. "What are you smiling about? Your days as a free man are over."

He cackled. "You're all dead"

"I think you're overestimating what your buddies in the hallway are capable of."

"You'll burn in hell, while we all are blessed with entrance into Jannah!"

Tanner tensed at the mention of the Muslim version of Heaven, by all accounts a paradise reserved for men where they could enjoy their 72 virgins. What a woman would want with 72 inexperienced men fumbling around struggling to find where to stick things, she had no idea. "What the hell are you talking about?"

The man's eyes darted up and she followed, cursing at what was revealed. An extensive network of wires leading to packages secured to the ceiling. Explosives. She activated her comms. "This is Echo Leader. This entire place is wired. Evac now. I repeat, evac now!"

Gunfire rattled in the hallway, drowning out her order as the stairwell teams engaged and her prisoner's laughter grew. She grabbed him, shoving him toward the window, gaining speed with each pump of her legs, then hurled him through. The curtains billowed then the glass shattered, his eyes bulging with surprise as she dove forward, shoving him into the daylight beyond.

He screamed in terror as she gripped his shirt, everything blocked from sight by the curtain enveloping them. There was a four-story drop, and she had to keep him between her and the ground if she hoped to survive unscathed.

Either way, this was gonna hurt.

Lyons gasped, exchanging a look with Lopez. "Everybody out!" he shouted as he followed his team lead through the window, Lopez on his heels as the gunfire in the hallway dwindled. The all-clear was announced over his comms as he launched himself through the shattered window, Control repeating Tanner's last orders, the stairwell teams acknowledging when a massive explosion tore at his heels, flipping him end over end with the force, giving him a view of the horror above as flaming debris blasted out the entire fourth floor of the residential building. And as he hurtled toward the ground below, saying a silent prayer for God to take care of his family should he not survive., Lopez shouted from above.

"This is gonna suck!"

And Lyons found himself laughing.

Indeed, it is.

Tanner hit the ground hard, but thankfully, she had managed to keep the meat cushion between her and the concrete, his cry of terror cut short at the moment of impact. Her knee smacked the ground hard, and she knew instantly it had been shattered. She was out of commission for a while, assuming she survived this. After all, there could be a building about to pancake on her ass.

Something hit the ground to her right, only a few feet away. The grunt, then the string of moaned curses, revealed it was Lyons. Another thud to her left was followed by nothing, and bile filled her mouth as she battled her way out of the heavy curtains, finally seeing sky. She stared down to find her target underneath her, his eyes wide with death. He hadn't survived, and right now, she didn't care that the mission was a failure.

Lyons groaned beside her and she pushed to her knees, glancing over at him.

"You okay?"

"I'll live, I think."

She spun to her left and scrambled over to Lopez, lying still on the concrete beside them, his helmet still firmly in place. She checked for a pulse. It was there, steady and strong. She smacked his cheek. "Yo, wake up." Nothing. She smacked it again. "Wake up, you lazy bastard. I don't wanna have to fill out paperwork on you."

There was a groan and she smiled, then gasped in agony as she fell to her side, her knee finally reminding her it was shattered. She lay on her back and activated her comms. "Echo Team, Echo Leader, report by the numbers."

There was a burst of static and Lyons reported in over the comms for the benefit of the others. "Zero-Two, reporting."

Lopez groaned.

"Zero-Three with me," she said on his behalf.

"Zero-Four reporting."

Then silence.

Tanner stared up at the flames and heavy black smoke billowing out of the fourth floor. "Zero-Five, report."

Still nothing.

Hogan had been at the door in the hallway. If anyone wasn't going to make it…

"Zero-five, report!"

Again, nothing.

"Does anyone have eyes on Zero-Five?"

A string of negatives.

"Control, this is Echo Leader. Do you have a status on Zero-Five?"

"Negative, Echo Leader," replied Leroux. "His helmet cam is offline as are his vitals. Our last image showed him running down the hallway toward the west stairwell when the explosion occurred."

She cursed, her chest aching. "Echo Team, continue sound off." Six through twelve rapidly reported they were still in the game, Foxtrot team following suit. Footfalls rapidly approached as sirens blared, the whine of a chopper powering up nearby reminding her of their highly volatile situation. "Echo and Foxtrot teams, secure the area. I want all evacuees corralled. Nobody gets out of here. Every single person in this building is a suspect right now. Control, notify LEOs of the same."

"Already being done, Echo Leader. What's your status? Your vitals are showing a very rapid heartbeat."

She rolled her eyes at Lyons, who had managed to sit up and remove his helmet, giving it a kiss before wiping the debris from it.

"I just jumped out of an exploding building, fell four stories, and used our target to save my ass. Unfortunately, my knee didn't get the memo. I'm gonna need medical attention."

"Copy that, Echo leader. How are Echo Two and Three."

Lyons held up his hand, wagging it side to side, and Lopez just stared up at her, still in a daze.

"Both are going to need medical attention."

"Copy that, Echo Leader. Local paramedics have arrived just north of your position. We're waiting for the scene to be secured before we allow them in."

"Copy that, Control. I think we're just gonna lay here for a while and hurt."

Leroux chuckled. "You do that. I hate to ask, but what's the status on our target?"

She rolled her head to the side, a large pool of blood staining the curtains still under the man. "Well, if you believe him, he's working on his first virgin."

"Understood, Echo Leader. You sit tight. We'll get help to you as soon as we can."

She gave a thumbs-up that her helmet cam should catch, then slumped back onto the ground.

Well, that was a Charlie Foxtrot.

Operations Center 3, CIA Headquarters

Langley, Virginia

Leroux stood as the inner door to the operation center hissed open and Morrison burst inside, his eyes immediately on the massive display. "What the hell happened?"

"It looks like they had the entire floor rigged with explosives."

"Status on our personnel?"

"Three injured including Echo Leader. I'm guessing bumps and bruises on a lot of the others, but at the moment we have no contact with Echo Five."

"Who's that?"

"Chuck Hogan."

Morrison cursed. "What do we know?"

"Helmet cam showed him running down the hallway toward the west stairwell when the explosion occurred. After that, nothing. East and west stairwell teams had already begun evacuating down the stairs when the explosion hit. It looks like it was designed to take out anybody in the apartments on that floor or in the hallway."

"Every apartment?"

"We don't know that yet. It looks like it was designed to not only kill themselves but to take out as much law enforcement as possible that might have been on their floor."

Child sat, staring at the display. "It's never gonna end with these people, is it?"

Morrison glanced back at the young man. "Right now, I don't see any way. All we can do is keep doing our jobs and hope someday they come to their senses."

Child scoffed. "Not in our lifetimes."

Leroux had to agree. This type of fanaticism would take decades, if not centuries, to stamp out if it ever could be. Until there was a reformation in Islam, it would never happen.

Morrison closed his eyes and pinched the bridge of his nose. "Status on our target?"

"They had him in custody when the detonation occurred. Echo Leader has confirmed he's dead."

Morrison cursed. "All right. For the moment, let's work under the assumption that anything incriminating was probably destroyed in that explosion, but we'll have our people go over that entire place with a fine-toothed comb just to make sure. But I think we can confirm at least one thing."

Leroux agreed. "He was definitely our mole."

"Absolutely. Now we need to figure out how the hell he got past all the security checks, and how it appears a rather large cell of Islamic fundamentalist terrorists managed to operate right under our noses, not fifteen minutes from what's supposed to be the most capable intelligence organization in the world."

En Route to Uzbekistan

Command Sergeant Major Burt "Big Dog" Dawson sat quietly on board the C-5M Super Galaxy, transporting his team and their equipment for a possible deployment into Iran. The prospect of killing some revolutionary guards excited him. These were brutal bastards who often killed for fun and certainly tortured for it. Yet despite how he felt, he had to keep those emotions in check as the commander of Bravo Team, in his entirely biased opinion, the best that America's Delta Force had to offer.

Officially, they were First Special Forces Operational Detachment-Delta, but it was fun to go by the moniker popularized by the great Chuck Norris and the legendary Lee Marvin. And while the team did enjoy the movie and its sequels, tearing them apart for their inaccuracies, he preferred Chuck Norris in classics like the Missing in Action movies, and Lee Marvin in the Dirty Dozen. The team was big on the classics, especially the action movies from the eighties, or more recent movies by the same stars. In fact, tonight they were supposed to watch Stallone in

Cobra and Schwarzenegger in Commando, Niner picking them because they both started with the letter C.

Much thought, indeed.

The TV on their C-5 was on the fritz, so the boys were acting out their favorite parts. He cracked his eyes and smiled to see Atlas holding Niner upside down by the ankle, reciting one of his favorite scenes from Commando, Atlas' impossibly deep voice making Arnold's seem feminine by comparison.

"I lied." Atlas released his grip and Niner hit the deck, feigning a fading scream as his character fell to his death over the side of a cliff, then Schwarzenegger climbed back into a Porsche that drove away with none of the damage from the previous scene. Continuity errors. They were the most fun to spot. A half-eaten bagel suddenly whole again, a cut in the cheek gone, an open curtain closed, or a Porsche with so much damage it would be written off, driving away in perfect condition.

Much more fun than finding technical errors.

No movie, no book, no TV show got it completely right, despite the best efforts of their creators.

His comms squawked and his commanding officer, Colonel Thomas Clancy, filled his ear. "Zero-One, Control Actual. Come in, over."

He sat up straight. "This is Zero-One. Go ahead."

"Zero-One, I have an update on your current mission. Details have been sent to your secure inbox. There's just been an incident in Virginia. CIA was tracking a possible mole involved in this situation. Turns out Echo Team stumbled upon a terror cell. One team member has been confirmed dead, several injured. An unknown number of terrorists are dead, and civilians are assumed among the casualties. It's a developing situation. However, it's Langley's opinion, mine as well, that this confirms there is nothing innocent or coincidental about Kiana Farzan's detention in Iran. It's now believed that the travel review approved by the CIA security branch was not approved in error, but was approved intentionally to get Farzan's family into Iran, likely to be used as leverage over him."

"Copy that, Control. Does this change the mission parameters?"

"Not at the moment. However, if this is part of some grand plan by the Iranians, be prepared for the extraction to be much more complicated than originally expected."

"Understood, Control. I'll read the package and brief the team."

"Copy that. Control, out."

All eyes were on him, the movie night substitute put on hold.

"What's up, BD?" asked Master Sergeant Mike "Red" Belme, Dawson's second-in-command and best friend.

Dawson opened the mission report on his tablet. "Update from the colonel. There was an incident outside of Langley. Echo Team was sent in on a mole hunt, ended up finding a den of fundamentalists instead. At least one of their team is dead, some are wounded, unknown number of hostiles and civilians dead." He continued to scan the file. "Looks like they had rigged the entire fourth floor of a residential complex. Looks like a real Charlie Foxtrot."

"So, what does this mean for the mission?" asked Sergeant Will "Spock" Lightman.

"It means none of this is coincidence, none of this is routine. These terrorists somehow managed to get a mole deep inside the CIA, who then okayed a travel review for a senior exec that never should have been approved. It means this whole damn shit show has been planned meticulously right from the get-go."

Atlas grunted. "So that means any extraction isn't going to be easy peasy."

"Exactly. We could be going up against the Revolutionary Guard with two children under our protection."

Niner sighed. "That doesn't sound like fun at all."

Imam Khomeini International Airport

Tehran, Iran

Kane cleared customs with little effort. Today, he wasn't an insurance investigator for Shaw's of London. That cover wouldn't work here. Instead, he was traveling on a diplomatic passport as a Swiss Embassy staffer. If the Swiss knew, they would be pissed. But what they didn't know couldn't hurt them.

If he had arrived sooner when Kiana Farzan had still been here, he would have done something to have himself flagged for further scrutiny. But now that she was gone, moved to IRGC Headquarters, there was no benefit to him remaining in the airport, one of the most heavily-secured buildings accessible to civilians in this totalitarian state.

Kiana was no longer his priority. The children were. But before he could address that situation, he had to solidify his cover. He had no doubt he was being followed. He hailed a cab, tossed his luggage in the trunk, then climbed in the back seat.

"Swiss Embassy, please."

The cabbie pulled away from the curb, and Kane pressed a finger against the left arm of his sunglasses, triggering a rear-facing camera embedded in the arm wrapped around his ear. The image displayed on the inside of the heavily-customized Ray-Ban Aviators, giving him a view out the back window. An unremarkable black sedan pulled out, staying several car lengths behind them, two men with thick mustaches in business suits in plain view. Their demeanor and lack of conversation blared state security, and when the passenger raised a radio to his lips, his suspicions were confirmed. He was being followed, though he was certain it wasn't because they suspected him specifically of being up to no good, instead because nearly every foreigner that entered, especially white males of his age, were as a matter of routine.

"Where are you from?" asked the driver as they merged into traffic on the Tehran-Qom Freeway.

"Switzerland. A little town you've probably never heard of called Lauterbrunnen."

"Switzerland. The Alps. I've seen pictures. Very beautiful. And you're right, I've never heard of that place. Are you here on business or pleasure?"

"A little bit of both, I hope. I'm going to be working at the embassy, temporarily, just a two-week assignment. Hopefully it'll lead to something more. Your English is excellent, by the way. Where'd you learn it?"

"My mother taught me when I was a child. She worked for a British family before the revolution. I took it in school as well. Then of course television and movies. A lot of the cabbies, we get together and speak

English to practice. Most foreigners who come here speak it, so it helps with our business."

"Well, keep it up. So, where can a European go here to find good food where he might be welcome?"

His cabbie glanced in the mirror. "I'm afraid things aren't very welcoming here anymore for foreigners like yourself. It's not that we Iranians necessarily have a problem with you. Some do, don't get me wrong, but most are afraid of the authorities, so a lot want to put on a show in case they're being watched."

Kane was surprised at the candor. The man was taking a risk by stating a fact the government wouldn't like expressed. "I don't mean to be indelicate, but should you be saying something like that to me?"

The man snorted. "If you were working for state security, they wouldn't be following us right now."

Kane faked a surprised look and made to turn his head when the cabbie hissed, "Don't look, you fool!"

"Sorry. Are you sure we're being followed?"

"No. *We're* not being followed, *you're* being followed. Don't worry, it's routine. As soon as I drop you off at the embassy, they'll return to the airport and follow the next young white male that hails a cab. I suggest you listen to your orientation briefing very carefully and follow all their recommendations. Your Swiss passport should protect you from men like that and the police on the street, but some of the more, shall we say, enthusiastic residents, will just see you as an American."

"Yeah, I suppose you're right. Maybe it's best I just stay inside the embassy and the apartment they've arranged for me."

The driver pointed. "The embassy's just ahead." He fished a business card out of a holder attached to the dash and handed it back. "My name is Dariush. You need to go anywhere, you call me. Anytime, anyplace. I'll make sure you're not harassed."

Kane took the card. "I appreciate that."

They pulled up to the front gate and Kane handed the man a wad of cash. Dariush took the money then extended a hand. "I hope you enjoy your stay in our country, my friend." He smirked. "Don't look now, but your shadow just parked down the street a bit. My guess is as soon as you're through the gates, they'll leave."

"Thanks for the advice." Kane climbed out and the trunk popped. He grabbed his bag and shut the lid with his knuckles before rapping twice, making certain he didn't leave any fingerprints should the security detail take a greater interest in him. Dariush pulled away and Kane approached the front gate, holding up his Swiss passport. He was allowed through then spent the next hour waiting in line to register himself as being in the country, as all travelers were recommended to do, but rarely did.

The detail assigned to him should be long gone, and if Iranian security at the airport ran his name, they would find it added to the list of registered embassy workers, Langley having inserted it before he arrived. There should be no reason for them to watch him, though, like Dariush had said, he still had to be careful. This was an extremely anti-American country, and why he had laid on a German accent. Thick. He had a Swiss pin on the lapel of his suit that he could tap and say "Soo-eess," the Farsi word for Switzerland.

He boarded the embassy shuttle parked inside the courtyard. It would take him to a residential compound reserved for foreigners where his local contact would meet him, then this op would truly begin.

One where he hoped the brain trust in Langley would come up with something more creative than bicycles to the border.

En Route to Farzan Residence

Tehran, Iran

To say Tara was miserable would be an understatement of colossal proportions. She hadn't even been here two days and absolutely despised everything about Iran. She didn't like the country, the people, the food, the smells, the sounds, everything. She hated it. She wanted to go home desperately, back to civilization. All morning, all she had heard were diatribes against her home, not only from her own relatives, her own family, but at the mosque where everyone had gone for morning prayers.

Prayers were over, and now they had joined a rally on the street. The chants of "Death to America" had her trembling with fear, especially when her family and her own brother joined in. Who was he? What had he become? It was terrifying to think he could change so much so quickly, and it wasn't an act—he wasn't one to just go along with something because it was expected of him. He always rebelled against such things, but here he was, embracing the hate, the zealotry. She could see the religious fervor in his eyes as he pumped his fist into the air, condemning the country that had given him everything he had.

He had drunk the Kool-Aid, as her father might say, and could no longer be relied upon to help her, to protect her. Her mother had been taken by the authorities, her brother by an interpretation of his religion no sane person could find reasonable. She was alone, terrified of what was happening. They were supposed to be gone for two weeks. It had taken them a day-and-a-half to get here, and the return would take the same.

She had a little more than a week left.

The question was, would they be allowed to leave? Would her brother even want to go? Would her mother be freed to come home with them? Would they even let her herself go, or were they intending to keep her here so she could be married off to one of these masochists? She had already caught Kaveh eying her, lust in his eyes. She was only sixteen. It was disgusting. She liked boys, was even curious about sex. Very curious. Some of her friends had already done it, but so far she had managed to remain a virgin despite society's pressures. For God's sake, what was wrong with America when a song called Wet-Ass Pussy reigned on the charts and was played live at the Grammys? Perhaps the Iranians had it right. Perhaps America should die, along with its already dead morals.

A gunshot rang out, then several more, the distinct rattle of a machine gun causing her to flinch. She didn't care how morally bankrupt America was. Right now, it was the only place she wanted to be. She wanted to go home with her mother and brother, home to her father, to her home.

The crowd cheered with renewed vigor as sporadic bursts of gunfire continued, machine guns raised into the air, and she was reminded of something her father had said once while watching a news report. "Don't these morons realize that bullets come down?" It had her wondering if somewhere in the city, somebody was getting killed by the bullets fired in celebration here.

She stared at her brother, catching his eye as he shouted, "Death to America," and he grinned at her before returning his attention to the crowd gathered ahead in a circle, burning an American flag. He was lost, and if she had to go home alone, she would, for she had no doubt he would abandon her if the opportunity arose. And her mother would want her to go. She had to take any opportunity to save herself from the insanity she found herself in.

She returned to her previous horrifying thought. Would they even let her go? They had her passport. They had her phone. They had her plane ticket. She glanced over at her grandmother, dressed head to toe in black, only her eyes visible and her bare hands, one of them clenched at her side, the other thrust in the air. These weren't the people her parents thought they were, not anymore. She was in serious danger here. She had to escape, but to where, and how? She squeezed her eyes shut, and reached up to wipe them dry, the unfamiliar clothing she was wrapped in feeling far heavier than when told to put it on this morning.

They've already made me look like them. How much longer will it be before I am one?

Diplomatic Quarters

Tehran, Iran

Kane climbed in the passenger seat and closed the door as his contact, Babak Shadmani, whom he had worked with in the past, smiled at him. Kane returned it. "Long time, no see. What's it been, about a year?"

Shadmani pulled away, merging into the light residential traffic. "At least. Good to see you're still alive."

"You too." Kane jerked a thumb at the blue plastic bag covering his window. "I seem to remember your car being in better shape."

"Ha! Poor man's window tinting. The window actually works. I just have it down and the bag in place so that nobody can see you from that side." He pointed at the bare pin of the window crank. "I just tell them it broke off. It's actually in the glove compartment if we need it."

"You're not worried that if you're searched that might raise questions?"

Shadmani shrugged. "My guess is they'd be more concerned about the pistol I have in there."

Kane snorted. "Yeah, that would probably make them forget the crank."

Shadmani jerked a thumb over his shoulder at the back seat. "Care package from Langley."

Kane twisted around and grabbed the backpack sitting on the seat. "Everything I requested?"

"Yes, I inventoried it myself. Do they really expect us to extract two teenage Americans?"

"Quite possibly. We're not sure yet what's going on. You've confirmed they're at the grandparents' residence?"

"Yes, visually this morning when the family went for prayers. I have some rather nice photos if you'd like to see them." Shadmani grinned at his phone, unlocking it, then handed it over.

Kane opened the photo app and started flipping through. He zoomed in on a shot of the daughter. "She doesn't look too happy."

"Not at all. And the way they were treating her tells me they're not too happy with her either. That grandmother's a tyrant, if you ask me. And look at how all the women are dressed. These are full supporters of the revolution, not those just keeping a low profile while they try to survive."

"My briefing indicated Farzan thought his mother was just saying what she did because she was afraid they were being listened to."

Shadmani dismissed the idea. "No, I think he's mistaken about his mother. I think she's gone fully over to the dark side, as has the entire family. The only one I'm not sure about is the grandfather. He's not with them, nor is any of his side of the family. It's all hers."

"So, you think he kept everything under control until he got sick?"

"That's what I'm thinking. My cousin lives not far from them. He said as soon as the old man fell ill, her family moved in. Apparently, it's the talk of the neighborhood."

Kane pursed his lips as they came to a red light. He adjusted the sun visor so it blocked most of his face from any cameras that might be at the intersection. "You know, this is sounding more and more like a set-up to me."

Shadmani snapped his fingers. "That's exactly what I was thinking. But how could they know Farzan is CIA?"

"They wouldn't. He didn't even tell his wife. She thinks he works at the power company. There's no way he'd tell his parents if he didn't tell her. My guess is, if they are as committed to the regime as you suspect, then they probably thought they could earn brownie points if they managed to get some of those who had left for America to come back. They may have even been told to do it, if my latest briefing is accurate."

"You mean that the Iranians might know he's CIA?"

"Exactly."

"Well, if that's the case, then this changes everything, doesn't it?"

"It does. We might have no choice but to extract those kids as quickly as possible."

"You haven't seen the son yet, have you?"

"Why?"

"Just take a look. There's no way in hell he's coming with us voluntarily."

En Route to Farzan Residence

Tehran, Iran

Tara couldn't help but tremble. She was terrified, afraid to say anything, afraid to look at anybody. The protest march was over and they were now walking back to her grandparents' home. But the cult-like insanity she had just witnessed continued to grip the group, including her brother. Eyes were wide, nostrils flared, and chests still heaved, the conversation loud and filled with hate toward America, the West, Christians, and Jews.

Every time someone spat out something about her home, glares were directed at her. She kept her head down, saying nothing, fearing any response, even eye contact, could trigger a physical rebuke. And her brother, participating fully, adding his own insults, broke her heart. Their cousin, Kaveh, had his arm wrapped around her brother's shoulders the entire way home. He was the problem. He was who had converted her poor brother.

And she feared it was already too late.

Ray would never listen to her. She could never reason with him, not when there was a chorus against her. Her father had called last night and they had spoken briefly, though before she realized what surrounded her. Last night, she had been scared for her mother, but not for a moment thought she was in danger herself, especially from her own family.

If he called again tonight like he promised, would they let her speak to him? And if they did, how could she tell him about what had happened to her brother, about the zealotry on display? How could she tell him of her suspicions that her own family had no intention of letting her go home? Her shoulders slumped. She had no way to communicate her fears. And would he even believe her? After all, they were simply fears. This was a different place, a different world, completely alien to her. Could she be seeing things that weren't there? Was it all in her head?

Her father had enough things to worry about, what with her mother being in the hands of the authorities here. Before she added to his troubles, she had to know for sure. And there was still time. But how could she figure out the truth? Perhaps the easiest would be to talk to her brother, to find out what he was thinking.

They reached the home, and as soon as they were inside, the oppressive outfits the women wore came off. Food was laid out, the men gathering around one service, the women another, though not before the men were served. This subservient society, when it came to women, was probably what disgusted her the most. She had been taught by both her mother and father that men and women were equal, and while things weren't perfect in America, when it came to equal rights, at least most were trying, despite recent evidence to the contrary.

She ate in silence. She was starving. She hadn't eaten much yesterday, her mother's situation killing her appetite. But today, her body demanded to be fed, and despite much of what was on offer being unfamiliar, she found herself enjoying the different flavors, some of them reminding her of dishes her mother would sometimes cook.

"So, what did you think of morning prayers?" her grandmother asked.

Tara's stomach flipped. She shrugged.

"Speak, child."

Tara flinched at the curt tone. "It was all right, I guess."

"All right, you guess? When was the last time you went to prayers?"

Another shrug. "I don't know, a couple of years ago, maybe."

Gasps erupted from the gathered women, her grandmother tilting her head back, begging Allah's forgiveness for her son's delinquency in her granddaughter's education.

"This is terrible! I knew my son had strayed, but I didn't realize how far. This is unforgivable." She smiled, patting Tara on the back. "But don't you worry. We'll make things right."

Tara took a chance, though with guardrails. "I'm eager to learn, grandmother, but I'm returning home soon with my brother and hopefully my mother."

"We'll see, child. We'll see."

Her chest tightened as her heart hammered, her stomach in knots. This was the confirmation. She wisely said nothing, instead grabbing some chelo kabab and stuffing it into her mouth, praying no one had noticed her trembling hand. These people had no intention of letting her leave.

But how could she possibly let her father know?

Outside the Farzan Residence

Tehran, Iran

Kane was not a hairy guy. He had it in the appropriate places, but he by no means was a Chewbacca like some men. Despite that, he could grow a good beard and mustache, but it took time. China preferred people to be clean-shaven, so when he was there, he made sure his face was smooth, which meant he had 24 hours of growth, not enough to blend in with this population. There were mad beards around here, but mostly mustaches, thick and luxurious, groomed for years with pride.

He was weeks away from anything respectable.

Instead, local attire, including a red and white checkered *chafiyeh*, similar to the Palestinian *kaffiyeh*, wide-rimmed sunglasses, and a good base tan was his disguise. Right now, he was smoking a cigarette with his contact, Shadmani, both of them leaning against a wall down the street from the Farzan residence. He took another drag. It was a disgusting habit that fortunately he had never become addicted to, despite sometimes being undercover in countries where everyone smoked. He just couldn't understand the appeal unless you were addicted, then it was no longer appeal, it was an insatiable need to satisfy a craving that you couldn't control, a thirst never quenched.

And why would anyone want to stink?

Smokers today, back home, stuck out like sore thumbs. You could smell it on their clothing. And he knew from experience, kissing a smoker was disgusting, no matter how attractive she was. Yet he wasn't one to judge. Everyone had their vices, their addictions, the things they would love to change about themselves. For years, between missions, he had drowned himself in alcohol and any number of drugs, in an attempt to escape a painful memory he had finally come to terms with after meeting and falling in love with Fang. She had helped turn his life around, and even if he lost her, like he thought he once had, he had no intention of returning to that lifestyle.

Though, as they say, the road to Hell was paved with good intentions.

A young man, perhaps in his mid-twenties, emerged from the residence, sporting a beard bin Laden would have been envious of. Kane tapped the frames of his sunglasses, taking a photo that would be transmitted back to Langley in case the video stream was interrupted due to a poor connection. "So, who do we have here?"

Shadmani lit another cigarette with his previous, Kane's contact here a chain smoker and a true addict. "That's the grandmother's nephew, Kaveh Jafari. He's a piece of work, full-on zealot. Mossad managed to hack the Iranian military personnel database last year, so we have files on pretty much anyone who served or is serving, thanks to our agreement with them. This guy served three years and was dishonorably discharged for beating his unit's Imam nearly to death. When they asked him why, he said the Imam wasn't forceful enough in his condemnation of Jews and Christians. Like I said, a real piece of work."

"And this is the one we believe the son's been corresponding with for about a year?"

"Yes."

"That explains the eyes that I saw in those photos. He's gone full Kool-Aid. And if this has been going on for over a year, a few minutes of reasoning with him is going to make no difference. We're probably gonna have to drug him and transport him like luggage."

Shadmani folded his arms, his cigarette dangling from his lips, bobbing up and down as he spoke. "That's doable, but it's going to make things more difficult, especially at the other end. Do we have any idea where the other end is yet?"

"No. Though I suspect it'll be in the Caspian Sea. The Gulf is too far from here. Get to the coast, rendezvous with a Zodiac, lifted out by chopper at sea, and back to Uzbekistan. Piece of cake."

"Sounds expensive."

"It is. And the only reason we would do it is because the CIA is afraid one of their own is or could become compromised. The shit Farzan knows could set us back years if he were to give an info dump to the Iranians in exchange for his wife and kids."

"My briefing didn't tell me what this guy did."

"Which means they don't want you to know."

Shadmani held up a hand. "I'm not asking what he does. The fact they haven't told me tells me it's something important and way above my pay grade. But I'll ask you this. Is all this worth it?"

"Absolutely. Forget who he works for or how important he is. These are kids. We're quite sure the daughter is 100% innocent. The son has been brainwashed and can still be saved. And the mother is innocent as well, despite her foolishness in allowing her children to come here. These are innocent civilians caught up in their government's politics. Every American deserves this kind of treatment, but unfortunately it can't be offered. Like you said, it's just too damn expensive."

"And if we're caught, it causes even more problems."

"In this case, we have no choice because of who Farzan is. Otherwise, they'd be left on their own and only diplomatic channels would be used because frankly, coming here is stupid. Even if the CIA said it was highly unlikely anything like this would happen."

A curtain moved on the second floor and Kane moved his head slightly, stroking the edge of the frames, the image zooming in, and his heart ached at the sight of a terrified Tara.

Don't worry, we'll get you out.

Farzan Residence

Tehran, Iran

Tara stared out the window, her entire body shaking. Everything before her was so strange, so different, so disconcerting, so unlike home. She was now certain they intended to keep her here. The street below was active, people going about their daily lives in the residential neighborhood, and it had her wondering if they were oblivious to how backward their lives were.

She spotted two men smoking across the street, one of them staring up at her. She was about to close the curtain when she spotted something unusual. Something different. The one staring at her held his hand against his stomach and pointed his index finger toward her, then traced a serpentine pattern across his stomach, then turned his hand downward, extending only his index and middle finger. He repeated the gestures two more times then turned away from her.

She stepped back from the curtain and lay down on her bed, confused. Was it a signal? Was it meant for her? It had to be a signal, and it had to be for her. But what did it mean? She repeated the motion on her own stomach. A finger pointing toward her. A serpentine pattern against his stomach. Two fingers, index and middle, pointing downward against the stomach. It had been repeated three times in the same manner. If it was a message, it was in three parts. It had to be some sort of sign language type of signal.

Unfortunately, she had no clue how to read sign language. But how many people actually did? Almost nobody. There was no way he would use sign language to send a message to her. And it didn't resemble any sign language she had seen on TV during COVID, where every press conference had somebody translating. No, this was something different. This was something improvised, meant to be something she could understand. If somebody were sending her a message and they pointed directly at her, what did that mean? That was the simplest one. It had to mean 'You.'

You what? You, a serpentine pattern, two downward fingers.

She still had nothing.

Her heart skipped. What if it wasn't the word 'you,' but the letter U? She gasped. U, then a serpentine pattern. That could be an S. Two downward fingers certainly made an A. USA? Could it be? She scurried to her feet with excitement and bolted toward the curtains, opening them again, but her shoulders slumped in despair. The men were gone. But she was sure the message was for her. And it said USA.

There was now hope.

Outside the Farzan Residence

Tehran, Iran

"That was kind of stupid, wasn't it?"

Kane shrugged at Shadmani. "You saw the look in her eyes. That poor kid is terrified. She's not going to tell anyone what she saw."

"But what if you were seen? Or what if she goes and tells her brother, and he tells someone?"

"That girl was desperate. If she continued to think there was no hope, she could have done something stupid. Now she's got hope."

"If she understood your message."

"Her file says she's a smart cookie. She'll figure it out."

"And if she tells her brother?"

"If he's as crazy as he looks to us, then she's seen the same looks, and won't tell him."

"I hope you're right. What are we going to do now?"

"Now, you're going to sit on this place and figure out how many people are actually inside. I'm going to go back to the residence just in case someone notices the White guy."

"Do you want my car?"

"No. I've got a ride already."

Shadmani cocked an eyebrow. "Oh?"

Kane grinned. "Don't be jealous. No one said we were exclusive."

Shadmani laughed. "Has this person been vetted?"

"Yes, by me." He gave Shadmani a traditional Persian embrace, then sauntered off, dialing his cabby's number programmed into his phone while waiting at the embassy. It was immediately answered. "Hi, Dariush. We met earlier today. You drove me from the airport to the Swiss Embassy. Does that offer for a ride still stand?"

"Of course, I remember you, and of course I can pick you up. Where are you?"

Kane gave him the street corner he was at.

"I'll be there in five minutes."

"Thanks. See you soon." Kane ended the call then squatted, his back against the wall of a bakery. He closed his eyes, picturing the girl in the window, and his heart ached for her. Getting her and her brother out would be difficult. He could only think of two ways. One was like he had already described. Get to the coast, get picked up on the beach, then taken out to sea for extraction. It was definitely doable, though it would be a challenge and expensive. Washington might approve it or they could just as easily say no and fire Farzan. But he would still be privy to everything he had been exposed to up to that point. He would then be truly desperate and could spill those secrets in exchange for his family. He was inclined to think Washington might approve the plan, though there was another possibility he had been mulling, another way out.

Tires screeched at the end of the street as a car careened onto the road he now rested beside. He rose as he recognized Dariush, the man grinning and waving at him. Kane climbed in the back.

"So good to see you!" Dariush looked about. "Kind of an odd place for you to be, isn't it?"

Kane chuckled. "For me, yes. But for one of my coworkers, not so much. I was invited to join him to have dinner with a local family, but he's not working tomorrow and I am, so I decided to call it an early night."

"Where can I take you?"

"Back to my residence." Kane gave him the address.

"Ah, I know this place well. We'll be there in fifteen minutes tops. Traffic's fairly light right now."

"Sounds good."

"What did you have for dinner?"

It was an innocent question, and if it were asked in almost any other country, it wouldn't have triggered alarm bells. But here in Iran, where no one could be trusted, he had to wonder if it was a test. Fortunately, he was well versed in Iranian cuisine, though he had to play dumb since his cover wasn't. His extensive knowledge, however, allowed him to be reasonably descriptive. "I'm not really familiar with the names, but we started with some sort of pita bread with a few different dipping sauces. What they were, I have no idea, but they were all delicious. Then the main course was some sort of lamb dish wrapped in grape leaves with a side of Basmati rice, I think. It's not that the foods were different, it's the flavorings. Your spices here are so aromatic compared to back home. It's delicious. I suppose if you eat that way every day, you get used to it, but it's a real treat. Back home, about the only food that has strong smells are our cheeses. I tell you, some of them can make your eyes water."

"I've heard stories about Swiss cheese. I hope one day, God willing, I'll be able to taste them."

"You're not lactose intolerant?"

Dariush shook his head. "Thankfully, no. My wife is, terribly. Any hint of dairy, and look out, I'm sleeping in a different bedroom."

Kane tilted his head back and roared with laughter. "That's hilarious! If I ever meet your wife, I'll be sure not to mention it."

Dariush glanced at him in the rear view of mirror, aghast. "Please don't! My God, could you imagine?"

They both broke out in more laughter. "Why is it that women want us to think they don't have gas?"

Dariush grinned. "I used to think it was the dog until I discovered the truth one day. I had to apologize for a week to the poor mutt." He checked his rearview mirror then his side. "You'll be happy to know you're no longer being followed."

Kane glanced up. "There are always drones."

"This is true. We are known for our drones. But my experience tells me if they're truly interested in you, they like the human touch."

"From your lips to God's ears."

Dariush pointed ahead. "This is your stop."

Kane handed another wad of bills over, including a generous tip.

Dariush's eyes bulged. "This is too much."

"Hey, you bailed me out of a long walk. Go home, relax, and who knows? You might hear from me in the next couple of weeks before I leave."

"Anytime, day or night." Dariush grinned. "This tip means I'll kick whoever's in my cab out to come get you."

Kane laughed. "Go ahead. Just leave my name out of it." He exited the cab, gave a wave to Dariush as he pulled away, then headed into the diplomatic compound, his ID checked and matched against the guest list. As he headed for the stairs, his CIA-issued and heavily modified TAG Heuer watch sent an electrical pulse through his wrist, undetectable to anyone but him. The coded pattern indicated it was a priority personal message.

He suppressed a frown, but picked up his pace slightly. He used his key pass to enter his room and closed the door behind him, performing a quick sweep to make sure he was alone. He tossed the backpack that Shadmani had brought him onto the bed then logged into his messaging app on his phone.

And gasped, suddenly sick to his stomach with what he had just read, a private message from Fang.

Her father was dead.

He dropped onto the bed, his shoulders slumping.

These were the times he hated his job.

Farzan Residence

Great Falls, Virginia

"Tell me everything you know about Poseidon's Trident."

Farzan's eyebrows shot up and his pulse pounded in his ears. Operation Poseidon's Trident was top secret, beyond top secret. Extremely compartmentalized. And the shock at hearing those words spoken by an Iranian agent caused him to slip up. "How the hell do you know about that?" He could almost hear the smile on the other end of the line.

"Thank you for confirming its existence."

Farzan muttered a curse. Perhaps Morrison was right. He was too emotionally distracted by what was going on. He had just committed a gaffe that even a raw recruit wouldn't. "Well, if you know about it, you also know it would have little to do with me. All I know is that it exists and that even I'm not supposed to know about it."

"You just lied to me, which means I'm going to order your wife beaten close-fisted for five minutes."

"No, wait!" He squeezed his eyes shut. "What do you want to know?"

"Everything you know."

"I wasn't lying when I said it has little to do with me."

"Little isn't nothing."

His eyes burned. If he told this man anything, he was committing treason. He could go to prison for the rest of his life. But they had his family. What could he possibly do? If he didn't tell them what they wanted, they would beat his wife mercilessly, perhaps even his children.

If he could only delay them. His last briefing had Dylan Kane in Tehran, his first recon mission of where his children were held already completed. The Swiss had made contact with the Iranians about his wife, but they were denying any knowledge of her being in their system. It was a standard tactic. They could believably be still processing the paperwork. Once the Iranians officially knew the American government was aware of what was going on, they might ease up on his wife and perhaps even let his children go.

But that would take time. Time he didn't have. Though perhaps he could buy a little to give him a chance to think. He had been prepared for all manner of questions concerning the ops under his command. It had never occurred to him they might ask about Trident, because it didn't involve Iran directly.

It involved Russia.

None of this made sense. Why would the Iranians be concerned with a Russian-focused op? They were obviously asking on the Russian's behalf. But why would that be their first question? And it forced him to wonder, was this just coincidence, or had his family been targeted and lured to Tehran in order to ask him specifically about this operation?

He needed time to think. He flipped over to the browser on his laptop, sitting in front of him, and one-finger-typed what just might buy him at least a few minutes, then tapped on the result, hoping it actually matched what he had searched.

A doorbell sound emitted from his speakers. "Somebody is at the door."

"What?"

"Somebody is at the door. I have to let you go."

"Nonsense."

"If I don't answer, they're gonna think something is wrong and they might call the police."

"Don't play me for the fool."

"It's a colleague from work. I'm expecting him. If I don't answer, he'll call a special team from Langley."

A string of curses erupted and the call abruptly ended. He sat for a moment, trembling, when the doorbell rang.

And he nearly soiled himself.

He checked his watch and frowned. It was far too late for polite company. That left a friend of one of his children, or something work-related. He pushed to his feet and headed for the door, surprised to see Morrison through the glass. The man had never been here before, and he had no idea why he would be here now. He wasn't directly under his chain of command, and they weren't friends. Morrison was an entirely different strata in the Agency.

They were colleagues, not peers.

He opened the door and forced a smile. "Sir, I'm surprised to see you."

"May I come in?"

"Of course." Farzan stepped aside, allowing Morrison to pass. Farzan closed the door. "Is there a problem, sir?"

Morrison's eyes ran over the entranceway. "I just wanted to bring you the latest update personally. And enough of this 'sir' nonsense. Outside of the office, I'm Leif."

"Yes, sir." Farzan smiled with chagrin. "Sorry, habit. Leif."

Morrison chuckled. "Don't worry about it."

Farzan exhaled loudly. "I'm sorry, Leif. Where are my manners? Come on in. Can I get you something to drink?"

"Absolutely."

Farzan led the man, who had authorized enough ops to probably have the blood of thousands on his hands, into the living room. "What can I get you?"

"What have you got?"

Farzan had danced this dance on many occasions with first-time visitors who knew he was Muslim. "Most of the usual. Apple juice, orange juice, pineapple juice."

Morrison eyed him. "Whatever you're having."

Farzan stepped over to their dry bar, opening up the doors, revealing a decent selection. "I was thinking an eighteen-year-old Macallan."

Morrison smirked. "Sounds good to me."

"Ice?"

"Sure."

Farzan lifted the lid off the ice bucket, filled every day by their maid at the end of her shift. He picked up a pair of tongs, lifting out one of the large, round ice balls. He dropped one in each of two scotch glasses, then poured doubles. He put the tongs down then replaced the lid to the ice bucket before carrying the glasses over to the couch. He handed one to Morrison, who waited for him to take a seat across from him.

His guest raised his glass. "To the safe return of your wife and children."

Farzan inhaled deeply, closing his eyes for a moment before lifting his glass. "To their safe return." He took a large sip, feeling the burn. As a Muslim, he had never tasted alcohol in his native Iran, but on his flight out all those years ago, as soon as they had announced they were outside of Iranian airspace, he ordered a scotch on the rocks from his flight attendant.

It had been disgusting, one of the vilest things he had ever tasted.

But it meant freedom. Freedom from an oppressive regime, freedom from an oppressive religion. He had always believed the Koran was a guidebook, not a rule book like too many in his religion thought. Demands not to drink alcohol, to him, were foolish. The real sin was abuse of alcohol. Having a drink every now and then hurt no one. Sometimes, you needed a drink to relax, to calm the nerves. How could Allah condemn something like that?

He sighed as the burn turned into a gentle warmth spreading through his body.

Morrison held up his glass. "I love these ice cubes. Is it a mold?"

Farzan nodded. "Yes. Basically a hollow ball. You fill it with water through a hole at the top, freeze it, and voilà, the perfect cooling mechanism for a drink. And, as you've just proven, a conversation piece."

Morrison laughed. "They are that, aren't they? I'll have to get myself some." He leaned forward. "Now, I have some news. It could be good, it could be bad. But I felt you needed to hear it from a friend in private rather than in a briefing room filled with people."

Friend. It was an interesting choice of words. He would never consider Morrison a friend, though he would certainly consider them on friendly terms. The fact was, he didn't really have friends at work except for perhaps Baxter, his deputy chief. He braced himself for what had to be bad news. "What is it?"

"Kane established contact with your daughter."

Farzan's eyebrows shot up. "Wait a minute, what? That wasn't part of the plan."

"It wasn't, but according to Kane, he spotted your daughter looking out an upstairs window of your parent's house, and she appeared extremely scared. He signaled her to reassure her that all hope wasn't lost."

"Why would he do that? That just puts her at risk."

"Trust me when I say, Kane wouldn't have done it if he didn't feel it was needed. He's my top officer by far. He would only do it if it was absolutely necessary. And from the report I read, he believed she might harm herself if she didn't feel there was hope."

Farzan slumped in his chair. "I don't understand. I can see her being upset about her mother, but why would that cause her to harm herself?"

Morrison frowned, placing his scotch on the glass tabletop with a clink. "I'm not sure if you're aware of this, but now that your family has the microscope turned on them, you should know that it appears they've become fundamentalists."

Farzan was taken aback by this pronouncement. "That's impossible. There's no way my father would allow it. He was always a moderate."

"It would appear your father's no longer in charge of the family. Your mother is."

Farzan pursed his lips. His mother had always been far more religious than his father. In fact, her entire side of the family were strict adherents to the Koran and the Hadiths. His father hadn't permitted that nonsense in their home when he was growing up, and he had never had any indication that his mother's Koran-thumping ways had been allowed.

"According to neighbors, ever since your father fell ill, your mother's become more domineering, and now several members of her family have moved in with them, including your cousin Kaveh, who is the one we believe recruited your son."

"Recruited? What do you mean, recruited?"

Morrison pulled out his phone and brought up a photo, handing it over. "Look at your son. This was coming back from morning prayers today."

Farzan's jaw dropped at the zealotry on display. He had never seen his son like this, and it was heartbreaking, terrifying, soul-destroying.

How had he let this happen? How had he let his job take him away from his responsibilities as a father? "I should have converted."

Morrison cocked an eyebrow. "Sorry?"

"When we arrived, we should have converted to Christianity so that the hatred would never be allowed in this household."

"That wouldn't have necessarily solved anything. Your son would have eventually figured out that you were originally Muslim, and his curiosity might have been piqued. And don't forget, a lot of the truly crazies are converts who grew up Christian. Don't blame yourself for this. Once we got your cousin's name, we ran it, and he's got quite the history, including a dishonorable discharge for nearly beating his military unit's imam to death."

Farzan's eyes flared. "I heard this story, but I couldn't remember who it was." He cursed. "If I had known, if only I had paid attention."

"You can look for who to blame later. Right now, we need to concentrate on your family. Which brings me back to your daughter. It's our fear that this was all a setup, that they somehow knew exactly who you were, that your mother, in cooperation with the authorities, hoped to lure you there, but instead settled for your family so they could use them as leverage against you. We believe your family has no intention of letting your children go home on their scheduled flight, and we believe it's possible your son never intended to return. It could explain why Kane felt your daughter appeared so desperate. She either knows that this is what's planned, or she suspects it."

Farzan downed his drink, placing the empty glass on the table with a loud clang. "What are we gonna do? What can we do? You have to save my children! You have to save my wife!"

Morrison exhaled heavily. "Your wife might be a lost cause left to the diplomats. We might be able to negotiate a release for her in exchange for some Iranian that we or one of our allies have in custody. The children, however, because they're outside the apparatus for now, we might be able to help, though your son could prove a problem."

"Then what do you propose?"

"Your son's eighteen. He's an adult, which means he can legally stay there if he wants. That's his choice. But I'm gonna ask you this, father to father, what do you want us to do?"

"Extract him! For the love of God, extract him! He doesn't know what he's doing. He's been brainwashed into a cult. I need to get him back here where I can deal with him, deprogram him. I don't care if he's eighteen. Treat him like he's twelve, because that's how he's acting."

Morrison regarded him for a moment. "Very well. I can't make any promises. If he threatens to compromise the mission, Kane might be forced to leave him behind. Right now, our focus is your daughter since she's an underage American citizen."

Farzan sniffed hard. "And my wife? If there's nothing we can do for her except wait for an exchange, that could mean years. She's a nobody. She's only important to me. There's no way Washington's going to agree to release anyone the Iranians might want in exchange for her."

"Well, don't lose all hope. The Swiss have agreed to a proposal, though they're none too happy about it."

Diplomatic Quarters

Tehran, Iran

"Secure relay now live. I'm disconnecting from the conversation now. Everything's totally private and is not being monitored."

Kane took a breath, preparing for the difficult conversation ahead. "Thanks, Sonya, I appreciate it."

"No problem, Dylan. And if you think it's appropriate, pass on my condolences. Pass on all our condolences."

"I'll do that. She'll appreciate it." There was a click as Tong disconnected from the conversation. "Hey, baby, how are you doing?"

There was a sniff and a burst of static as Fang sighed heavily. "As good as can be expected, I suppose." The control she had managed so far failed her, and she erupted into tears. "Oh God, Dylan, he was so young! No one should die that young!"

His chest ached at the anguish in the voice of the woman he loved. He should be with her, holding her in his arms, comforting her, helping her through one of the most difficult times in her life —in anyone's life— the loss of a parent. "You're right, babe, he was way too young, but his suffering's over now. When I saw him, he was in pain, though he hid it well."

"You're right. I saw it as well. I suppose that's the bright side of it. That's all over now. I just feel horrible for mother. She's all alone now."

Kane smiled. "Sweetheart, I was there. That woman is never alone and I can guarantee you she's surrounded by friends and family who will take care of her in her time of need. If you want, we can arrange another conversation."

Fang dismissed the idea. "No, not right now. It's too dangerous. I got to say goodbye to my father, and my mother now knows the truth." Another heavy sigh as control returned. "I'll be fine. It's just going to take time."

"I know, babe, you take as much time as you need, and I'll be there before you know it."

There was a beep in his ear, a warning from Control that he had less than thirty seconds left. They couldn't risk the Iranians detecting the signal. "Okay, babe, I'm gonna have to let you go. You take care of yourself and if you need anything, you know Chris and Sherrie will do anything for you."

"I know. Sherrie's actually here right now."

"Hello, Dylan!"

"Hey, Sherrie."

"You just take care of yourself and get home. I want to hear every detail about your visit."

"Don't worry, babe. I already wrote a report so I wouldn't forget anything."

A double beep indicated ten seconds.

"Okay, they're about to yank me off the stage. Love you, see you soon."

"Love you too."

He ended the call and sat on the edge of his bed, his shoulders slumped, his heart aching for poor Fang. His parents were around the same age as hers, though both were in decent health, though so was her father a year ago. Cancer was a bitch. It didn't care how old you were, how healthy you were, how rich or poor. It didn't discriminate. Where things were different was in treatment options. Some countries covered it. Others forced you to pay out of pocket, and it had him wondering if her father lived in America, could he have been saved?

Sometimes, no matter how much money you had, no amount was enough. Sometimes people were just too far gone, the cancer simply too aggressive and far too often someone's personal circumstances simply couldn't be worked around. Her father lived in China. There was no way her family could ever leave there.

He had won the lottery being born in the United States. To him, it was the greatest country in the world, despite its problems, and he just prayed America didn't throw it all away out of stupidity influenced by social media algorithms that didn't care about what was good for the country, only what was good for the shareholders.

He sighed as his watch indicated a priority message from Langley. He accessed it by pressing around the face in a coded pattern.

Meeting approved. Details in your secure messenger.

He cocked an eyebrow, surprised at how rapidly the Iranians had approved the request, and he had to wonder why. He suspected they were curious as to why the Swiss were so quickly involved. They likely were approving his fishing expedition so they could do a little themselves. Whatever was going on, at least it would make tomorrow that much more interesting. It would at least take his mind off the problems back home and, if he were lucky, expedite his return.

Ministry of Foreign Affairs Building

Tehran, Iran

The Swiss hadn't been pleased, though had agreed once the situation was explained to them in detail, and they realized their embassy staff had already been infiltrated. A hissy fit had almost broken out, and he didn't blame them, but the president himself had called the Swiss president and asked him for a personal favor. "I'll owe you one," was apparently what sealed the deal, so now Kane, already in Tehran as a Swiss Embassy employee with credentials approved and vetted by the Iranian authorities, was in an embassy car being driven to the Ministry of Foreign Affairs Building to negotiate on behalf of the American government for the release of Kiana Farzan.

Herman, his assigned driver, brought them to a halt in front of the building and put the car in park. He twisted in his seat. "Have you ever been here before?"

Kane truthfully shook his head. "I can't say I have."

"Be careful. These people don't live by the international rule of law. Just because you have diplomatic credentials doesn't mean they'll be honored. I'm sure you've already been briefed, but let me tell you as someone who's worked here for over twenty years and seen countless people like you go in then when they got out, told me what had happened inside. Be prepared for anything. The Iranians expect to be respected. Oh, and expect to be made to wait. It's a power move on their part. And if they're going to treat you properly, be prepared for rather strong tea. Whatever you do, don't grimace, don't refuse it, and drink it all."

Kane regarded the man. "What if they poisoned it or drugged it?"

It was only a half-serious question, since if it was, the Iranians had already decided on what they intended to do with him, and avoiding a cup of tea wasn't preventing that.

"Then you're already screwed."

Kane chuckled. "I like you. Will you be here when I get out?"

"I'm not going anywhere until either you're back or I'm ordered to leave."

"Good to know." Kane gripped the door handle. "Well, wish me luck, and thanks for the advice."

"Don't mention it, and good luck. Hopefully you won't need it."

Kane opened the door and stepped out into the oppressive sun, the entire area, covered in concrete, well on its way to scorching temperatures—he just hoped the IRGC believed in air conditioning, otherwise, what he suspected would be a long day would be all the more difficult. Yet just to have the chance to possibly negotiate the release of

Kiana was worth any amount of suffering he might endure, though as he walked through the doors, he had no doubt his efforts would be futile.

There was no way the Iranians were letting her go.

Conference Room 4F, CIA Headquarters
Langley, Virginia

"Operation Poseidon's Trident is a go."

Smiles filled the room and Leroux joined in, everyone having worked on this for months, some of them for almost a year. It was a bold plan, something they hoped could cripple the Russian economy once and for all. Too many countries were illegally purchasing Russian oil, avoiding sanctions by not purchasing it directly. Massive transfers of millions of barrels were being performed at sea, millions more through third party ports. Poseidon's Trident could theoretically put an end to that.

He glanced across the table at Farzan, his smile as broad as any, the first time he had seen the man show any positive emotion since his personal crisis had begun.

Morrison, chairing the meeting, held up a hand, quieting everyone. "Our operative is already in place at the Hilton in Saint Petersburg, about two hours from the Primorsk oil distribution center. He'll be given the go code as soon as I'm out of this meeting. And if this works, we'll be able to seriously diminish the amount of Russian oil on the market, and hopefully help bring an end to this damn war."

Applause and desk pounds were the response, then Morrison headed out of the room. The good mood continued into the hallway, though any chitchat was stowed the moment the door opened. This was a highly classified operation. If the Russians caught wind of it, it would end their plan quite rapidly.

Jack—just Jack—was in position to contaminate the oil distribution terminal responsible for over a million barrels of oil a day, with an isotope trackable by satellite and drone. It was a recent DARPA breakthrough Washington was eager to deploy. The isotope was trackable, yet unless the Russians knew to look for it, their standard scanners wouldn't pick it up. It meant any oil that left that terminal and ended up in countries that were taking advantage of the situation by buying black market oil through third parties, could be identified and sanctions leveled against them.

If they could starve the Russian treasury of money, they might be forced to end the war. It was a long shot, but if they could prove that countries like India and Turkey were knowingly purchasing this oil, then refining it into products they then resold to other countries without identifying the original source, the mere threat of sanctions should put an end to it. And if it didn't, the actual sanctions could be crippling. This was a war that had to be won. How anybody could be so naïve as to not understand that was beyond him, but too many today listened to those they worshipped rather than investigated the facts themselves.

Leroux headed for the elevator, finding Morrison holding it for him. He jogged to close the final few feet, boarding the crowded car, a few annoyed expressions delivered toward him, no one daring to say anything to the Chief.

"Sorry, folks, priority. If you knew why, I'd have to kill you."

Chuckles greeted the Chief's apology.

They were at the basement level containing the operation centers within a few minutes, and Morrison led the way to Operations Center 3 to deliver some unpleasant news to Leroux's team, for what was about to happen wasn't at all what had just been announced in the meeting.

Operation Poseidon's Trident was not a go, not as long as one of those on the inside was compromised.

The two guards on either side of the entrance to the ops center acknowledged them as Morrison placed his hand on the scanner, followed by Leroux. The door opened, and they stepped inside. Morrison pressed a button on the wall, and the door closed behind them, the inner door automatically opening, preventing any stray signals from getting in or out of the room.

Tong rose from her seat at the sight of Morrison, bowing her head slightly at them. "Sirs, what's the word? Do we have an op?"

Her question was reasonable. After all, it wasn't every day the Chief came here for no reason, and the team had been placed on standby before the meeting had begun.

Morrison smirked at Leroux. "I'll let you deliver the bad news."

Leroux rolled his eyes with an exaggerated sigh. "Okay, fine." He stood in front of the room, Morrison just behind him, to the side. "If I can have everyone's attention, please." It was unnecessary. He already had it. "The bad news is, we're all going into comms isolation effective five minutes from now. I don't know how long it's going to last, but if there's anyone here who has a pressing situation where they can't commit to the next seventy-two hours, like you're donating a kidney or something, this is your chance to bow out. No judgment. We all have lives, and this is unexpected."

No one moved.

He smiled. "Good, because I need every single one of you, and the Chief here would've fired anyone who walked out that door."

"He's not lying," said Morrison with a grin.

Chuckles rippled through the room, everyone knowing it wasn't true.

"Contact your loved ones now. Just let them know you might not be home for the next three days. They know the drill. They've been through it before. Apologies for any plans that get screwed up, especially you, Randy, I know you had Comic-Con plans."

Child spun in his chair, his arms outstretched as if he were Jesus on the cross. "The things I sacrifice for my country."

Therrien hurled a customary insult. "I would think you'd be more concerned about not getting a weekend with this imaginary woman you keep telling us about."

Child's outstretched hands turned into fists then birds as everyone laughed. "I've got pictures." He dropped a foot, killing his spin, then tapped at his keyboard. The massive display arcing across the front of the room updated, showing Child dressed as Captain Kirk and what could be a woman standing beside him dressed as a Gorn, the costume so elaborate her entire body was covered.

Packman scoffed. "That's not proof of life. For all we know, that could be a dude you ran into at the comic book store."

More laughter, more birds.

"You're all assholes."

Packman leaned over and patted Child on the back. "Yes, we are, and don't worry, so are you."

Leroux checked his watch. "Two minutes, people. Make sure you get your calls in because we're going radio silent. For the next three days, all cellular relays and external lines will be cut, phones will be checked. The switchboard will relay any urgent messages from outside." He smacked his hands together twice. "Now, let's go!" A flurry of activity was the result, and he faced Morrison. "Do you think this is going to work?"

"Hopefully. Unfortunately, the only way to know for sure is if things go wrong, and if they do, it means I could be sending a man I shared a drink with last night to prison for the rest of his life."

Ministry of Foreign Affairs Building

Tehran, Iran

Kane didn't bother checking his watch. The standard black on white round office clock mounted to the wall near the door revealed the time. He had been waiting for hours, exactly as predicted, but he was prepared for this, and trained for it as well. As an expert sniper, he was accustomed to long waits where he couldn't move without potentially revealing his position. This was the same thing.

His prey was watching him on one of several cameras in the room, only one visible to the naked eye in the corner to his left. However, he had already spotted several others, including in the clock that predated the revolution. The key to appearing unaffected was to minimize body movement since that would reveal his discomfort, to minimize watch or clock checks, to keep his facial expression neutral, and to avoid heavy, impatient sighs.

Eventually, they would tire of his lack of reaction and the show would finally go on. The delaying tactic was working, however, on some in the room. A few others were making valiant attempts to control themselves, though none as successfully as him. Those few others likely had been through this many times before and picked up on what was going on.

The door to what lay beyond the waiting room opened and everyone lifted their head expectantly.

"Mr. Keller."

Kane rose with a smile then bowed his head, walking toward the man. He stepped through the door, not bothering to offer to shake the man's hand, as all who had done so had been left hanging. The door closed behind him and Kane stepped aside, allowing his escort to lead the way. He was shown into a room where a man in a business suit sat behind a large desk. He rose with a smile.

Kane stuck to his cover, extending his hand. "Peter Keller, temporary attaché to the Swiss Embassy."

The man took Kane's hand and shook it firmly. "Navid Yazdani, Deputy Chief for Immigration Control. It's a pleasure to meet you."

"Likewise."

The man indicated a chair in front of the desk and Kane sat as his host returned to his own. "I understand you want to speak about one of our citizens who's been detained."

Kane played dumb. "I'm sorry, there must be some confusion. I'm here to speak about Kiana Farzan, an American citizen who's been detained."

The man smiled. "Now, I know you're not that naïve, Mr. Keller. You're well aware that we don't recognize non-Iranian citizenships for those born here. One of our own returned home without the proper documentation and without properly declaring herself. She was flagged and taken for interrogation, and now is being held awaiting trial."

"What are the charges?"

A file folder was opened in front of the man, a piece of paper handed over. "I've had it translated into English for you."

Kane smiled. "I appreciate that. German or French would've been fine as well."

Yazdani regarded him. "Not Italian?"

Kane chuckled. "No, never saw the need. I'm from Zurich, born and raised, mostly German and French around there."

"Yet your English is excellent."

"Most people in Europe who want to be successful learn it as a child." He quickly read the list of nonsense charges, then handed back the piece of paper. "Since neither of us is naïve, let's be frank with each other. You and I both know those charges are nonsense. Former citizens come in and out of here all the time, including American. For some reason, you targeted her. Now, we both know this has nothing to do with her and everything to do with her husband."

"Oh?"

Kane eyed the man. "Now who's being naïve?"

Yazdani smirked slightly. "Why don't you tell me about her husband?"

Kane took a chance. None of this would be happening if they thought Farzan worked for a utility company. "The Americans tell me he's an executive at the local power utility. But I did a little digging on my own in preparation for this meeting, and I call bullshit on that. Just like you must have."

"You don't believe he works for the power utility?"

"No, I don't. And neither do you. Who he does work for, I'm not sure, though I'm quite certain you either know or suspect something, which is why you're holding her. Here's the thing. I wouldn't be here so quickly if her husband was a paper pusher at a public utility. There's only one reason favors were called in to get me here so quickly, and that was because her husband is something much more. What he is, I don't care, though I'm sure it's important to you. My question for you is this, how long do you need your leverage?"

Yazdani stared at him, his fingers steepled in front of him, the tip of his chin resting on his middle fingers, a move Kane had seen countless times performed by Morrison. "An interesting question, which implies Mr. Farzan has knowledge we wish to acquire."

Kane shrugged. "I'm not implying anything. And we can dance around the truth all you want and waste each other's time, or get to the truth. Am I going back to my embassy and contacting Washington and telling them not to worry, she'll be put on her return flight, or am I telling them that she'll be held much longer?"

"You're different than most of the Swiss Embassy that I deal with. Usually, they don't dare say what they're really thinking. They merely relay what Washington told them to say, and nothing more."

Kane smirked. "And does it work?"

"Never."

"Exactly. You and I both know what's going on here. Let's be really honest with each other. I don't care about this woman. I don't care about her children. I obviously don't want anything bad to happen to them, but they're nobody to me, and as far as I'm concerned, they should have known better than to come here if Farzan is who you and I both think he is. Why the man let his family come here is beyond me. It was stupid, it was asking for trouble, and now they found it. What are your intentions when it comes to the children?"

"Are you here about them?"

"No. My understanding is everyone's working under the assumption they'll be allowed to leave on their return flight with or without their mother. Can you confirm that?"

"We have no interest in the children. They're American citizens born in America. They're here legally with proper visas. As much as the American government and press would have you believe, we're not monsters."

"That's good to hear. Do I have your permission to inform Washington of this?"

"You do."

"Good. Then that only leaves the wife. Will she be leaving on that flight with them?"

"That, I cannot say."

"So, I should tell Washington that negotiations will be necessary?"

"Yes. If they want the return of Mrs. Farzan, they'll have to offer us something substantial enough to make us want to give up one of our sisters who has returned to us."

"And should you get what you want from her husband?"

Yazdani rose and Kane followed. "That, I'm afraid, is beyond both our pay grades." A hand was extended. "Until we meet again, Mr. Keller."

Kane smiled. "I'm looking forward to it." He shook the man's hand then headed for the door. He stopped, turning back. "Would I be able to see her to report back to Washington on her condition? I have no doubt they fear the worst."

Yazdani smiled broadly. "You do have brass balls, as I understand the Americans might say. And the answer is no. You may not see her."

"Is she being properly cared for?"

"She is being provided with food, water, shelter, and medical care."

Kane cocked an eyebrow. "Medical care? Has she been injured?"

"She fell. And because she was handcuffed, she landed on her face. There was some damage. She's being treated."

Kane frowned. "I think we both know the Americans won't like that."

Yazdani snorted. "What do I care what the greatest threat to mankind thinks? She's being cared for. That's all they need to know."

Kane gave a firm nod of his head. "Understood." He opened the door and stepped outside, his escort already waiting for him. He walked briskly out of the building and found his ride where he had left it all those hours ago.

Herman stepped out then opened the rear door for him. Kane climbed in and the door was closed. Herman sat behind the wheel and moments later they were underway. Nothing was said until they cleared the gates. The windows were tinted but the windshield wasn't, and the cameras aimed directly at them might allow someone to lip read what was said.

"Any luck?"

Kane grunted. "Nope. But he has agreed to another meeting, which I suppose is promising." He pulled out his phone, his thumbs flying as he wrote a report for Langley, confirming what they already feared. Kiana Farzan was being tortured as leverage over her husband.

And Farzan was already compromised, or soon would be.

St. Petersburg, Russia

CIA Operations Officer Jack—just Jack—lay relatively comfortably on his bed in a dump of a hotel down the street from his original digs. His laptop sat on his legs as he watched the feed from the camera set up in the window, aimed down the street at the Hilton where he had stayed until this morning. Today was to be the launch of Operation Poseidon's Trident, but instead of receiving the go code, he had instead been contacted a few hours ago and instructed to move.

Something was afoot.

The fact they had him setting up surveillance on his own hotel suggested they expected a raid, and there was only one reason for that.

He had been compromised.

The question was, how? There had to be a leak somewhere, and that pissed him off. This op had been in the works for almost a year. He had been in and out of Russia repeatedly in preparation for it, laying the groundwork for what would hopefully cripple the Russian war machine. Was there a leak from inside? Had he slipped up, compromising the mission himself? He was confident the screw-up didn't come from his end, though anything was possible. He wasn't as perfect as he told the ladies. He smirked. Well, he was pretty damn near perfect in that department. Broken hearts the world over could attest to that.

The sound of cars racing past the front of his new hotel had him sitting up as the camera caught the first of over a dozen vehicles screeching to a halt in front of the Hilton. He cursed. The mission was compromised. Now the question was, how badly and by whom? All he was certain of was that if they couldn't get this mission back on track, the Russian war machine would continue to be funded by countries like China, India, and Turkey, content to allow thousands to die, and millions to suffer as long as they saved a few bucks a barrel on oil.

He shook his head as scores of security forces swarmed his former hotel. His mission was about to be scrubbed.

Months of work down the drain, because someone couldn't keep their mouth shut.

Operations Center 3, CIA Headquarters

Langley, Virginia

Leroux cursed as Jack radioed in what they had already watched on satellite. "I can't believe he did it." His voice was low, the rest of the room not privy to what was going on.

Morrison folded his arms. "Don't be too hard on him. Family changes the equation, though I would have hoped he would approach me and tell me what was going on so we could feed him false intel."

"But isn't that what we just did by having him in the briefing, telling him where Jack was staying and that the mission was a go?"

"Oh, we did play him, there's no doubt about that, but we could have played it better if he had stayed on our side of things. I'd have preferred to set up a patsy, but unfortunately there was no time for that."

"What do we do with the operation now?"

"It's on hold. Right now, we don't know what he's told them. If he's smart, he's playing both sides. Revealing where Jack was and that the operation had been approved means little if he didn't tell them how the operation worked."

"How can we know?"

"Well, if we see the Russians crawling all over their distribution center with scanners, then we'll know. But if he played dumb and didn't tell them how Trident worked, then we might start things up again in a few weeks. But until then, this operation is dead in the water."

Leroux frowned. "All that damn work ruined because some idiot sent his family into one of the most hostile regimes in the world."

Swiss Embassy

Tehran, Iran

"No doubt about it, you picked up a tail as soon as you left. Have you lost your mojo?"

Kane scoffed at Leroux's jab. "Well, we were kind of expecting that now, weren't we?"

"I suppose. What do you plan on doing about it?"

"Nothing. A few of us from the embassy are going out. I'll deal with them after I've eaten."

"You saw the update about the operation?"

Kane frowned. The news that Operation Poseidon's Trident had been compromised was disappointing, to say the least. He had provided input on the mission and recommended Jack to execute it. He was relieved when Morrison had agreed, as he had no desire to spend weeks, perhaps months, in Russia, waiting for a trigger to be pulled. There were too many other missions to do, and Jack was perfectly capable and content to be on his own.

Kane now preferred shorter missions that allowed him to swing back home and spend some quality time with Fang. Weeks or months apart were now torture. His new situation had him seriously contemplating retiring from the operations game. It would allow him to settle down with Fang, perhaps get married, perhaps start a family. But what the hell would he do? He was an adrenaline junkie. He loved his job. What he did was important. There was nothing that compared to it. Taking on a desk job at Langley held zero appeal, and even if he went as a private contractor, that would mean weeks or months away regardless, just for a lot more pay and a little less risk.

His serious thoughts had eventually been dismissed. This was his life, at least for now. If he were injured on the job where he couldn't recover to his former self, or he just grew too old, then that would be the time to reconsider. Fang had already told him she was fine with things the way they were. She understood the itch. She lived it. She had been Special Forces herself, part of China's elite Beijing Military Region Special Forces Unit. Each time he came back from an extended op, she would arrange some adrenaline-fueled activity for them, and he loved it. He wished she could be on ops with him. It would be a blast.

There was a tap at the door of the secure communications room at the Swiss Embassy. "Gotta go. That's my date."

"We'll continue to monitor. Don't eat anything too spicy. We don't want a repeat of Jakarta now, do we?"

Kane grimaced as he gripped his stomach, memories of a bad night flooding back. "I'll try to take it easy, but you and I both know that wasn't the spiciness, that was food poisoning."

"Whatever it was, I recommend you avoid repeating it."

Kane smirked. "If I was just repeating, it wouldn't have been a problem."

Leroux laughed. "Talk to you soon. Control Actual, out."

Kane pressed a button next to the comms unit, indicating it was clear for someone to enter. It opened and Heike, another one of the new arrivals, poked her blond head inside. "You ready?"

Kane smiled. "Absolutely. Let's go try this restaurant I've been hearing so much about." He joined her in the hallway and wrapped an arm over her shoulders, and she smiled up at him.

"I think this is going to be a fun assignment."

Kane returned the smile. Adding to his cover as a single womanizing Swiss lothario determined to play while on a temporary assignment, might just make his tail deem him to be less of a threat.

He just had to make sure things didn't go too far.

After all, he was spoken for.

Sepah Command Center

Tehran, Iran

Kiana scurried into the corner of her cell, curling into a ball as the lock slid aside and the door swung open. Her interrogator stood silhouetted in the doorframe. She couldn't make out his face, but she would recognize him anywhere now, the amount of pain, the amount of terror caused in the past couple of days, overwhelming.

"Something curious happened today."

She didn't respond. He was just toying with her.

"A man I suspect was an American agent, pretending to be working for the Swiss, was in my office inquiring about you and your children."

This piqued her interest, though she remained silent. Her husband had said if anything were to go wrong, to contact the Swiss Embassy as they were America's liaison in this godforsaken country. She obviously hadn't contacted them, but her husband must have, or perhaps her family here did on her behalf.

"I see you're not interested." He reached for the door.

She couldn't help herself. "What happened?"

He chuckled. "Curiosity is an overwhelming emotion, isn't it? He admitted that your husband doesn't work with the power company. He didn't confirm what we already knew, that your husband works for the CIA, but he implied it."

It was devastating. If the Swiss were saying her husband was CIA, or at a minimum not an employee at the utility company, then perhaps everything this man had told her was true. She caught herself. Unless this was also all a lie, all part of the games being played. "I don't believe you."

"Then perhaps you should listen to what was said." He placed a micro recorder just inside the door then left, its tiny speaker playing a meeting conducted in English, and as she listened, her heart broke, as she had no idea who was telling the truth.

Her husband of over twenty years, or this man who had just beaten her hours earlier?

She stared up at the heavens and prayed for the first time in years.

Allah, please save me.

Farzan Residence

Tehran, Iran

Tara sat in the corner, ordered out of her bedroom by her grandmother. It had given her a chance to spend some time talking with her grandfather. He seemed like a nice man, a reasonable man, so unlike her grandmother, whom he flinched at every time she snapped at him. There was a dynamic here she didn't understand. She had always been told that men ruled here, not women, yet that clearly wasn't true in this household.

"Forgive me, my child, for I must rest."

He had left after a particularly long diatribe on the state of the house he was leaving her grandmother with, and he was now in his room resting, though she suspected it was more an escape than anything else. Whatever the reason, it left her alone among the insanity that surrounded her.

Her brother sat against the opposite wall with several of the men, including Kaveh, who continued to leer at her. It was disgusting. Not only was he far too old for her, he was revolting looking. His hair was a wreck, his beard was wild, he had a large mole just to the left of his right eye, and a mouth full of teeth that were barely hanging on.

He grinned at her, showing them off. She twisted away and laugher erupted on the other side of the room.

Her aunt, sitting beside her, swatted her arm. "You two would make a good match."

Tara spun toward the woman, her mouth agape. "What?"

"You two would make a good match. He's a good man. He would make a good husband."

Bile filled her mouth at the thought. "That's disgusting!"

Her aunt's eyes narrowed. "In what way?"

"First of all, he is way too old for me."

The woman batted away the concern. "Nonsense. Women younger than you get promised all the time."

A queasiness rippled through her. "Not to mention the fact he's my cousin. We're related."

"Cousin, but not by blood. We adopted him when he was a baby."

She suddenly remembered who she was talking to. This was Kaveh's mother, or adopted mother. Whatever, it didn't matter. She had to be careful. "I'm not interested. I'm leaving here soon."

The woman scoffed. "We'll see about that."

She had to take a chance. She had to find out what was happening. "What do you mean?"

The woman dismissed the question. "It's none of your concern. Your family knows what's best for you."

"My family is my mother and father, not you people."

The woman's hand darted out, smacking her across the cheek, the stinging admonishment shocking. Her parents had never hit her. Not once in her entire life, nor her brother, despite him desperately deserving it sometimes. Corporal punishment was so alien to her, she burst out crying, resulting in more laughter from the other side of the room.

She stared at the piece of garbage they wanted her to marry, and her brother who had betrayed her. Yet for a brief moment, she could swear he was as shocked as her before he joined in, avoiding eye contact with her. She had to get the hell out of here, but where could she possibly go? And what about the man on the street who had sent her the signal? He was obviously here for her, wasn't he?

A horrible thought occurred to her. What if he wasn't? What if he was just a man on the street who knew she was American, so made the sign not to give her hope, but to warn her he knew? She hugged her knees and turned away from the others.

She truly was all alone, and she would rather die than marry that thing sitting across the room.

Staff Bathroom, CIA Headquarters

Langley, Virginia

Farzan hugged the toilet bowl, retching yet again. His guilt had given him barely a moment's respite since he had revealed the location of the asset assigned to Operation Poseidon's Trident. At least he still had a conscience, but he had still betrayed his country. Yet he would gladly face prison for the rest of his life if it meant saving his wife and children. The man on the other end of the line, whose name he didn't know, hadn't provided him with any relief when he had asked if it meant they would set his wife free.

"We'll see, but I'll promise you this. No one will touch her for twenty-four hours."

"And my children?"

"They aren't our concern. They're American citizens born in America. If they choose to stay here, then that's their choice."

"They would never choose to stay. Their home is here."

"Are you sure of that?"

The question had challenged his beliefs. He was certain his daughter would never want to stay. She was a young American woman. Living under an oppressive, masochist regime would never be acceptable to her. His son, on the other hand, he wasn't so sure about anymore. "When will you make your decision?"

"Not before I confirm your intel."

The call had ended, and he had vomited into his waste bin in his office. What he had hoped was a one-off wasn't, having him in and out of here for hours. What he had done was so wrong, so against everything he had ever believed in, the guilt and shame were overwhelming. But what else could he do? Yes, Kane was in position, had already seen his children, and apparently made contact with his daughter. He had also met with a representative of the Iranian government to discuss his wife, but nothing had come of it.

There was only one way she was getting out of this, and that was if he cooperated. Yet he still needed the CIA to get his children out, should it become necessary.

The bathroom door opened, somebody rushing inside. "Cyrus, you in here?"

It was Baxter.

Farzan spat in the toilet then flushed it. He checked himself to make sure he didn't have anything on him, then opened the door.

Baxter was about to say something then stopped. "You look like shit."

"I feel like shit."

"Something you ate?"

The suggestion gave him a reasonable explanation that hadn't occurred to him. "Something I drank."

Baxter cocked an eyebrow. "Something you drank? I didn't think you were a drinker."

"I'm not. That's why it upset my stomach. A single shot of scotch nursed over an hour, that, I can tolerate. A couple of doubles in an hour with Morrison is an entirely different story."

Baxter snickered. "Yeah, I've heard he can put them back. You know he used to be an operations officer?"

It was Farzan's eyebrows turn to jump. "Really?"

"Yeah. Probably why he's so good at his job. Are you gonna be okay?"

Farzan shrugged. "Eventually."

"Well, good. You've got an emergency meeting."

"What's up?"

"Poseidon's Trident has been compromised."

Farzan darted toward the toilet once again.

Malek Cafe & Restaurant

Tehran, Iran

Heike was a bundle of fun, and if Kane were single, he would be already heading home with her. But he wasn't, and bedding her wasn't necessary to the mission. The meal was fabulous, and he was gaining a new appreciation for Persian cuisine. He excused himself and headed for the bathroom. He took care of business and sent a text to Shadmani, arranging a meet-up. His contact responded a moment later, confirming the rendezvous.

He stepped out of the bathroom and into the hall to find Heike standing there. She grabbed his hand and hauled him into the women's bathroom, locking the door behind her. She shoved him against the wall and began an assault on his mouth. He played along, something that wasn't hard to do. She was gorgeous, after all. But when she reached down and gave junior a squeeze, he gently pulled her hand away.

"Not now."

She stared into his eyes, lust written across her face. "Why not?"

"First of all, if we get caught in here, you know it's gonna cause problems for both of us. And besides, if we're gonna do this, I wanna do it right."

"Tonight?"

"Absolutely."

"My place or yours?"

"My place is a room."

"So is mine."

"Okay. Your room or mine?"

She grabbed him by the back of the neck, pulling his ear toward her mouth. "Mine. It's probably cleaner."

He gave her a look. "I haven't even been here two nights. Just how much of a pig do you think I am?"

She grabbed him by the sides of his face, staring back into his eyes. "I hope you're filthy."

He smirked. "As filthy as you want me to be." He kissed her again then gently pushed her away. "You go first. If we go back together, people might talk."

She gave junior another squeeze. "Let them." She patted the responding little guy. "Something tells me you should wait here a few minutes. Otherwise, questions could be, you know, 'raised?'"

He grinned. "You're terrible, but I think I like that."

"Good. See you tonight."

She left, leaving him alone, when he remembered he was in the women's bathroom. He made a hasty escape and checked both ways down the hall, nobody noticing. He headed for the rear exit, sending Heike a text. "Just got a message. Have to leave. Sorry. Going out the back. You know why." He followed it with a grin emoji. She responded with a laughing emoji and a kiss.

He left the restaurant, stuffing his phone in his pocket, wondering how he would get out of tonight's scheduled rendezvous. As much as the old version of him would love to ravage this woman, he had everything he wanted or could need at home waiting for him, her heart broken with the death of her father.

Shadmani pulled up in front of the alleyway and Kane jogged over, climbing into the passenger seat. They pulled away as Kane yanked the seat belt in place. "Anything new?"

"Yeah, I'm thinking of putting a taxi meter in this thing and charging you for these rides."

"Knock yourself out, as long as you provide receipts. Langley's footing these bills, not me. Just remember that old saying, 'Don't bite the hand that feeds you.'"

Shadmani considered the idiom for a moment. "Yeah, I guess that makes sense, doesn't it?"

Kane regarded his friend. "So, anything new?"

"Nothing really. They seem to be sticking to their routine. They went for morning prayers as a family. The father remained behind. Then they joined in an anti-America, anti-Israel rally, then returned home. Those that work headed to their jobs."

"And the kids?"

"The son appears to still be a zealot, and the daughter, from her body language, looks broken. There was one new development, however."

Kane's eyebrows rose. "Oh?"

"Yeah. The grandmother and a couple of other women went to the market with the daughter. They're there right now."

"Interesting. That suggests they're not keeping her prisoner."

"No. I doubt they'll let her out on her own, but it does provide us access."

"If we try to grab her, we'd have to neutralize those with her. But if they're gonna start letting her out, we might be able to slip her a message."

"Is that wise?"

"We have to let her know that there is hope, and to be ready when the time comes."

"And the brother?"

"I still think we're gonna have to take him against his will. Have you seen him out?"

"Other than prayers, no. But if he's truly turned, it's probably just a matter of time. Any word yet on an extraction plan from Langley?"

"Yes. Basically, grab them, throw them in the trunk if we have to, drive them to an extraction point where they'll be smuggled to the coast, just like we talked about. It works a lot easier if the son's on board."

"I don't think that's happening."

"I agree. Where are we headed?"

"The market. There's a chance they could still be there."

"Good." Kane pulled a small pad of paper out of his pocket and began scribbling a note. He tore it and a blank page off then folded them together. "Do you have a pencil?"

"Glove compartment."

Kane opened it and found an imitation Hilroy. He snapped it in half and wrapped the pages around it.

"Hey, why'd you do that?"

"A full pencil is harder to conceal. And besides"—he held up the second half before tossing it back into the glove compartment—"you can still gnaw this into something usable."

"Uh-huh." Shadmani pointed ahead. "Here's the market." He pulled to the side of the road and Kane activated his comms. "Control, Fly Guy. Come in, over."

"This is Control. Go ahead, Fly Guy."

"What's my tail doing?"

"Scratching their asses, by the looks of it. Your dinner party has left for the embassy just a couple of minutes ago. Looks like your tail's not sure what to do."

"Have they gone in yet?"

"No, but I expect they will any minute now."

"How was the exit?"

"Chaotic enough that there is a chance they might think they just missed you."

"Let's hope so. Keep me posted. Fly Guy, out."

Shadmani eyed him. "Fly Guy?"

"I wanted Pretty Fly for a White Guy to honor The Offspring, but I was overruled."

"Thank God."

Kane wrapped a chafiyeh around his face. It clashed with his off-the-rack suit, but he had seen plenty of men wearing similar attire. As unnatural as it felt, it should still allow him to blend.

They made their way through the bustling market, both their heads on swivels, searching for the family, made all the more difficult by what they normally wore outside. Then again, their black head-to-toe garments allowed him to rapidly eliminate most of the crowd.

"Two o'clock," murmured Shadmani.

Kane turned his head slightly and spotted three women in the traditional garb, and young Tara wearing something more appropriate to her age, though still very conservative. Her chin was pressed against her chest, her shoulders rolled inward, a mouse among a clowder of cats. "I'm gonna make contact. You distract them."

"No problem."

Kane wove his way through the crowd, Shadmani on his heels, his message and the pencil palmed in his hand. Tara's relatives were haggling with a fruit vendor as the poor girl stood meekly nearby. Shadmani passed him, making a beeline for the same stall. He leaned over, placing his body between Tara and the others, loudly demanding the price for three Persian melons.

Kane walked up to Tara and, as he brushed past her, pressed the note and pencil into the palm of her right hand. She gasped and turned to say something, but he warned her off. "Don't react." And he was gone, cutting between two stalls, Shadmani still boisterously interacting with the vendor, the female customers' agitation with his cutting in, growing.

Kane wandered back to the car, praying the young girl was collected enough to hide the message and the pencil away before being caught. Shadmani casually joined him, three melons cradled in his left arm, one split by the vendor, half-eaten. "Want some?" he asked, raising his occupied arm slightly.

Kane grabbed a few wedges. "Did you get a good deal?"

"The best. The key is to make them think they're gonna lose their other customers if they don't quickly seal the deal."

"Let's just hope you don't prove too memorable. Otherwise, those women are gonna spot you from a mile away when you're watching their place."

"I have one of those faces that nobody remembers."

Kane eyeballed him. "It's true. It's a miracle you got married."

Shadmani shrugged. "Yeah, I was surprised too. I'm pretty sure she thought she was marrying someone else but realized it too late, so decided, 'What the hell? Let's give him a try.' Seems to have worked so far, but I don't know if I'll ever get used to the name 'Samir' while we're making love."

Tajrish Bazaar

Tehran, Iran

Tara didn't dare look down as her heart hammered. Something was in her hand. She didn't know what it was, but it felt like paper and something hard. The man had spoken English, warning her not to react. But how the hell was she supposed to avoid that? She couldn't recall being more terrified in her life, yet the man had spoken in English. He sounded American, perhaps Canadian. Could it have been the man from across the street who had signaled USA to her?

She had caught a glimpse of him in a business suit, dramatically different clothing than the man yesterday. But that meant nothing. She had to hide what was in her hand. She couldn't be caught with it. She bent down and tightened her shoelaces, and as she stood, drew her robe up with her hand and shoved whatever had been passed to her into the pocket of her pants before letting the garment fall back down to her side.

She couldn't wait to get home now.

Ugh.

She couldn't believe she had just thought of it as "home." It wasn't her home. It never would be. Her terror was slowly giving way to excitement, to curiosity. What was it? If it was indeed paper, it was probably a message. Who was it from? It had to be her father, but how? How would he ever get her a message? He was a nobody. He worked for the power company. How colossally boring was that?

Yet she was an American. Her mother was being held. Maybe the government had become involved, though she highly doubted that. They were a family of nobodies. They had come here voluntarily. Why would some man be slipping her a message like he was a spy? Her father had said there was no American Embassy here. She had to think if there were efforts being made to bring them home, it would be through official channels. Families like hers didn't merit special attention.

She spotted one of her aunts eying her. Her instinct was to quickly turn away, but instead she gestured at the oranges. "Can I get one?"

Her grandmother turned. "How much for six of those?" she asked the vendor, and more haggling ensued. Soon they were heading back to her grandparents' place, laden with heavy fruits and vegetables, but the weight didn't bother her as whatever had been passed to her burned a hole in her pocket.

Her grandmother picked up on her distraction. "What's going on with you?"

"Huh?"

"You're off in another world."

Tara was already prepared for the question, and gave the answer she always did. "I'm just worried about my mother."

"Stop worrying about her. She'll be fine."

Tara bit her tongue. How the woman could be so dismissive was beyond her. Her grandmother was cruel, mean, and if she ever did get out of here, she had no desire to ever see or speak to the woman again. She never wanted to even think about this country again. This wasn't her home. Never would be, never could be. Yet she had to adapt, at least temporarily, for every indication was they had no intention of letting her go.

Yet that wasn't her biggest concern. Her biggest concern was Kaveh. He terrified her. It was clear he was attracted to her, clear the family wanted them to be married, and she feared he might take advantage of that and rape her. And her brother, who had to know what was going on, seemed fine with that.

They reached the street where her grandparents lived, and she surreptitiously searched for the man who might be her savior, but couldn't spot him. It didn't matter. She had whatever he had passed her buried deep in her pocket. They passed through the door then up the stairs to the main floor of the home. "I have to use the bathroom," she said.

Her grandmother scowled. "Such lack of control. Be quick about it. There are chores to be done."

"Yes, Grandmother." She scurried to the bathroom and closed the door. She took care of business first, as going again could raise suspicions. She finished but didn't flush, instead reaching down into her pants pocket. She retrieved what turned out to be a piece of paper rolled around the stub of a pencil. She stuffed the pencil back into her pocket then unfolded two small pieces of paper. One was blank, but the other had writing on it, and the words had her heart racing with hope.

I work with your father. Don't tell anyone, even your brother. Write your answers to my questions, then when you have a chance, crumple it up and drop it out your window.

She gulped as she read the questions.

Do you believe your brother has become radicalized?

Will he leave willingly?

Are you in danger?

She pulled out the pencil and quickly began scribbling her answers when there was a rap at the door. "What's going on in there? Hurry up!"

"I'm almost finished," she yelped.

"Well, hurry up!"

"Yes, Grandmother." She finished the answers then stuffed the two pieces of paper and the pencil back into her pocket and flushed the toilet. She washed her hands, staring at herself in the mirror. Her cheeks were flushed, and her heart still pounded from the excitement. She had to keep control, and sticking to her story of being worried about her mother would hopefully continue to work.

She dried her hands then returned to the kitchen, wondering when she would get a chance to deliver her answers to the man her father had sent. And now a new question preoccupied her.

How did her father, a pencil pusher at the power company, ever manage to get someone to help her in a country like Iran?

Outside the Farzan Residence

Tehran, Iran

Shadmani bent over and brushed some non-existent dirt off the cuff of his pants then picked up the crumpled piece of paper tossed out the window only moments before. He continued down the street as Kane started the engine and shifted the car into gear. He pulled away from the curb, rounding the residential area and coming out the other side where Shadmani hailed him. He climbed in the passenger side, then Kane pulled back into the light residential traffic.

Shadmani held up the crumpled paper. "Shall I do the honors?"

"Knock yourself out."

He flattened out the small page, and Kane glanced over to see the printed words, cursive a skill lost to a generation due to short-sighted educators. It appeared hurried and shaky. "Yes, my brother has become radicalized and I don't think he would willingly go. Yes, I think I'm in danger. I'm afraid my cousin Kaveh will rape me. I don't believe my family plans to let us go, and they're talking about me marrying him. Help me, please." He held up the page. "There's three exclamation points, and that last sentence is underlined."

Kane sighed. "Well, at least that confirms a few things that we suspected or feared. She's scared, possibly in danger, and wants to leave. Her brother is radicalized and probably won't leave willingly. Her family apparently has no intention of letting her leave, and is already making plans for her future. So that means getting them out through the airport on their regularly scheduled flight is a no-go. And since he's been radicalized, even if we tried to get them out on false identities, he wouldn't cooperate."

"So, that leaves Langley's original plan." Shadmani grimaced. "Which I don't like."

"Neither do I."

"We don't really have a choice now, do we?"

"Not that I can see."

"What do we do now?"

"We prep for the extraction."

"And just how do you plan on doing that? The family's always around. And the only time I see the two kids together is when they go for prayers."

It was a problem Kane hadn't stopped thinking about, and it was a question he had little time to find an answer to.

If the underage Tara was afraid she might be raped, there was no time to waste.

Tajrish Bazaar

Tehran, Iran

Kane, this morning dressed in more appropriate garb, spotted young Tara with her grandmother, the other female relatives not here this morning for some reason. He casually strolled toward her, chatting with Shadmani about a soccer match his friend had watched last night, and that Kane had read a summary of provided by Langley. It was a sport he was slowly getting into, most of the world crazy about it, including parts of the world he operated in. Sports and pop culture were great covers and easy conversation starters that might get lips moving, hopefully, eventually in the direction you wanted them to. But today it was a great cover for two men walking in a market, mostly filled with women.

"Did you see that save by Hosein in the fourth quarter? It was unbelievable."

Kane agreed. "Saved the game, for sure."

"Definitely."

They were only ten paces away from Tara. She turned her head, and they briefly made eye contact. Kane gave her a slight wink and her eyes bulged then redirected toward the ground as her head tipped forward. Kane crossed between her and her grandmother, passing her a note, this time without a pencil, hoping the young woman was wise enough to have hidden it away somewhere so she could reply to his questions.

Kane continued on as Shadmani bumped into the grandmother, making no apology, a loud harrumph the reply though no words spoken. In Iran, a good Muslim woman never spoke in public to a male that wasn't a relative.

Kane continued past the stalls, eying several street food carts. His stomach grumbled, and he turned to Shadmani. "What's good here?"

Shadmani grinned. "Everything."

"I'll be the judge of that. Pick your favorite because we might not get another chance. Langley wants them out ASAP. Once she answers those questions, we'll have all we need to do the extraction tonight."

Shadmani gestured ahead at a food cart with no line. "This is the one."

Kane's eyebrows rose. "Really? The only one with nobody in line?"

"It's not because the food's not good, it's because the owner's an asshole."

Kane chuckled. "And so are you, so I suppose you two get along great."

"Horribly. I took Jack here once."

"Just Jack?"

"That's the one. And he said the guy reminded him of the soup Nazi. What's a soup Nazi?"

"Too hard to explain."

"Huh. That's what he said."

They walked up to the food truck and the exchange that followed mimicked the famous Seinfeld episode so closely it had to be staged. Kane opened his mouth to say something when Shadmani subtly shook his head. Apparently, there was no talking in the line.

What line?

Shadmani paid, and they were handed their wraps assembled in front of them from piles of delicious fresh vegetables, most marinated or pickled, the meat he presumed to be lamb, shaved off a vertical spit. It reminded him of a traditional Lebanese donair.

Shadmani led them away and jerked his chin toward Kane's wrap. "Tell me what you think."

Kane folded the wax paper out of the way, first inhaling the aroma then groaning. "Smells good."

"Wait till you take a bite."

Kane bit down, tearing off a mouthful, then chewed in bliss. "Holy shit, this is good!"

"Told you. Have you ever had better?"

Kane swallowed. "I know you're gonna hate to hear this, but there's a little food truck run by an old man named Mr. Wu in China that beats this"—he held up his thumb and forefinger, separated by an eighth of an inch—"but only by this much. This is fantastic. What's it called?"

"Kebab Torki. Turkish Kebab."

"And is it always this good or is it just this guy?"

"This is my favorite. Probably like your pizza back home. There's good, there's bad, some are just godawful. But this asshole's is consistently good." They leaned against the side of a building and enjoyed their meal. "So, Langley has given up on the possibility they could be sent home with their plane tickets?"

Kane swallowed. "Yeah. They're not willing to risk it. This is looking too well organized. One of my updates has a terror cell that was operating just outside of Langley involved with an inside man, a mole at the CIA."

"I thought you guys were too good for that."

"So did we, but apparently not. We have no idea how they got inside and made it through the screening process, but they did. And it looks like they're the ones who got Farzan's travel review approved. The mole is the only reason the family's here, because he falsely cleared it as safe. Now that the terror cell has been taken down, they know we're on to them."

"Then why are we waiting until tonight?"

"It takes time to put these things together, especially when one participant is unwilling. Also, Langley is confident no move will be made until it has to be made, which means we probably have until their departure date."

"That gives us over a week yet you're going tonight?"

"Absolutely. My gut tells me we can't risk waiting.

"And the wife, we're just going to leave her to rot?"

"For now, she's in the hands of the diplomats, and you know how well that works in these situations."

Shadmani lowered his wrap, a frown creasing his face. "She's in for a hell of a lot more pain."

Sepah Command Center

Tehran, Iran

Kiana lay in the corner of her cell, curled into a ball, her face swollen and bloodied, barely able to see through her fluid filled eyelids. She struggled to breathe, certain at least some of her ribs were cracked. This was the worst beating she had received since her imprisonment. It was brutal. Vicious. The entire event had been recorded, each volley of blows punctuated by her masked torturer whose voice she recognized as that of her interrogator, spitting at the camera, admonishing her husband for the deaths of his Islamic brothers.

She had no idea what the hell he was talking about, but it was clear a message was being delivered. Something had happened, something resulting in the death of people this man seemed to know. It was once again clear that they blamed her husband for whatever had happened, still convinced he worked for the CIA. Could people like this make such a mistake? She had her doubts. They seemed so certain, and now they had committed an atrocity, a violation of human rights, and had recorded it. She had no doubt with what was said during her beating that it would be sent to her husband.

It meant the proof of their crimes would be out there.

Why would they do such a thing? It seemed foolish, yet this wasn't America. If someone did this back home, they would face prison time if it were discovered. Here, they would probably get a parade. A spark of resistance flared and she inhaled slowly, deeply, expanding her lungs as far as she could manage while gripping at the agony. She wasn't letting her old country win. She was American. She was free. And if her husband did work for the CIA, which would both piss her off for lying to her for all these years, but fill her with pride that he was helping in the fight to free their former home, he and those he worked for might just manage to free her. She had to hang on for her children, for her husband, but most of all, for herself.

She was not dying in an Iranian prison cell. She had too much to live for.

Farzan Residence

Tehran, Iran

Tara didn't dare risk heading for the bathroom a second day in a row. She instead helped with unpacking what they had bought then cleaning and preparing the fruit and vegetables for the meals later in the day. When they were finally done, she turned to her grandmother. "May I go to the bathroom now?"

Her grandmother stared at her inquisitively. "You don't need permission to go to the bathroom."

"But yesterday…"

"Yesterday you had chores to do. When you're finished your chores, you're free to do what you want."

"Oh, I understand."

Her grandmother gave her a hug and Tara returned it, not questioning whether there was any love behind it. There wasn't. Her grandmother let her go and Tara headed for the bathroom, struggling to control herself, her eagerness to see what was written on the message passed to her, threatening to betray her. She did her business as she had last time, though this time she read the note while doing it. She didn't want to be in here any longer than necessary.

Tara, it won't be much longer. Please answer these questions using the numbers.

1. Have you seen any guns in the house?

2. Are you able to walk out the front door or is it locked or blocked in some way at night?

3. How many adult males and females do you think will be there tonight at midnight?

4. Do you expect your brother to be there tonight?

Be prepared to leave at midnight. Don't tell anyone including your brother.

She closed her eyes, her chest heaving with panic and relief. She would be rescued tonight. It was almost over. They would get her, and by the sounds of it, they would take her brother whether he wanted to go or not. She was worried sick about her mother, but there was no doubt what the woman would want for her. She would want her children safe, and cooperating with whoever this man was, was the key to that.

Once they were free and back in America, there would be no shutting her up. She would go public with what had happened to her and to her family, and wouldn't rest until her mother was freed.

She flushed the toilet and washed her hands, joining her grandmother in the kitchen. "I'm going to take a nap."

"That's fine. I'll wake you in an hour. I want your help preparing dinner."

"Yes, grandmother." She entered her room and closed the door, finding it empty. Most of the household was at work or school. Ray had gone with Kaveh, and she was pretty sure it was just her and her grandparents in the house.

She fetched her pencil, hidden at the bottom of her toiletry bag, then began scribbling the responses to the questions from her savior, when the door opened. She gasped at the sight of Kaveh standing there, glaring at her.

"What are you doing?"

Her stomach flipped, her mouth watered, then a hint of resistance from her American upbringing asserted itself. "None of your business! Get out of my room!"

He stepped deeper inside and she scrambled to her feet, crumpling the paper behind her back, surreptitiously shoving the page with the questions into the palm of her other hand, squeezing the pages together as she backed toward the window. "Get out of here! This is my room! It's not appropriate for you to be in here!"

He closed the door behind him, his eyes roaming her body, the look in his eyes terrifying, animalistic, primal. "What were you writing? Tell me, woman!"

Her bum bumped into the windowsill and she tossed the crumpled papers out the window. Kaveh rushed toward her, rage replacing the lust. He grabbed her by the throat and pulled her away from the window then peered outside. "What was that?"

"It's none of your business! Now let go of me!" She struggled against the iron grip on her throat that continued to tighten. "Let go of me!" she screamed, but the air was being cut off. She clawed at his face and he cried out as she drew blood, but the response was a fist to her nose. The pain was overwhelming, and she slumped in his grip for a moment. He threw her onto the bed then approached her slowly as she sobbed.

"We are to be betrothed. You are to be my wife." He unbuckled his pants. "I don't think we should wait for our wedding night. You're going to be taught what it means to be a good Muslim wife, a good Muslim woman." He undid his pants then zipped down his fly, shoving them to the floor, revealing he wore no underwear.

She recoiled in disgust at the sight of her first man. She squeezed her eyes shut. She wasn't ready for this. She was too young. She wanted to have sex, but with a boy she loved, a boy who loved her. Whether that was when she was 16 or 26, she didn't care. All she knew was this wasn't what she wanted. This was never what any woman wanted. She was about to be raped, and she did the only thing she could think of.

She screamed for help.

And he laughed in response.

"I'm the man of the house. No one's going to save you." He stepped forward, closer to her. "Get on your knees."

"What?"

"Get on your knees. Open your mouth."

She clamped her jaw shut, shaking her head as the tears rolled freely. She folded her arms, covering her breasts, covering anything that might sexually stimulate this beast. He stepped closer and she could smell him.

It was revolting. Was this what it normally smelled like, or was he just an unbathed pig?

"Open your mouth."

She shook her head again, her teeth clenched, her lips pressed together. He smacked her, the sting as bad as the punch.

"Open your mouth!"

Again, she refused, and this time he reached down and punched her in the stomach. She gasped, her mouth opening, and his hips thrust forward, but she twisted her head in time. "Help! Please, Ray, help!" Why wasn't her brother helping her? He had to be here. He had been with Kaveh when they left this morning. Surely he was here. Surely he heard her.

Kaveh grabbed her by the chin, glaring down at her. "This is your last chance, or else I'm going to beat you so badly you'll be begging for me to marry you." He clenched his fist and raised it. "Do you understand me?"

She did. She was going to lose. Her brother had gone so far to the dark side, he was no longer willing to help his little sister. She was all alone. Her life was over, and this was her future, servicing a beast for the rest of her days.

He jerked the fist back, preparing for the punch. "Do you understand?"

Her shoulders slumped, and she nodded.

"Now open your mouth."

She did and squeezed her eyes shut as the grip on her chin loosened, his hand moving to the back of her head, pulling her closer.

Oh God, please kill me!

The door burst open and Kaveh spun. She opened her eyes to see her brother standing there, shock on his face. "What the hell is this?"

"Get out of here, my brother. This is between a man and his woman."

"She's my sister!"

"She's to be my wife. You know this. You supported this."

"But she's only sixteen!"

"Age is but a number. Now get out of here. She's already agreed to this."

Her eyes bulged as she shook her head rapidly, pleading with her brother. "Help me!"

Ray stared at her then Kaveh, confusion on his face. Yet how could there be? There was only one choice here. He had to help her. How could there be any debate? She was his sister. He was her big brother. He was supposed to protect her.

"Get out of here now!"

Ray's head slumped and he stepped backward.

"Close the door!"

Ray reached for the door and she screamed as it closed. Kaveh grabbed her head with both hands. "Now, where were we?"

The door flew open, smacking against the wall as Ray roared. Kaveh turned and her eyes shot wide with joy as her brother rushed in, a kitchen knife raised high.

"Kill him, Ray! Kill him!"

Kaveh reached for the knife but it was already on the downswing. Her husband-to-be cried out in agony as the tip of the large weapon pierced his palm, the downward motion shoving the blade all the way through. Kaveh dropped to his knees, wailing in agony as Ray pulled the knife free.

"Kill him!" she urged, and Ray, his eyes filled with blind fury, shoved the blade forward once again, catching the kneeling Kaveh in the throat at an angle, slicing through the jugular. Her assailant flopped onto the ground, gurgling his final moments, and Ray stepped back, the knife clattering to the floor. She burst from the bed and into his arms, sobbing. "Oh, thank you! Thank you!"

He slowly regained his senses and hugged her back. "Are you all right?"

"I am now, but we have to get out of here."

Footfalls down the hallway added credence to her statement.

"Oh my God, what have you done?" It was her grandmother.

Tara was about to respond when her brother beat her to it. "He was trying to rape her!"

Their grandmother stared at him. "Then you let him! He's to be her husband! Those things are between man and woman."

They both stared at her in horror. "But she's only sixteen! She's still a child! He's ten years older than her! And shouldn't it be her choice?"

Their grandmother dropped to her knees, staring down at her nephew, her hands outstretched though not touching the body, uncertain as to what to do. "Did he teach you nothing? I thought you understood our ways."

Ray, his arm over Tara's shoulders, squeezed her tighter. "I thought I had too, but if this is your way, I want nothing to do with it."

Their grandmother pushed to her feet. "I'm calling the police. They'll deal with you two infidels!"

"You'll do no such thing."

Everyone spun to see Grandfather in the door. He glared at his wife. "Kaveh was a pig and deserved to die. And you disgust me! Your whole family disgusts me! I had no idea what I had married until it was too late." He turned to his grandchildren. "Clean yourselves up, get that blood off you, then leave. You can't be here when the rest of the family returns."

"Where are we going to go?" asked Ray.

"Try to get to the Swiss Embassy. It's on Yasaman Street. Hail a cab. Ask them to take you to that street. Don't ask them to take you to the embassy. Remember, you both look Iranian and you both speak Farsi, so you want them to think you're one of us."

"What about our passports? Our phones?" asked Tara.

"In my bedroom, top drawer of the nightstand. That's where she's put them. Now, get out of here. There's not much time before her family comes back."

Tara rushed into his arms and the old man hugged her.

"I'm so sorry for this. I should have been stronger."

She stared up at him, her eyes filled with tears. "You were strong when it counted."

Her grandfather's eyes glistened, and he smiled down at her as his lip quivered. "I'm so happy I met you. I will die content with the knowledge that my granddaughter is a strong, independent woman who knows what she wants." He stretched out an arm toward Ray. "And my grandson is a courageous warrior who defended his sister's honor and couldn't be led astray by the twisted words of a hateful family." He gave them both strong hugs. "I love you both. Now go and tell my son, your father, that I love him and that he raised two amazing children. Tell him I'm extremely proud of him, even if he does work for the CIA."

Tara's jaw dropped, as did Ray's. "The CIA?"

Her grandfather smiled at them. "I think when you get home, your father has some questions to answer."

"But how do you know if we don't even know?"

The old man sighed, shooting daggers at his wife. "That's a question you'd have to ask your grandmother, but there's no time for that. You must leave now. The others will be back any minute. You must go."

Tara gave him another squeeze then let him go, rushing down the hall toward the bathroom, her brother on her heels. Ray cursed as he saw himself in the mirror, arterial spray staining his clothes.

"Go to your room. Get some new clothes."

He rushed from the bathroom and she washed her face and hands then straightened her clothes. Her nose was slightly bloodied. Her cheeks were red and would soon bruise, but she was alive, though how long that would last if the family returned, she had no idea.

They had to get out of here. Now.

Outside the Farzan Residence

Tehran, Iran

Kane scooped up the crumpled piece of paper, finding it a little thicker than expected. A girl screamed and he twisted around, staring up at the window. He heard the distinct sound of a fist impacting flesh, followed by another cry. It had to be Tara. But what was happening? Had she been caught writing her responses? Was she in a fight with her brother, with her cousin Kaveh? The two had entered the home only minutes ago. It had to be Kaveh. He was a true zealot. Her brother might be headed down that road, might even have reached the destination, but Kane couldn't imagine him beating his own sister.

Yet anything was possible.

He fired a message to Shadmani.

Bring the car now!

He couldn't let this go on. It had to be stopped, and that meant intervening. It likely meant killing Kaveh, incapacitating Ray, and carrying the boy out over his shoulder, which meant he needed a car. He sent another message to Leroux.

Activate the network. This is going down now.

Two messages pinged back, Shadmani indicating he was three minutes out, and Leroux replying with a message he expected.

Acknowledged. We'll do our best.

He fired a thumbs-up back as the shouts above continued, Tara screaming for help, screaming for her brother. He wanted to go in, to put an end to this now, but he had to wait. Once he committed, that was it, everything had to move like clockwork. He would be in, up the stairs to her bedroom. Kaveh would be dead inside of three seconds. He would put her brother in a sleeper hold. He would be out in less than a minute. Then all three of them would be down the stairs and directly into Shadmani's car.

But it had to be here. They couldn't be standing on the street for the entire neighborhood to see in broad daylight. It had to be timed perfectly. He checked his watch. Shadmani should be two minutes out. It was time. Another voice joined the shouts. It sounded young. It had to be Ray. He held off. If Ray was involved, it meant the dynamic of the current situation had changed, the immediate urgency of saving Tara from imminent rape, gone, though perhaps only for a moment. Everything depended on how Ray would react to seeing his sister about to be taken by his mentor in extremism. Would he protect his sister, or would he submit to the will of the Svengali currently gripping him?

The shouting subsided. More screams erupted then Ray bellowed. Kane headed for the front entrance, shoving open the door, answering one of his questions. Did they keep the front door locked or blocked?

Apparently not.

He rushed silently up the stairs as the shouting continued, then calmed. He stood waiting, listening, an old man now talking. It had to be the grandfather, and it was clear whose side he was on, that of his grandchildren, not his wife and her fanatical family.

They didn't have time for this conversation. Minutes counted. But if they knew he was involved, it could change the situation. He edged his way down the stairs. They would come out any minute now. As long as the family, especially the grandmother, believed the children were headed for the Swiss Embassy on their own accord, that would help send the authorities in the wrong direction.

He cracked the door open as the conversation above continued. He peered out, finding it clear, and stepped outside, closing the door carefully behind him, though without making it appear too obvious he was doing so. Shadmani pulled up, gently applying his brakes. Kane climbed into the passenger seat.

"What the hell's going on?"

"Change of plans. Something happened up there. I think the cousin tried to rape the daughter and the brother intervened."

"So, this is on now?"

"It is, in some way, shape, or form. This could turn into a total Charlie Foxtrot, or our lives could have just become a whole lot easier."

"How's that?"

The door swung open and Tara rushed out with her brother Ray.

"That's how."

Tara, still a jumble of emotions, stepped out into the sunlight holding her brother's hand, a brother who had saved her, a brother who had come back to her. The door closed behind them and she stared up and down the street. "Which way do we go?" But her question was answered for her as the door of a car parked in front of them opened.

"Get in the back, now."

Ray took a step back, but she immediately recognized the man as her savior. She grabbed the handle of the rear door and yanked it open. "Get inside."

"But…"

"Just get inside."

Ray acquiesced, scrambling into the back seat, shuffling over to the other side as she climbed in and closed the door. The car pulled away slowly, which she supposed made sense, since they didn't want to draw any attention. The man who had passed her the notes twisted around in his seat to face them. He smiled broadly at her and repeated the USA symbol he had delivered that first time she had seen him. She returned it, and he extended a fist and she bumped it.

"USA!" He turned to Ray. "Nice to meet you, Ray. Can I assume you're back from the dark side?"

Ray snapped out a quick nod, clearly confused and scared.

"My name is Dylan. I work with your father and I'm here to get you two back home. Can I assume you both want that?"

Ray was much more certain this time, his head bobbing vigorously as Tara threw her arms around him, giving him a tight squeeze. "Yes. More than anything!" she cried.

"Then good. I have one rule."

"What's that?"

"That you do exactly what I say, when I say. No questioning. No hesitating. No asking why. Nothing. When I say to do something, you do it immediately without question or people die. Understood?"

They both nodded, the reality they weren't free yet setting in.

"Good. Then let's get the hell out of this shit hole."

The driver took offense. "Hey, this shit hole is my home."

The man who had called himself Dylan patted the driver's shoulder. "Sorry, man. Just trying to make a point. I'll try better next time."

"Words can hurt."

Dylan flashed a grin at them and winked, and she immediately felt more at ease than she had since her mother had sent them through those doors at the airport.

"What about my mother?"

Secure Flex Space 6C, CIA Headquarters

Langley, Virginia

Leroux entered the secure flex space, not to find excited team members, but instead concerned ones. Deeply concerned. "What did you find?"

Packman replied. "Nothing good. After we found the mole, we kept digging like you said to, and found some disturbing, I don't know, coincidences? So, we dug a little deeper and I think we might have a much bigger problem than someone messing around with travel reviews."

Leroux sat. "Run it down for me."

"Well, we started digging into our dead mole, Ali Hassan, but there wasn't much to find beyond the personnel files that we already reviewed. But when the photos started to come in from Echo Team, we started running those, and would you be surprised to find out that three of them applied for jobs here over the past six months?"

Leroux popped an eyebrow. "Really? Though I suppose I shouldn't be. If one applied and got in, then so could others."

"Yeah, but that's what's interesting. The others applied before him."

"Why were they screened out?"

"Mostly automated. Bad credit checks, lack of employment history, too many traffic violations, standard stuff that screams unreliability. But get this. Whatever the previous one was screened out for, the next one wasn't. It was like they were probing the system to see what the red flags were and then correcting them for the next applicant."

"Did they use different addresses?"

"All the same building but different apartment numbers."

"And that didn't raise any red flags?"

Child shrugged. "I guess not. Everyone was screened out for other reasons by the computer."

"But one made it through." Leroux paused. "Please tell me only one made it through."

Packman confirmed it. "As far as we can tell, the only person working at Langley from that building was Hassan until he resigned."

"Were there any more applicants after that?"

"No."

"Interesting. That suggests they were working toward a purpose."

"Just to approve a travel review?"

Leroux folded his arms and leaned back as he chewed his cheek. "It seems ridiculous, but let's piece together what we know, working backward. Operation Poseidon's Trident was compromised. Fortunately, we suspected it would be, so we warned our officer and he's safe. The intel that was released in the briefing was classified top secret, and less than a dozen people on the planet knew what hotel Jack was staying at, and that includes people like me and the Chief. Within minutes of that meeting, Farzan made a phone call to a number we traced back to Tehran, so we're quite confident he was the leak on that operation.

"However, there's no evidence to suggest he was providing them information before the situation with his family occurred. That means they're using them as leverage against him. The only way they could use them as leverage is to get their hands on them, which means they had to get them to Iran. The only way they could get them to Iran was to plant the seed that they needed to. They used Farzan's father's illness as the lure. That lure was cast when they had their man in position to do something about it. Farzan filed the travel review request. Hassan received it, approved it, paving the way for Farzan to then allow his family to visit his father before he died, but because it denied his travel, it kept him here." Leroux paused. "When did these job applications start?"

"Six months ago."

"Six?" Leroux squinted. "Exactly when?"

"February seventeenth."

Leroux grunted. "There's no way that's a coincidence."

"What do you mean?" asked Packman.

"Poseidon's Trident has been in the works for almost a year. Two days before that first application, Farzan was partially read in on the file because we needed to know how it might impact other petroleum producing states. If we took Russian oil off the market, we could be inadvertently helping the Iranians."

Packman leaned forward. "Wait a minute. You're saying we have this op, highly classified, Farzan gets read into it, and two days later the Iranians start trying to get people on the inside. How the hell would they have found out if Farzan wasn't working for them?"

Leroux scratched at his chin, puffing out his lips with a blast of air. "I'm not sure either. Either we're wrong about Farzan and he always has been playing for the other side, or somehow the Iranians became aware of the op."

"But we have no evidence of that."

"Well, we're gonna have to keep digging just in case."

Child spun in his chair. "But why Poseidon's Trident? Why are the Iranians so hot and bothered by that? It has to do with the Russians, not them."

Packman wagged a finger. "No, remember, they're allies now. The Iranians are supplying a significant number of the drones those bastards are using in Ukraine. If they stumbled upon something that could prove useful to their allies, they'd run with it."

"Why not just tell the Russians?"

"Maybe if they caught wind of it, they might want to find out what was going on to curry favor with Moscow. They might also be trying to see how it could play in their favor. Remember, if Russian oil is taken off the market, prices could skyrocket worldwide which would benefit Iran, but if Moscow loses the war, Iran's lucrative drone business dries up. They're always playing both sides."

"Except when it comes to us," muttered Child.

Leroux chuckled. "True. They only play one side with us, but let's think this through. The Chief of Iranian affairs gets read in on a top-secret file involving the Russians that could impact the Iranians. Two days later, the Iranians start to try to get a person inside. Were all those positions in the travel review office?"

Packman nodded. "Yes."

"So, they knew exactly what they needed very quickly."

Child leaned back. "How could they have figured that out so quickly to put a six-month plan in place in a matter of forty-eight hours?"

"My guess is they already had this scenario gamed out. They just didn't have a target. As soon as they knew their man was Farzan, they ran with him."

"But they would have to have known he had a family."

"Oh, I'm quite certain they have files of every American who was born in Iran."

"But the sick father?"

Leroux thought for a moment. It was a good point. There were just too many coincidences here. An idea occurred to him and he leaned forward, grinding it out. "All reports we've had indicate Farzan's family has gone full nutbar on the mother's side. What if his father isn't sick, or has been made sick?"

Child eyed him. "What do you mean? Like bad cooking?"

Packman swatted him. "No, you idiot. Poison."

Child rubbed his shoulder. "That could make sense."

Leroux agreed. "You've got this family, extremely loyal to the regime. The regime is suddenly interested in a family member. One of them is brought in, talked to, perhaps Farzan's mother. She's given a poison to slowly feed her husband to make him sick. And while they get their man in position here, the father gets progressively sicker, the calls go out to the son, and the push begins to get the family there."

"But I thought the briefing said they tried to get him there at first."

Leroux dismissed the point. "They would know he'd never be approved. It wouldn't be believable for even a fake travel review to indicate it was safe for him to go. Even if we thought his cover was intact, it just wouldn't be risked. He knows too much."

Packman drummed his fingers on the conference table. "So then, what we're saying is, six months ago, Farzan gets read in on Poseidon's Trident. Within two days, applications start flowing in one after the other, each refining their attempts to get a man on the inside. Farzan's father falls ill either coincidentally or by design, either the old man lying, or the wife or someone else in the family poisoning him. Urgent calls go out to Farzan saying Dad's dying, you have to come home. Meanwhile, they get their man Hassan in position to issue a false travel review saying it's not safe for him, but it's safe for his family. They then make the push to get the family over. They snatch the wife, leave the kids with the family, and force him to tell them more about Trident. He tells them where Jack's staying in exchange for something, maybe going easy on his wife."

Leroux's head bobbed. "It's thin but it's plausible, though there are a few holes."

"What?"

"First, if Farzan is innocent in all this, how did the Iranians find out he had been read in on Trident? And second, how did Hassan actually get the job? Coming from outside the Agency and getting a job in security isn't an easy thing and…" Leroux thought for a moment. "Those two questions have to be answered." He tapped the desk. "For Farzan to be read in and two days later for the Iranians to be taking action means there's another mole. It's either Farzan himself or someone close to him."

"Who?"

"Well, we can eliminate anyone who already knew about Trident. Otherwise, the Iranians would have acted sooner. And we can eliminate anyone who doesn't know anything about Trident. Trident is the key here. There's a mole and I'm willing to bet it's in Farzan's inner circle."

"His family?" suggested Child.

"No. We already know he didn't tell his wife, so he certainly didn't tell his kids, and he's claimed he hasn't told anyone in Iran about his job, which makes sense. No, it's someone in this building." His jaw dropped, a queasiness flooding through him. "Wait a minute. How did Hassan get the job?"

Packman's eyes narrowed. "What do you mean?"

"He applied for the job, made it through all the automatic screenings. But how did he actually get the job? He had to interview, right? His references had to be checked."

Packman pulled his laptop closer and began pecking away at the keyboard. "Yeah, it looks like he passed the automated checks. Personnel reviewed his résumé and it fit the requirements. References checked out fine and…" Packman's eyebrows shot up. "Holy shit!"

"What?"

"He had an internal reference."

"Who?"

Packman tore his eyes away from the screen. "Deputy Chief Kyle Baxter."

Deputy Chief of Iranian Affairs Office, CIA Headquarters

Langley, Virginia

Kyle Baxter sat behind his desk, a desk assigned two full years before Farzan was parachuted in to the Chief position after his predecessor retired. It was to be his job. He had worked his way up through the ranks over the years, made it to Deputy Chief, a proud day at the Baxter household, his wife trusted enough to keep a secret. And when the Chief retired, the man had recommended him to be his replacement. It was nearly a fait accompli, when, out of nowhere, Farzan was given the job.

The man had been at the Agency for only a few years at the time. Ridiculous. Farzan was an affirmative action hire and nothing more. The idea he could help because he was born in Iran was ridiculous. The man hadn't been there in over twenty years, and the country had changed entirely during that time. He was sick and tired of this nonsense. Equity, diversity, inclusion. Everyone deserved a job unless you were a straight white Christian male.

America was going to hell, and this woke nonsense was at the root of it.

The best qualified person should get the job, whether they were white, black, gay, straight, Catholic, or Muslim. It didn't matter. He had been robbed by the system, robbed by those he had trusted, robbed by those he had served. Shit like this had been happening to him his entire life, whether it was in high school and not making the team because they needed to balance out the racial profile, not making it into a club because they needed an equal number of boys and girls, or reading job applications that basically said white men need not apply.

He was tired of it.

He had kept his head down, worked hard, never said anything about it except to his wife and a few buddies, all of whom were in agreement with him. He had anonymously vented on message boards and social media about how the system was broken. When you hired by checkbox rather than qualifications, the quality of the work went down. It was why productivity was so low, why so many stupid decisions came out of public offices and large corporations where these policies were forced upon them. The country was in trouble and he was sick of it.

He had decided to fight back.

If his country didn't care about him, then he didn't care about his country. He would look out for his family and that was it. That was what was truly important. Family, friends, neighbors, but not the country. Screw the country. So, when approached in a mall parking garage a year ago by a man in a dark suit with darker sunglasses, he hadn't been as dismissive as he should have.

"I've been reading some of what you've been posting."

"Oh? And just what have I been posting?"

"Daily screeds about the state of your country."

"My country. Not *our* country?"

The man had smiled and handed him a business card. "Contact me if you want to talk."

The man had left, leaving him confused. For one thing, how could the man know what he had been posting? It was all anonymous. Yet somehow someone had managed to find out. It wasn't good. It meant he had been compromised. If word got out, he could lose his job.

He had been convinced he needed to find out the truth, so had arranged the meeting. Much to his horror, it was exactly as he suspected. One of the social media sites he used had been hacked, his personal information revealed. He had no doubt he wasn't the target of the attack. It was the entire user list.

The info was probably posted on the Dark Web or sold to various groups to exploit, in this case the Iranians, and they had him over a barrel. He was shown hundreds of his posts, all linked back to him.

"If you don't cooperate, the CIA will receive an anonymous package. You'll lose your security clearance and your job, your pension, everything. You might even go to prison the way your justice system works, all for just expressing an opinion. One we agree with, by the way."

"We?"

The man had smiled. "We share your opinion, and from now on, you work for us."

"Bullshit."

The printouts were wagged at him. "You work for us or you'll work for no one. You'll never get another job in Washington again. You'll be blacklisted. You'll be serving up fries at McDonald's just to make ends meet. Work for us, and we'll put aside money in a bank account of your choosing for every bit of intel you provide."

"You're asking me to betray my country. I can't do that."

"Your country has betrayed you. Besides, you already have betrayed your country."

"How?"

One of his postings was shown to him, one where he bitched about his new boss. "This is of particular interest to us."

He closed his eyes, already knowing the answer, but asking the question anyway. "Why?"

"You said your new boss is Iranian born, and by hacking your home computer, we know you're the Deputy Chief of Iranian Affairs at the CIA. That means your new boss is the Chief of Iranian Affairs, and he's Iranian born. What's his name?"

"I can't tell you that."

His address was read off. "That's correct, isn't it?"

His shoulders slumped. "Yes."

A photo was held out showing his wife herding the children into the car in front of their house.

"Beautiful family."

"What are you saying?"

"I'm saying nothing, Mr. Baxter. And I'm asking very little. What's your boss' name?"

"Cyrus Farzan." He had almost vomited when he gave up the name, but it was his family. He couldn't risk their safety, not for a man he despised.

"Now, that wasn't so hard, was it? The next time we meet, you provide me with a bank account number. I highly recommend something private, outside of the country, like the Cayman Islands, and I'll wire fifty-thousand-dollars into it. You keep providing me information, and you'll continue to receive deposits."

"What kind of information?"

"Anything I ask, anything you might happen to come across that you think we'd be interested in. You'll know it when you see it. Have a good day, Mr. Baxter."

The meeting had ended abruptly, and his life as a traitor had begun. Yet it was surprisingly easy to justify, for the man was right. His country had already betrayed him, so payback was a bitch. Yet he controlled the flow. The man might ask a question, and if he deemed it too deep of a betrayal, he would make up some excuse that it was above his clearance level, or there was no way for him to get access to that information without tripping a security flag.

He had given them very little so far, mostly tidbits about things that might link back to Farzan. If a mole was discovered, he wanted his new chief to go down for it, not himself. And when read in on Poseidon's Trident, he had decided it was his key, not only to a massive payday, but to the end of all this. He already had a million dollars in his bank account, with a negotiated two million more promised when Trident was successfully stopped.

Farzan had already compromised himself. The man was on the way out, and he had spent the past six months scrubbing every corner of the Internet and Dark Web of anything that might compromise him, creating fake trails suggesting there was someone else impersonating him out there having stolen his identity. When Farzan went down, it was his intent to apply for the job again, and if anything came up during the vetting process, he could point to the stolen identity. He should be in the clear. He should get the promotion he deserved, then he would move on with his life, with an extremely comfortable retirement in place.

And should things go south, he had an escape plan for him and the family. Everything had been thought of, everything taken care of except for one thing.

He couldn't get access to Ali Hassan's personnel file. But he was prepared for that.

There was a knock at the door. "Come in."

It opened and Morrison entered.

Baxter rose, surprised. "Chief, what can I do for you?"

Two armed security entered the room, their hands on their holsters.

"I'm afraid I'm gonna have to ask you to come with us."

He involuntarily stepped back, bumping into his chair. "What? What do you mean?"

"We know who you're working for. It's over."

He held up both hands in front of him. "Wait a minute, you don't understand. It wasn't me, it was Farzan."

Morrison pursed his lips, staring at him as his head slowly shook. "Trying to throw an innocent man under the bus is not the way to curry favor with me. You're the one who got Ali Hassan in here. You're the one who informed the Iranians of Operation Poseidon's Trident as soon as you were read in. You're why they've always been a step ahead of us."

"That's not true! I didn't compromise Trident! I knew almost nothing about it!" He directed a shaky finger at Morrison. "That's right! It couldn't have been me! I didn't know where our asset was! How could I have compromised the operation? It couldn't have been me!"

Morrison smiled. "No, it couldn't have been you. You didn't know where our operative was. Yet you also couldn't have known that was how the operation was compromised, unless someone told you. And that's classified. Almost no one in this building knows what happened, yet somehow you do. I think we're gonna go find a nice place deep underground where we can have a chat, so you can tell us what's going on and how you've been communicating with the Iranians, who obviously were the ones who told you about how Trident was compromised, an operation they only knew about because of you."

Baxter slumped against the wall, defeated. There was no point denying anything now, Morrison knew. "My family?"

"You won't be seeing them for a long time. Then when you do, it'll be from behind bars." Morrison waved a finger and the two security personnel moved in. "Your life as you know it is over."

Tehran, Iran

Kane inspected the passports and visas, along with the airline tickets the teens had managed to retrieve thanks to the intervention of their grandfather. He tapped his ear, indicating his hidden earpiece. "And I might have some good news on your grandfather."

Tara's eyes widened. "What do you mean?"

"There's a theory running around back home that your grandmother was poisoning him. If we get to him in time, we might just be able to stop it and save his life."

Tara exchanged an excited glance with her brother before returning to her original question. "What about our mother?"

Kane frowned. "Unfortunately, at the moment, there's nothing we can do for her, but I assure you, all diplomatic channels are being used. Once we get the two of you out of the country, then that removes most of the leverage they have over your father, and that should help."

Ray stared at him, wide-eyed. "Is it true that our father is CIA?"

"You didn't hear that from me. That's a conversation to be had when we get you home. But for now"—he wagged the passports then handed them back—"these are your identities. If we're stopped, our chauffeur here is your cousin Babak Shadmani, and you don't know who I am, just that I'm a friend of his. But don't worry, the chances of us being pulled over are next to nothing. We'll be in this car for a few more minutes, then we're gonna say goodbye to our friend here and meet someone else where you'll be given new identities and we'll be taken north in a new vehicle. Understood?"

They both nodded.

"Good. Now, let's try to keep smiles on our faces."

Forced grins appeared.

"You're not members of the Insane Clown Posse. Normal, pleasant smiles. No need to show teeth. You just need to try to get that fear out of your eyes."

Ray snorted at the Posse reference, though it was clear Tara had no clue what he was talking about.

"Now, just relax. We'll have you home in no time."

"Yes sir," said Tara.

Kane turned back in his seat, his eyes narrowing. "Where the hell are we?"

"Construction. I had to take another route."

Kane caught sight of a street sign and bristled. They were heading in the wrong direction. This was no detour. He jerked his chin to the left. "What the hell is that?"

Shadmani spun to look and Kane retrieved the man's pistol from the glove box and aimed it directly at his friend's head. Tara cried out in fear as Kane cocked the hammer for effect, not utility.

"What's going on?"

"I'm sorry! They picked up my family last night. They must have spotted me watching the Farzan residence. I don't have a choice. If I don't hand you over, they're dead."

"Pull over."

"I can't. They'll kill them."

"They'll kill me and these kids."

"No, they won't. They said they'll let the kids go. They don't need their father anymore. They'll let the mother go too. It's over, Dylan."

"And I'm sure they said they'd let me go too."

"I'm not gonna lie to you. I've never lied to you. But no, you, they're going to keep for obvious reasons."

"And you?"

"They're probably going to torture me for months just for fun then execute me as a traitor. But at least my family will be left alone."

"You hope."

"Hope is all I have." Shadmani stared at him, tears filling his eyes. "I'm so sorry. I never meant for this to happen. I've always considered you an honorable man, my friend. But this, it's my family. It's my wife, it's my children, my parents, everyone I love. I have no choice. You know how they are."

"I understand." Kane cold cocked him, knocking him out. He gripped the steering wheel as he dropped the gun into his lap. He lifted

Shadmani's right foot off the pedal and the car slowly decelerated, the manual transmission shuddering in the wrong gear. Kane guided them to the side of the road then hauled up the emergency brake, bringing them to a jarring halt. The engine stalled and he turned off the ignition.

"Let's go."

"What's happening?" asked Tara.

"What did I say? No questions. You just do what I say when I say it."

He climbed out, wrapping his chafiyeh around his face, indicating for Tara and Ray to cover their faces as best they could before getting out of the car. He grabbed his bag and slung it over his shoulder, then hustled them down the side of the busy street, heading for the nearest cross street. Shadmani was out cold, but that wouldn't last long. They had to get out of sight before he recovered and began searching for them.

He felt for the man, and might have done the same if the roles were reversed. Family was everything, and there wasn't anything he wouldn't do for those he cared about the most. But there had to be a better way than throwing two other children under the bus.

They reached the corner and turned right. Kane glanced back to see Shadmani still passed out, then continued forward at a reasonably brisk pace, not wanting to draw too much attention. At the next intersection, they crossed the street and continued straight. Zigzagging their way across the massive city wasn't an option. In order to save his family, Shadmani would no doubt call in what had happened, and this entire area would be swimming with security personnel in no time. Every person in uniform within sight would be notified to be on the lookout for an American with two teenagers.

He activated his comms. "Control, Fly Guy. We've been compromised, over."

Leroux responded. "Fly Guy, Control Actual. What's your status?"

"I'm on foot with the two targets. My contact betrayed us. He said they picked up his family last night. Burn him. Let's see if there's anything we can do to help his family out. We need a pickup, and we need it now. I knocked him out, but it won't last long. We have to get out of the immediate area. Over."

"Copy that."

Kane could hear fingers snapping and other voices in the background. Leroux cursed, and Kane's jaw clenched, already knowing what his friend was about to tell him.

"We just tried to make contact with your extraction team, but they're not responding."

It was Kane's turn to curse. "Shadmani knew the drop-off location. He must have told them. What do we do now?"

"We need to activate a new contact, and that's gonna take time, at least thirty minutes. Then we have to reassemble the network. These are all locals. If they get wind of what's going on, they'll disappear into the woodwork."

"Send them into the wind. If the first part of the chain has been captured, they know where the second part is, and will eventually break. Scatter it, set it up again, then contact me when you've got a way for me to get these kids out of the city."

"Acknowledged. Good luck, Fly Guy."

"I don't need luck. You're forgetting, I'm pretty fly for a white guy."

Leroux laughed and Kane killed the comms as he spotted two police ahead, one on his radio, both heads on swivels. He grabbed the teens by the hands and hauled them into an alleyway, both terrified.

"What's going on?" asked Tara.

"Do you know what a Charlie Foxtrot is?"

She shook her head, but Ray nodded. "It's a military term for Cluster Fu—"

Kane cut him off. "That's the one. But don't worry, I've been in a lot of these before, and I always figure my way out."

"Really?"

Kane grinned. "I'm here, aren't I? I have to be honest with you two. My contact in the car, you heard what happened. He betrayed us because they took his family. We can blame him all we want. It doesn't matter. It is what it is, and we're now in the situation we're in. But because he was the first part of a series of steps that would get us where we need to go, the entire network has to be dismantled. Otherwise, he tells where the next group is, they get tortured, tell where the next group is, and so on. So now we need to set up a new network, but that will take time. My friends back home think thirty minutes. Unfortunately, we don't have thirty minutes."

"So, what are we gonna do?"

"I'm not sure yet, but we have to keep a low profile."

"Can we get another ride? Like rent a car? Steal a car?"

Kane smirked at Ray. "This isn't Grand Theft Auto, kid, but you have given me an idea."

Chief of Iranian Affairs Office, CIA Headquarters

Langley, Virginia

Farzan sat in his office, pulling at his hair, the stress of the situation overwhelming. Baxter had just been taken into custody. He thought the man was his friend, but apparently, he was the one responsible for everything. The operation was underway to extract his children, but he wasn't privy to what was going on. He would have thought they would allow him to sit in and observe, but the vibe he had sensed when Morrison had told him about Baxter, suggested the man no longer trusted him.

And he didn't blame him. He had betrayed his country. He had already decided that as soon as his family was safe, he was turning himself in. It was the right thing to do, and maybe they would be lenient with him. Trident had been compromised when he informed them of the hotel their asset was using as his base of operations, but when they had pressed him on what Trident was, he had pled ignorance. It was clear they only knew what Baxter knew, and he knew very little. He was only aware of its existence, and the fact it involved Russia and the war in Ukraine.

Baxter hadn't been read in yet on the details that involved the tracking of Russian oil exports. Right now, the mission could still be completed, though it would be delayed. With an operative known to be in the area, the Russians would increase security at all vital assets, including the oil terminal. Jack would have to wait, or more likely, another officer would be moved in since Jack's face could be on surveillance cameras at the raided hotel.

He sighed, checking his watch. It hadn't even been half an hour since he was told the extraction had begun early, and Morrison had instructed him to remain here. His cellphone vibrated with a call. He leaned forward and his heart raced. Unknown caller. He closed his eyes, uncertain as to what to do. His children should be safe soon, though their extraction had likely been reported already, as he had no idea how Kane could retrieve the children without his parents knowing.

He should ignore the call, just in case they weren't aware of the extraction yet. There was a possibility that even if they were aware the children were missing, they could think they had run away on their own accord.

He couldn't risk them knowing the truth.

He stared at the photo. They had his wife. Did it matter if they knew about the extraction, that it was CIA run? Perhaps if they knew, they would accept the fact there was nothing they could do about it, and just let them go, let his wife go.

His shoulders slumped. He had no choice. He picked up the phone and swiped to take the call. "Hello?"

"Next time I call you, you answer right away."

The anger was obvious, but he already had an answer prepared for this eventuality. "I had to get to my office. Obviously, I can't have this conversation in the hallway, where it might be overheard."

There was a grunt, hopefully accepting the explanation. "There's someone here who would like to say hello."

He gulped, thinking of only two possibilities. His wife, or his recaptured children.

"Cyrus, is that you?"

He cried out at his wife's voice. "Yes, yes, it's me! Are you all right?"

"Don't worry about me. The children. Are the children all right?"

He had to play stupid. "Of course they are. They're with my parents."

There was a loud sound and his wife sobbed with pain, the man's voice returning. "Every time you lie, I hurt her."

"I'm not lying! The children are with my parents!"

"You know very well that your children are no longer with your parents, that they're with an American agent, on their way out of the city. If you don't stop this extraction, I'll have your wife beaten and raped every day for the rest of her life. You'll never speak to her again, but every day I'll send you a video of what we're doing to her, and it'll all be because of you."

Tears flowed as he pictured his wife tied to a table, men lined up to take their turn. It broke his heart, but it also enraged him, giving him the spark to think straight. The children were leverage over him and his wife, but only as long as they were in the country. If Kane could get them out, and that fact proven to the Iranians, then any threats involving them were neutralized. He could turn himself in to Morrison, and that could be made known to this piece of shit, then there would be no need to hold her, as he would no longer be in a position to help them. And because he would be in custody, they wouldn't even have a way to reach him.

But it was all contingent upon the children escaping.

"I have no idea what you're talking about. As far as I know, my children are with my parents. If the CIA is extracting them, they haven't told me. They just arrested my deputy, and they're probably about to arrest me. They're going to see these phone calls you've been making to me, and the call I made to you, and they're going to figure out that I betrayed my oath."

Another loud sound, another cry. "You've lied to me again."

"No, I haven't! I swear to you, I don't know anything about this extraction. But if the CIA is behind it, you know it can't be stopped. They're too good. Why don't you just end this now? Let them all go. I'm of no use to you anymore. Even if they don't suspect me, because of what happened, I'll lose my security clearance. Any operations I've been involved with will be either scrubbed or changed, so that anything I might have told you, or might tell you in the future, is worthless. This is over. Just end it now. Just do the right thing."

"Do the right thing? I'm not the traitor here! You are! You betrayed your own homeland, and you betrayed your new one. But more importantly, you betrayed your family. I'm going to find your children and throw them into prison with their mother. And I'm going to make your son watch as his sister is violated. And I'm going to make them both watch while their mother is violated. You've just signed your family up for a lifetime of suffering. Only you are to blame here. No one else. This is your last chance. Tell me what Operation Poseidon's Trident is, and I'll halt the pursuit of your children. Don't, and I will find them. And your wife's new life begins the moment I hang up this phone."

His head drooped as he struggled to control his emotions. Part of him desperately screamed to tell the man what he wanted to know, but that would just be the beginning. They would want more and more, and the operation was too important. Thousands, perhaps millions of lives rested on its success. Were all those lives unimportant just because they weren't his family? They were someone's family. Every soldier that died on the front was someone's son or daughter, whether they were on the Ukrainian or Russian side. Did those families deserve to suffer just so he could save his wife?

If Kane had his children, they would be safe soon. It might take hours, it might take days, but it would be soon. He had faith in the man, and the sooner they were out, the sooner the leverage was gone.

A line had to be drawn.

He ended the call then turned off his phone and tossed it in his top desk drawer. He pushed back, the chair hitting the wall as he gripped at his hair again, his pulse pounding as he prayed he hadn't just condemned his wife to unbelievable horror.

Tehran, Iran

Kane squatted behind a large garbage bin in the alleyway they had taken refuge in, Ray and Tara trembling by his side. He peered through the gap between the bin and the wall of the restaurant it belonged to, and sighed with relief when a taxi pulled up, Dariush leaning across the passenger seat, peering toward them.

Kane rose and gave him a wave. "Let's go. Quickly, quietly, the two of you get in the back seat. Ray, you first, then Tara, you're in the middle. I'm getting in the back seat with you."

He led the way, Dariush's eyes widening for a moment at the sight of the two teens. Kane opened the back door and Ray climbed inside, followed by Tara. He didn't bother checking for police. That could be a suspicious movement. He simply climbed in and closed the door.

Dariush stared back at them. "Friends?"

"Yes. Let's call them family. I need your help. *We* need your help."

Dariush stared at him for a moment then faced forward, putting the car in gear and pulling away from the curb. Within moments, they were in the flow of traffic. "Where do you need to go?" he asked, remarkably calm.

"Can we trust you?"

Dariush shrugged. "Can anyone really trust anyone these days in this place? You don't work for the Swiss Embassy, do you?" He adjusted his rearview mirror so he could see Kane without turning his head. "CIA?"

"The less you know, the better. But right now, all my credentials are valid and indicate I work for the Swiss Embassy. And at the moment, my job is to get these two American citizens to safety."

"American, huh? Let me guess. The father's Iranian, decided he wanted them to live here in our wonderful country rather than back in the corrupt America?"

"Something like that."

Dariush sighed. "You know, I have family too."

"I have no doubt. And if they were in a similar situation, what would you want? Some kind and caring—"

Dariush held up a finger with a smile. "Don't forget good looking."

Kane chuckled. "And good looking taxi driver to do the right thing?"

Dariush exhaled loudly. "My wife is going to kill me if she finds out about this." He tilted his head. "But then again, I probably won't survive, so the end result is the same."

"I'll make sure you're handsomely rewarded. Biggest damn tip you could ever imagine."

Dariush shifted gears. "I should hope so. I've had my eye on something with real class to drive my customers in. Something British."

"If it's got a leaping jungle cat on the hood, skip it. It'll only break your heart."

"So my friends tell me." Dariush muttered a Farsi curse. "Oh well. Now, where do you need to go?"

"Word's probably gone out already, so the sooner we get out of this area, the better. Head north, out of the city."

"Ultimately, where are you heading?"

"You don't need to know that. Not unless you're actually taking us the entire way."

"Time is of the essence, I would assume."

"You would assume correctly."

"If you're heading north, I'm guessing the Caspian. Someone's going to pick you up there?"

"In a manner of speaking."

Dariush grinned. "It's like a spy movie. Who do you think will play me?"

"Someone very handsome, no doubt. An Iranian Brad Pitt."

Dariush's head bobbed. "I like the sound of that. Then I suggest you get on the phone with Hollywood. I'm going to activate this meter for what's going to be an extremely expensive ride that if I survive, I can finally buy my wife the new washer and dryer she's been harassing me for."

Kane smirked. "Trust me, my friend. When your tip arrives, you'll be able to remodel the entire house."

"I like the sound of that. Now you kids settle in. At this time of day, it's going to take a few hours to get there because of traffic. And another thing," said Dariush as he readjusted his mirror to see out the back window.

"What's that?" asked Kane.

"Try not to look so guilty."

Kane glanced over at the teens, both terrified. "How about we play the sleeping game?"

Operations Center 3, CIA Headquarters

Langley, Virginia

Child held up his hand as if he were in high school, though at least this time didn't wait to talk. "I've got something. Their equivalent of an APB has just gone out giving Kane's description along with the children and a last known location." He smiled. "It says here they're believed to be on foot."

Leroux stared at the map showing Shadmani's car now underway, circling through the neighborhood, and Kane's newly acquired ride, a taxi driven by a man who had given him several rides since he arrived, already on the freeway, heading north, out of Tehran. If the Iranians really wanted the children, it was only a matter of time before they locked down the city and activated the checkpoints already in place on every route leading out of the metropolis.

He turned to Tong. "ETA on them getting past the final checkpoint?"

"Based upon their current speed and traffic along the route, the computer estimates nine minutes."

"I want updates every minute."

"Copy that."

"And bring up their projected route. We might be able to take advantage of this. Nobody's gonna be looking for them in a taxi unless they were spotted getting into it." He turned to Packman. "See if you can pull any footage from that area, any security cameras we might have access to. Check the satellite feed as well. See if you can tell if anyone paid particular attention to them, and monitor the police in that area and their chatter. I wanna know the moment someone reports they got into a cab, because that's when they'll have to transfer." He turned toward the back of the room. "And Marc, start reassembling the extraction with this new reality in mind. Try to get the front end of it to provide escort from a distance, just in case they get in trouble."

"You got it, boss," replied Therrien as the door to the operations center opened and Morrison entered, joining Leroux at his workstation at the heart of the operation.

"Status?"

"Kane and the children are in a taxi driven by the man who picked him up at the airport. Kane has used him a couple of times since he's been there."

"They struck up a friendship, I take it?"

"Apparently."

"Can he be trusted?"

"We had him checked out, seems clean, no ties to the regime, just a cabby trying to do his job as far as we can tell."

"Why isn't Kane with Shadmani?"

Leroux brought him up to speed on what had been happening and Morrison cursed. "Nothing ever goes smoothly, does it?"

"It's what keeps our job interesting."

"Sometimes a dull day would be nice." Morrison lowered his voice. "Farzan received another call. We monitored it with the listening devices we placed in his office after we began to suspect him, and he behaved himself. The Iranians know about the extraction and they're demanding he stop it. He claims to know nothing about it. They also asked him about Trident, threatening to beat and rape his wife for the rest of her life and send him video of it, and do the same to his daughter if they caught her, but he told them nothing. He's pretending he only knew where Jack was and that he knows nothing about the nature of the mission. And then he terminated the call."

Leroux's eyebrows shot up. "Really? That's ballsy."

"I think he was afraid he was about to give in, so he ended it, then turned off his phone."

"What are you going to do about him?"

"Nothing for the moment. I'm going to let him stew in his office while we wait to see what happens with his children."

"But you're going to have him arrested?"

"I have no choice."

"What if he turns himself in?"

"Well, that might change things. As far as we know at the moment, all he's told them is where Jack was staying. That's fairly egregious, but he had the presence of mind to not tell them the true nature of Trident."

"There's a chance he might have suspected we were listening in because of the situation."

"True, but did he do anything any of us wouldn't have done?"

Leroux sighed. "Sometimes I'm happy I don't have children."

Morrison chuckled. "It does simplify life somewhat, but don't let a situation like this influence your decision. Trust me, 99.99% of us parents go about our daily lives without worrying that the Iranians are going to kidnap our children." He moved back on topic. "I just observed the initial interrogation of Baxter. This guy's a piece of work. He started spilling his guts the moment we began recording him. Apparently, he was recruited by the Iranians about a year ago. They've been paying him for minor stuff. He gave us the account number for where they've been depositing his money. He has over a million dollars stashed there."

"How did they recruit him?"

"Apparently, he wasn't too pleased at not getting promoted to the Chief's position, so he's been ranting on social media under assumed names. One of those platforms was hacked and their entire user list released. The Iranians used that to find out who he was, thinking they might be able to use him because he had identified himself as a government worker in one of his rants about employment equity. Once they identified who he was, it was pretty easy to put together that he worked at the CIA. They apparently threatened to reveal what they knew to us, meaning he'd lose his security clearance and his job, be blacklisted from ever working for the federal government again, so he started cooperating and named his boss. They figured out who Farzan was, and Bob's your uncle. They had their mole. They knew who Farzan was, and they put their plan in motion as soon as the existence of Trident was revealed to them by Baxter."

"And we're assuming Farzan mentioned it to him?"

"We'll confirm that later, but that's the assumption we're working under. From what we know so far, he would've told them little beyond the name of the operation and that it involved the Russians. That would be enough to get the Iranians interested."

"What are we going to do to him?"

"Oh, the book will be thrown at him, for sure. He has no excuse other than being a disgruntled employee." Morrison jerked his chin toward the ongoing operation. "I want you and your team to focus on this. Get those kids out. As far as I'm concerned, we've plugged the leaks here. We'll let the Justice Department figure out the appropriate punishment. Let's just help these innocent victims. They didn't do anything to deserve this."

En Route to the Caspian Sea, Iran

From what Kane had been told, the sleeping game didn't work on teenagers, only small children, but it appeared that was only partially true. It worked on terrified teenagers. At first, they had pretended, but the steady breathing from the back seat told him they were sound asleep, which was perfect.

Dariush pointed ahead. "We're coming up on the final checkpoint. I suggest sleepy time for you too."

Kane agreed. The traffic continued to move steadily, though had noticeably slowed, likely because there were men with guns sitting idly by. Kane nestled into the corner, resting his head against the window and tucking his chafiyeh into place, covering the bottom half of his face. He closed his eyes and instead listened to everything happening. The sound of the car, the road, engines around them, brakes with pads on their last legs, then the change in the ambient noise as they passed through the gates, the noise changing once again as they were clear. Yet he didn't open his eyes. The gates might not be the end of the security zone.

An alarm sounded and he stifled a curse. It was in front of them rather than behind, but the Doppler effect revealed they were rapidly passing the source.

"Everybody stay calm," said Dariush, Tara and Ray stirring.

"What's going on?" asked Tara.

"Keep pretending you're sleeping," said Kane calmly. "We're past the checkpoint. Just stay calm."

The alarm faded as they put distance between them and the checkpoint, traffic speeding back up to normal, perhaps a little quicker with what had just happened, as everyone separated themselves from whatever security operation was underway.

"All right, we're clear," said Dariush.

"Everyone stretch as if you just had a good nap. Nobody look back." Kane stretched, as did the teenagers, and he leaned forward. "What did you see?"

"The alarm went off just after we cleared the gates. A lot of guards rushing around, the gates closing. There's no way to know for sure whether it's about you guys or not, but we should assume it is."

Kane's comms squawked in his ear but he didn't react. It was one thing for Dariush to suspect he was an American spy, it was another thing to confirm it by having an entire agency in his ear. He couldn't risk panicking the man, no matter how much on their side he appeared to be at the moment.

"Fly Guy, Control Actual. If you can talk, talk. If not, just listen. We're showing you clear of the last checkpoint in Tehran. They've just shut the city down. Our intercepts are showing they're looking for you and the

Farzan children, but there's no indication yet that they know you're in a cab. The shutdown appears routine. We're arranging for an extraction vehicle to provide backup just in case something goes wrong. They should be in place within fifteen minutes. Right now, we're recommending you continue with your current mode of transportation. Our SME here indicates it's quite common for taxis to be taken from Tehran to the Caspian Sea, so you shouldn't attract any undue attention. We'll monitor for any changes. Acknowledged, over?"

Kane grunted once.

"Copy that, Fly Guy. Extraction will be in place once you reach the coast. Good luck. Control, out."

Kane checked his watch, noting the heavy traffic traveling significantly under the speed limit. "How long do you think?"

"Like I said, this time of day, three, three and a half hours. If we're lucky, two and a half but I doubt it."

"And what are the chances of checkpoints ahead?"

"They don't like to do them unless it's absolutely necessary. This is a major transport artery for goods to and from Tehran and the Caspian Sea. Shut this down and start checking vehicles one by one, and it affects the economy. Let's just hope they think they shut the city down in time. If they do, then hopefully we'll get there with no problem." Dariush adjusted the mirror once again so he could make eye contact with Kane. "If we do get screened, however, and they're looking for a man with a teenage boy and girl, we're not making it through."

"That's fine. If we are pulled over, you just tell them we flagged you down and paid you to take us to the coast. You've never met us before and just assumed we were tourists because we showed you proper ID with visas."

"Sounds good to me. It would be nice to see my wife and kids tonight."

Kane reached into his bag, removing a wad of cash from an envelope. He handed it forward. "Maybe I should pay you in advance. It would fit the story more."

Dariush took the cash, his eyes bulging. "It's too much."

"No, I want you to have it."

"You don't understand. It's too much. If they find this on me, they'll ask why I wasn't suspicious." He handed it back. "Half that, make it more believable." He grinned in the mirror. "But I want fat stacks just like that slipped under my door one day."

Kane laughed. "You've got it."

Karshi-Khanabad Air Base

Kazakhstan

Dawson entered the rec room reserved for his team at what was once known as K-2 in Uzbekistan as they waited to be activated for Kane's extraction mission. Unfortunately, they were being activated, though not according to plan. He closed the door, the laughter and chatter falling silent as his team turned toward him.

Niner jabbed a finger at him. "See, that's his Charlie Foxtrot expression. Every time he has that, it means the mission's gone south before we've even got boots on the ground."

Atlas' impossibly deep voice seconded the observation. "He's got you there, BD. Last time I saw that was when we ran out of hamburgers at the barbecue last week." The big man spun towards Spock, a meaty finger extended. "J'accuse!"

Spock cocked an eyebrow and rolled up a middle finger. "I was told it was stag. Somebody else"—an accusatory finger was directed at Red—"changed it to a family event."

Red shrugged. "My kid wanted a hot dog. It's not my fault you don't check your email."

"Text! My God, who uses email anymore for urgent messages. You're like my dad."

Red dead-panned him. "That's not what your mother said."

"Ouch!" winced Niner, pulling up his knees as if to protect himself from any secondary burns.

Spock gave Red a look. "My mother's a very nice woman. I hope you treated her right. Her favorite color is yellow and she likes tulips. I better see a dozen the next time I'm over."

Red stared back at him. "I already sent her purple ones. Next time I'll know better."

Heads turned to see what Spock's response would be, the tennis match having everyone's attention.

"She likes purple also. I think it'll be okay until next time. Bring a bottle of scotch for my father, though. He likes a double after sex. And make it a good bottle, at least twelve years old, preferably eighteen, because he's got his work cut out for him making her forget the disappointment she experienced with you."

Hoots and hollers erupted and Red held up his hands in surrender, turning to Dawson. "BD, I think you had something to say, if that Charlie Foxtrot face meant anything."

Dawson dropped into a free chair. "That depends. Are we done here?"

Red and Spock nodded. "Yep."

"Good." Dawson leaned forward, smirking. "And forget the tulips, boys. I always just send her a dozen red roses."

Groans and guffaws filled the room as Spock stared at him. "Et tu, brother? How the hell did my mother get pulled into this, anyway?"

More laughter before Dawson calmed the room. "Okay, here it is. You're right, Niner. It's a Charlie Foxtrot already. We were supposed to go in tonight for a nice extract under the cover of darkness, but shit went south when the cousin tried to rape the daughter. Apparently, he's dead and the children escaped on their own. Kane managed to grab them, but half of Iran is looking for them right now, and the other half soon will be. Top that off with the fact Kane's contact betrayed them. Apparently, the authorities picked up his family the night before. The whole network has collapsed."

"Where are they now?" asked Red.

"If you can believe it, they're in a taxi heading north toward the coast. How long that will last is anybody's guess. Right now, they're two hours out, depending on traffic. So far, there's no indication they're looking for them outside of Tehran, but it's only a matter of time. We're going to have to go in, possibly during daylight."

"Son of a bitch!" exclaimed Niner. "Isn't that kind of like suicide?"

"Langley's looking for a secluded spot now, and this coastline isn't monitored as closely as the Persian Gulf. It is what it is, gentlemen." He smacked his hands together and stood. "Let's get a wiggle on. Control wants us in position off the coast so we can go in at any time."

Niner shuffled past him, his head shaking. "Always a Charlie Foxtrot." His ass belched with its own commentary, and the room groaned.

"My God, Niner. See a doctor. No healthy human should make a smell like that," cried Sergeant Gerry "Jimmy Olsen" Hudson.

Niner raised his hands. "Don't blame me. Blame the milkshakes for being so good."

Dawson rolled his eyes. "I thought I told you to get some Beano."

"Have you ever tried asking around the Unit for Beano while producing your own mustard gas? It's not often a successful mission. People get a little testy."

They filed out of the room as Niner let loose again with a one-cheek squeak.

"Gas! Gas! Gas!" shouted Jimmy as everyone dove and took cover, leaving only Niner standing plus others in the hallway who had no clue what the hell was going on.

Niner held up a finger. "Does anybody have any Beano?"

Operations Center 3, CIA Headquarters

Langley, Virginia

Tong, her station within Leroux's line of sight, raised her arm and tilted her head forward, pointing at the main display. "We've got activity ahead."

Leroux looked up at the satellite image showing a temporary roadblock being set up, northbound traffic rapidly coming to a halt. "Zoom in. What are we dealing with?"

Tong complied, the image updating. "It's not one of their regular checkpoints. This is just two pickup trucks, four guards."

Leroux cursed at the one blocked lane, a single open lane slowly moving as a guard on either side of the road peered in the windows then waved them along. This clearly wasn't any type of operation to detect smuggled goods or a specific individual. They were profiling, likely searching for a Westerner with two teenagers, anything that didn't fit the description waved through.

He fit his headset into place. "Fly Guy, Control Actual. We've got a problem ahead. There's a makeshift roadblock. Looks like they're searching for you, over."

"Acknowledged, Control. Details?"

"Two pickup trucks, four guards, one on either side of the road looking in windows, one slowing cars down just ahead of the blocked lane, the other waving them through when cleared."

"Weapons?"

"Looks like sidearms only. Anything heavier must be in their vehicles."

"Understood. Where's our shadow?"

"Two cars behind you."

"Are they clean?"

"As a whistle. Why?"

"Time to take one for the team." Kane relayed what he needed then Leroux folded his arms, leaning back.

"I'm not sure they'll agree to that. They might be on our side, but I've always thought of them as in it more for the money."

"Tell them double if they do it, quadruple if they're caught. Otherwise, I'm killing these four guards."

Leroux stared at the image. Kane had no options left. They couldn't turn around without being spotted, and turning around meant heading in the wrong direction. They had to get to the coast. They had to get to the rendezvous with Bravo Team. If the shadows weren't willing to take the risk, this entire op could be blown.

Four dead soldiers would redirect the entire Iranian search operation in the proper direction.

He sighed. "I'll run it by them."

"Well, do it quick. We're almost there."

"Copy that. Control, out." He turned to Tong. "Connect me to the shadow vehicle."

Tong tapped at her workstation then gave a thumbs-up.

"Here goes nothing."

En Route to the Caspian Sea, Iran

Dariush cursed, immediately gaining Kane's attention. "What?"

"I lost my cellphone connection. It's usually pretty good on this road."

Kane checked his own phone and found it dead. "Cellphone jammer?"

Dariush glanced at him in the rearview mirror. "Definite possibility."

Kane frowned. He had satellite comms that wouldn't be impacted by the jammer, but he didn't know about their shadow. He doubted they had encrypted satellite comms. If they got caught with them, there was no way in hell they could explain it away. Same with sat phones. But cellphones? Everyone had one.

"We're next," said Dariush, now privy to the fact Kane was much more than he had originally thought, the conversation with Leroux essential. "What do you want me to do?"

"No more than we discussed before."

"Who are you people? What have you got me into?"

"They're innocent kids, just caught up in something they have no control over. They're nobodies."

"Nobodies?"

"Yes. But their father isn't."

"He's important?"

"Yes."

"Like a politician?"

"No, important because of the job he holds and what he knows. He's no better than you and me, but his kids have been caught up in something that isn't their fault."

"If you shoot these guards, they'll be coming after us."

"Absolutely."

"Can you get me and my family out?"

"Possibly, but I can't make any promises. Listen, Dariush, I know you wanna help. You're a good man, a brave man. Most, as soon as they found out what was going on, would have pulled over and kicked us out, but you didn't. Just tell them we're a fare from Tehran that hired you to take us to the coast. Stick to that story, that you didn't know there was any trouble, we didn't give you any reason to suspect anything, and you should walk away from this."

Dariush sighed as he pressed gently on the gas, the guard ahead beckoning them forward. "This is it. It doesn't look like your friends got the message."

Kane was about to agree when an engine revved behind them. The guards all stared as a horn blared. A white box van blasted past them, careening around one of the pickup trucks parked on the side of the road, then wobbled back onto the pavement, its engine gunning as it picked up speed. Kane exchanged fist bumps with Tara and Ray as the guards scrambled into their trucks and gave pursuit.

"Punch it, Chewie!"

Dariush stared at him in the rearview mirror. "Huh?"

"Hit the gas! Stick just slightly over the speed limit like you normally would, but we have to take advantage of this. We don't want them reestablishing the roadblock ahead. Let's let them think they've got their man, and we might just get out of this alive."

Dariush pressed on the gas, accelerating, though not insanely. This wasn't a Fast and Furious movie, but it also wasn't Driving Miss Daisy. The pickup trucks had quickly caught up to the box van, but it was swerving back and forth on the road, blocking them.

"What do you want me to do?" asked Dariush, gripping the steering wheel, his knuckles white.

"Move into the left lane. Drop your gear. Get ready to gun around them on my mark."

"Are you crazy? He's all over the road!"

"He's setting it up for us. Just wait for it."

The box van swung all the way to the left then abruptly cut right, their pursuers following. "Hit it!"

Dariush floored it, the engine protesting as they rapidly accelerated, the tachometer climbing toward the red as the box van slowed. They whipped past and Kane smiled at the teens.

"Okay, easy there. Back to normal. You're just a taxi driver getting around a problem, not someone trying to escape."

Dariush's foot lifted off the accelerator, and the car slowed before they hit a respectable cruising speed. Kane leaned over and checked the speedometer. "Add ten kilometers per hour to that. Nobody's gonna get suspicious of a cab driver trying to make up a little time on an open road." He turned and stared out the rearview mirror to see the box van once again accelerating, swerving around. An SUV cut from the opposite direction and through the grass median separating the two sides. The van careened to a halt, the pickup trucks blocking it front and back, oblivious to the danger approaching.

The SUV stopped and two men stepped out with assault rifles. Muzzle flashes were followed by four guards dropping, then their shadows jumping out and climbing into the SUV. It peeled away, heading toward them.

"Stay to the right. Pay them no mind."

Dariush edged them a little closer to the shoulder, the SUV blasting past less than a minute later. He had a death grip on the steering wheel as he no doubt figured out this was as real as it got. "Was that part of the plan?"

"Killing four men just doing their job is never part of the plan. That's why I wanted them to just be a distraction. Go around the roadblock, try to stay ahead of them as long as possible, then pull over and claim you were just impatient. You had a pickup that you couldn't be late for."

"I guess they had their own plan."

Kane flicked his wrist toward the road ahead. "How much longer?"

"This will save us a lot of time. I'd say we're about an hour out."

"All right. There were witnesses to what just happened. Everyone will be on the lookout for that SUV since the occupants are responsible for four deaths. Right now, the locals are gonna forget about us. We're a Tehran problem that they were asked to look into. Our shadows got us through that roadblock, and they just might have got us all the way to the coast."

On the Caspian Sea

Dawson stood at the prow of the Kazak ship as they idled off the coast of Iran in the landlocked Caspian Sea. A lot of favors had been called in now, Washington desperate to preserve the integrity of a mission he wasn't privy to. It had to be important. His team was here, using a former US military base in landlocked Uzbekistan, and now they were on a navy ship provided by Kazakhstan, in exchange for looking the other way on their oil swaps for Iran, at least temporarily.

It was a waiting game now. The latest update from Control, their mission run by the CIA not the Pentagon, was that local assets had just killed four Iranian highway patrol officers. Right now, the entire security apparatus, from the point of the incident all the way to the coast, had activated, which normally wasn't a good thing. But they were all after the occupants of a black SUV, not an American with two teenagers in the back of a cab. At least not until the two situations were connected.

Unfortunately, it meant a heightened alert status across the entire area, and that made their lives more difficult, especially if they were forced into a daylight extraction. Langley had located an isolated stretch of the coastline, free from regularly prying eyes. While that didn't mean someone wouldn't happen upon them, this mission could head south in a hurry if just a single person spotted them on the beach.

"Can I come out of the doghouse now?" whined Niner from the opposite end of the boat.

Atlas, standing nearby, jabbed a finger at him. "Fifteen minutes without farting."

"It's been at least that."

Spock, leaning against the railing, his arms folded, cocked an eyebrow. "Wait a minute, when did you have that milkshake?"

Niner shrugged. "Dunno. These time zones have me all screwed up. A day or two."

"And you still have gas from it?"

Niner took a bite of something and chewed. "What can I say? I'm an enigma."

Atlas leaned forward, peering at what was in Niner's hand. "What the hell is that?"

"Some sort of snack I found in the galley."

Atlas growled. "That better not be cheese."

"No idea, but it sure doesn't taste like cheese." He grimaced as he swallowed another bite. "Tastes like shit, actually."

"Don't let our hosts hear that," said Dawson. "They might toss you overboard."

Atlas shook a fist. "You son of a bitch, you've been eating dairy this whole damn op, haven't you?"

"Is there a law against that?"

"There ought to be." The big man turned to Dawson. "Permission to toss the sergeant overboard?"

"Granted."

Atlas grinned and spun toward his friend, advancing rapidly. Niner scurried backward but had nowhere to go, the railing blocking his way. "It's just peanut butter and crackers!" he cried, holding it out.

"Stand down, Sergeant," ordered Dawson, and Atlas reluctantly came to a halt, snatching the package from Niner's hand. He held it up to the others.

"It is. So, you haven't been eating dairy?"

"I never eat dairy on a mission. You know that."

"Then why the hell have you been farting like crazy?"

Niner rolled his eyes. "I thought we covered this. I'm a pig, remember?"

"To hell with it." Atlas grabbed Niner by the shirt and belt, then raised him over his head. "In you go." He tossed Niner over the railing, but only let go of his collar, keeping hold of his belt. As Niner shouted, Muscles gripped him by the ankle and held him over the gentle seas below.

Niner looked up at him as several ration packs fell out of his pockets and into the water below. "You bastard, there goes my dinner!"

"You call that crap you're eating 'dinner?'"

"Better than nothing. But I do have a question."

"What's that?"

"Do farts float up?"

"Why?"

Niner released some ass thunder.

And Atlas let go.

Sepah Command Center

Tehran, Iran

Navid Yazdani, definitely not the Deputy Chief for Immigration Control, peeled the bloody gloves off his hands, finished with the latest beating. He was a senior interrogator. He didn't need to deliver punishment personally anymore, but he couldn't give it up. He just enjoyed it too much. He stared down at the bloody pulp in front of him, yet another prisoner that had outlived their usefulness. Sometimes Command ordered them released, other times killed, sometimes killed horribly. The video of this particular death would be sent to the family, a message delivered to make certain no one else dared resist the regime.

He wasn't entirely sure of the effectiveness. Some people, it did scare straight, others it merely inspired them to continue their rebellious ways. He didn't really care. There were always dissidents, always people who needed interrogating, and he was always happy to deliver the beatings.

He tossed the gloves in the trash then stepped out of the room. He jerked his chin toward his handiwork. "Dispose of the body, the usual routine. Make sure copies of her death get put on the official record and are sent to her family, and send me a copy too for my personal files. This one was particularly satisfying."

The young guard smirked. "She was rather attractive. I know we sure enjoyed her. She was a fighter."

Yazdani chuckled. "Yes, she was, wasn't she? Her husband should be proud. She never cracked, never gave him up."

"Perhaps she didn't know anything like she said?"

"Perhaps. But that's what they all say at first. I'll be in my office. Let me know when the next one's ready, but give me an hour." He flexed his fingers. "I need to give these guys a rest."

"Yes, sir."

He headed down the corridor, his hands throbbing, though the pain felt good, satisfying, like a good workout. And it was a good workout. Beating someone to death wasn't easy. It took strength and stamina, both of which he had plenty of. He could do this all day, and he intended to.

He stepped through the door to find his aide rushing up. "Sir, there's been an incident."

"What?"

The young man lowered his voice. "Four Rahvar Police were shot and killed an hour north of here. They had set up a checkpoint to search for our missing Americans."

Yazdani smiled. This changed everything. With blood on their hands, no amount of diplomacy was getting them out of this situation. "Do we know who did the shooting? Was it our American spy or one of the children?"

"None of them."

Yazdani eyed him. "Wait a minute. If it wasn't one of them, then who the hell shot our people?"

"We don't know. Early reports are sketchy. We should have video of the incident shortly. But initial reports are that they set up the roadblock and a delivery vehicle tried to circumvent it. They gave chase, brought it to a halt. then a black SUV arrived. The occupants shot our people, then everyone escaped in the SUV."

"So, wait a minute. The Americans weren't involved?"

"Only tangentially, sir, in that our people were only there because of them."

Yazdani cursed as he resumed heading for his office at a brisk pace. "What's the status of the search for them?"

"The SUV or the Americans?"

"I don't give a damn about the SUV. They have nothing to do with this. They're just…" He stopped. Or did they? "What's happened to our search?"

"It's still underway in the city, but it's taken a back seat to the search for the SUV."

Yazdani cursed. "You tell them the priority is still the missing Americans."

His aide's phone pinged and he held it up, tapping at the display. "I've got the dashcam footage from one of the vehicles used for the checkpoint."

Yazdani glanced at it as they boarded an elevator, the torture chambers deep underground, away from prying eyes and ears. "Advance it to the incident." He peered over the young man's shoulder as he dragged his finger across the display, the video from what appeared to be a truck parked on the side of the road facing the opposite direction so it could get a good shot of anything approaching, sped ahead before it suddenly changed. His aide slowly dragged his finger back. "Show me a few minutes before." His aide complied then handed him the phone. Yazdani watched the cars slowly advance, then smiled as the box van cut out of traffic and sped past.

But that wasn't what had him smiling. It was a taxi approaching, three passengers in the back. He couldn't make them out, but his gut told him it was who he was after. He tapped the phone, pausing the video, and handed it back. "This is what we're looking for."

"Sir?"

"They're in the back of that cab. Put the word out. I want that cab found. I don't give a damn about the SUV. That cab is our priority."

En Route to the Caspian Sea, Iran

Kane stared at his phone, the map guiding them toward a set of GPS coordinates provided by Langley, where he had been assured no one would see them and they might hole up until nightfall. It could mean a calm, quiet extraction by boat.

A siren sounded behind them, and Dariush checked his mirror, cursing. "Police!"

Kane pressed the muzzle of his pistol against the man's right kidney.

"What are you doing?"

"Don't worry, I'm not gonna shoot you. But this is what you tell the police when they arrest you, that I had a gun on you the moment you realized there was trouble."

Dariush eased off the gas. "And here I was thinking I was going to have a perfectly normal day."

Kane grinned. "Odd, I was just thinking this was a perfectly normal day."

"I really hope you are a spy, because if this is a normal day for an American, then being Iranian doesn't seem so bad."

"Control, Fly Guy. A little help here, over."

Tong replied. "Fly Guy, Control. There's an alley just up on your right. If you go in there, it comes out to a road just north of you. It gives you an opportunity to partially box them in."

"Good enough for me." Kane pointed ahead. "Turn right into this alley." Dariush complied. "Now keep going twenty meters, then slowly stop, and put your flashers on."

Dariush guided them deeper through the narrow lane then gently came to a stop, putting the car in neutral before yanking on the parking brake and activating his four-ways.

"You kids stay down. Dariush, get ready to floor it."

"You're the boss, apparently."

The siren stopped, though the lights continued to flash. The front doors opened and two men stepped out. Kane leaned out his already rolled-down window and emptied his mag into the engine block, steam hissing as the men shouted and ducked for cover. "Hit it!"

Dariush, already having released the parking brake and shifted the car back into first, popped the clutch as he floored it. They surged ahead, down the alleyway, as Kane returned to his seat.

"Turn left," ordered Kane. "And watch your speed."

Dariush cranked the wheel and they careened onto another road. He regained control as Kane checked the GPS again. They were five minutes from their destination, but they had just confirmed to the entire Iranian regime where they were and what they were driving. This area was about to be blanketed by security forces.

"Control, Fly Guy. We're about to get swatted. Deploy Bravo Team now."

"Acknowledged, Fly Guy. Already deployed. ETA seven minutes."

A helicopter thundered overhead and everyone instinctively ducked.

"Tell them to expect stiff resistance. M4s aren't gonna be enough."

On the Caspian Sea

Dawson stepped onto the UH-60M Black Hawk, executing a pinnacle maneuver on the end of the Kazak naval ship. He had changed the plan long before Kane's last update, switching the insertion from sea to air. Zodiacs, when daylight was involved, were too slow. "Let's go! Let's go! Let's go!" he shouted, and the pilot of the massive helicopter gave a thumbs-up before they lifted off.

Dawson took a seat beside Red as he activated his comms. "Control, Zero-One. We're in the air, over. ETA—"

"Seven minutes!" called the pilot.

"—seven minutes. Status on our cover?"

"Inbound now."

"Copy that. Keep us posted of any changes on the ground. Zero-One, out."

Niner, peering out one of the windows, grunted. "Our Kazak friends appear pretty eager to get the hell out of here."

Dawson glanced out the window to see the water heavily churning behind the naval vessel as it headed home. If the intention had been to use a helicopter the entire time, there would have been no need for the Kazaks to be so close to Iranian waters. But the plan had always been a nighttime extraction. The helicopter was quicker, but it was much harder to hide than a couple of Zodiacs at night, especially with the motors the Spec Ops models used. They could have slipped in, grabbed Kane and the children, then slipped out, the chances of anyone noticing slim. But in daylight, they would be sitting ducks.

Speed was now key, but so was avoiding detection by enemy radar.

Niner stared down at the waves below then grinned at Atlas. "If this thing had balls, Prince Caspian would be licking them right now."

Atlas gave him a look. "Is everything sex with you?"

"Only when I'm around you. Strange, eh?"

Spock cocked an eyebrow. "Very strange. So, what you're saying is you're never sexual around Angela?"

Dawson held up a finger, cutting off any response from Niner as he tilted his head, as if listening to a comms report.

Niner tapped his earpiece. "Have my comms failed?"

Dawson dropped the finger and grinned. "Nope. Just wanted to leave that one hanging out there."

Laughter erupted and Niner cranked up the bird. "If you didn't outrank me, I'd kick your ass."

Jimmy scoffed. "Now that's something I'd pay to see."

"It can be arranged," said Dawson, deadpan.

Niner smacked his hands together. "Let's do this. Who's putting their money on who?"

In unison, the team replied, "BD!"

Niner appeared crestfallen. "Really? Nobody's putting money on me? Now I'm really hurt." He threw his arms around Atlas and squeezed. "Especially that you would bet against me."

Atlas grabbed Niner's entire face with his hand and shoved him away. "Dude's got forty pounds of muscle on you. He'd break your skinny ass in two like a wishbone."

"There you go, talking about my ass again. I think it's on your brain."

Atlas fell back in his seat, staring up at the heavens. "Lord, what the hell did I ever do to you to inflict so much suffering on me?"

Niner held up a finger. "I think you gotta go Old Testament on this one, dude, and ask God. I don't think Jesus is in the punishment game."

Sardab Rud, Iran

Kane cursed as a second chopper roared overhead, this one banking and circling back. "Control, Fly Guy. I think we've been made in the air. ETA on that evac?"

"Four minutes."

He checked his phone. They were two minutes away, but it might already be too late. "Anything you can do about those choppers?"

"Not at this time. We recommend you continue to proceed to the evac point. By the time you get there, choppers and support will be in position, over."

"Copy that, Control." Kane held his gun up against Dariush's head so those on the street could see it clearly. He had to give the man a good cover story that plenty of witnesses could attest to.

"I really hope this is for the show," sputtered the man as he guided them toward the rendezvous point just outside of the city.

"It is. Just tell them the truth. That I held a gun to your head and told you where to go. As soon as we get out of the car, you leave and flag down the first government vehicle you see, and turn yourself in. We'll have someone check in on you with an envelope."

"Thick, big, brown. No small letter mail type thing. As a matter of fact, make it a duffle bag."

Kane chuckled. "Done. Just don't spend it all at once or people are gonna ask questions."

Dariush pointed ahead. "This is the access road. It goes straight to the beach, but I can't take it. It's too rough. Look."

Kane cursed at the massive potholes visible the entire length. "That's fine. We'll get out here. You just do exactly what I said."

Dariush slammed on the brakes, bringing them to a rapid halt. "Good luck, my friends."

Kane climbed out then helped Tara and Ray, before pointing toward the Caspian. "Run! Now!"

They didn't have to be told twice. Ray took his sister's hand and they sprinted away from the taxi.

Kane held his weapon out, aiming it directly at Dariush. "Good luck, my friend and thank you. Now go."

Dariush hammered on the gas and pulled away, then Kane followed the teens as sirens approached rapidly and a helicopter thundered overhead. For the moment, he didn't expect them to shoot. He had no doubt Tehran wanted them alive, but as soon as the Black Hawk arrived, that would change. It would be open season. They needed that cover to arrive, or no one was getting out of this alive.

He caught up to the teens quickly and glanced over his shoulder to see a police squad car racing into view, followed by several more security vehicles. Ray appeared fine, but Tara was struggling with her shoes. Kane raced up behind her and grabbed her, throwing her over his shoulder. She yelped but there was no time for apologies or comfort. They had to get to the beach. Ray sprinted ahead and Kane followed as shouts echoed behind them. They crested the rise and Kane leaped over the edge, passing the more tentative Ray. His feet hit the sand and he slid down the rest of the way to the beach below.

"Let's go!" he shouted, and Ray followed, tumbling head over heels as he lost his balance.

"Control, where the hell is our ride?"

"Thirty seconds. You should see them now, due north, your twelve o'clock."

He peered into the distance and spotted a black dot hugging the waves as it raced toward them. Shouts approached on the ridge above and he drew his weapon. He fired two shots into the air. He wasn't winning in a gunfight, but he had to buy time, and the seconds he just did could mean the difference between freedom and imprisonment, or worse, death, as their pursuers regrouped, now aware he was armed.

"Control, patch me through to the extraction team, over."

"Comms unified. You're good to go."

"Zero-One, Fly Guy. You there?"

"Go ahead, Fly Guy" replied Dawson, a man whose team he used to be on before the CIA recruited him. A man he had absolute faith in and considered a good friend.

"Be advised the LZ is hot. We've got two choppers overhead, assumed armed, and an unknown number of hostiles on the ridge above."

"Copy that, Fly Guy. Be prepared for shock and awe."

"Give them something Bernie Shaw would be proud of."

Dawson laughed. "I've got one word for you."

"What's that?"

"Duck."

Contrails on the horizon came into view. Air-to-air, and air-to-ground missiles launched by incoming MQ-9 Reapers and other airframes, filling the sky. Kane lowered Tara to the ground, face down, then grabbed Ray, hauling him down beside them before he draped his body over both. "Hang on, kids, this could get a little bumpy. As soon as that chopper lands, you get on. You don't wait for anything. You don't wait for me. You get on. No matter what you hear or see, you get on. Understood?"

"Understood!" they both echoed, terror in their voices.

And he didn't blame them. If he hadn't been through this scores of times before, he too would probably be shitting his pants.

A massive explosion overhead had him turning to see one of the choppers falling to the ground, but beyond the ridgeline where it couldn't do them any harm. Another explosion, this one farther away, indicated both helicopters he had spotted had been downed. Tara screamed with each loud noise and Ray huddled closer, wrapping an arm and leg over her body, protecting his little sister as his own tears flowed.

"Don't worry!" said Kane reassuringly over the noise. "That's two of their helicopters being taken out. That's gonna slow them down!"

More rockets streaked past, hammering the ridge line behind them, and Kane pointed. "Look!"

They both lifted their heads to see the Black Hawk racing toward them, the nose tilting up as the pilot brought them to a rapid halt then dropped onto the sand.

"Let's go! Let's go! Let's go!" shouted Kane as he shoved to his feet. He yanked them both up then pushed them toward the chopper as he followed, checking over both shoulders to catch a glimpse of what was happening with the Iranians behind them. But all he could see was smoke and flame, the carnage beyond his line of sight.

"Let's go!" shouted Dawson, and Kane turned to see the Delta team fanning out to provide cover.

Ray reached the chopper first, but refused the hand held out to help him inside, instead waiting for his sister.

That kid is gonna be all right.

He still had some humanity left. They had reached him in time and the horror of the past day would likely cure him of the fundamentalist nonsense programmed into him over the past year. It would take time, but he was part of that family again.

Tara disappeared inside the chopper and Ray followed. Kane leaped inside with a single bound, reaching up and grabbing a handhold experience told him was there, bringing himself to a rapid halt.

"Let's get the hell out of here!" shouted Dawson as the team piled back inside, the pilot never having powered down. Dawson, as was his habit, was the last one off the ground. "We're clear!" he shouted the moment his boot left the sand, and the pilot acknowledged him.

They lifted off, finally giving Kane a view of the ridgeline. At least half a dozen vehicles were aflame, the Iranians running around in a panic, but more were arriving and reports of this had no doubt gone out over the radio.

There would be a naval and air response for certain.

Dawson scrambled forward to the cockpit. "Hug the waves. Push this thing beyond its limits. We've got to reach that twelve-mile limit before they can scramble. That's where our air cover's gonna be."

"You don't have to tell me twice!" said the pilot as he sent max power to the engines. More friendly rockets blasted past as the copilot launched countermeasures just in case the Iranians managed to get a shot off.

The rapid pops of the chaff was a sound Kane loved. Unfortunately, it was usually associated with a FUBAR mission, but that was fine. He could live with that. It was the children he was worried about. They held each other, strapped into their seats, the terror on both their faces, especially young Tara, reminding him of the young Yazīdī girl years ago during an evac from an ISIS attack.

Children should never go through shit like this. What the hell was wrong with the world? What advantage was there to being the asshole on the block? Iran, China, Russia, North Korea. Four countries that caused so much havoc, so much pain, so much suffering. Why? What was the point other than hate, greed, narcissism, megalomania?

"Zero-One, Control Actual. We've got inbound on your position. Two MiG-29s."

"Control, Zero-One. Acknowledged. ETA on inbounds?" replied Dawson.

"Four minutes, but their missiles can get there sooner."

"Any evidence they actually have a bead on us, or are we still off their radar?"

"No evidence they have a lock either way, but the fact they haven't fired suggests they don't. Stay low. Keep heading for that twelve-mile limit. F-18s are inbound. They'll take out anything that fires on you once you're past that limit."

"Acknowledged, Control." Dawson climbed forward. "We've got inbound fighters four minutes out. Their missiles will be a hell of a lot earlier than that. ETA to the limit?"

The copilot pointed at a map on the console, a dot indicating their position and a line they were rapidly approaching, showing the 12-mile limit. "Seconds."

"The moment you cross that, broadcast live on an open frequency that we have crossed the twelve-mile limit and are in international waters. You keep repeating that."

"Roger that," said the pilot as they thundered past the line. He jerked a thumb at his copilot. "You heard the man, let the world know."

The copilot gave a thumbs-up and began broadcasting as Dawson returned to his seat, the airframe continuing to vibrate violently as the pilot pushed the massive beast past its design limits.

A threat alarm blared as Leroux calmly reported what the system had already detected. "This is Control. You have one inbound missile. I repeat, you have one inbound missile."

The pilot banked hard to the left, chaff and flares once again erupting in a desperate attempt to avoid the incoming ordnance. Two Super

Hornets roared past and Kane got a glimpse of missiles launching from each, the Iranians about to be splashed. The chopper continued to bank hard, the thuds of the countermeasures continuing the entire time, when an explosion rocked them. Tara screamed, even Kane gripped on a little tighter as the Black Hawk rocked hard, away from the detonation, the blast wave threatening to tilt them over.

The pilot battled hard as everyone held on, Tara and Ray screaming, Niner in Atlas' lap, holding the big man tight, ever the comedian, even in death. But Atlas held his friend, and Kane had to wonder, was Niner putting on a bit, or was there genuine fear there?

Alarms joined in with the threat alarm, warning indicators lighting up the cockpit as the pilot continued to struggle. The temptation was to ask what was going on. Would they be all right? Were they going to die? But the man was doing everything he could to regain control, and distracting him would just get in the way of that.

"I got it!" shouted the pilot, the chopper finally banking back toward level. Cheers erupted as they recovered then gently turned north.

"This is Control. Your Iranian fighters have been splashed. Two naval vessels en route to your position are bugging out. It looks like you're clear."

More cheers and fist bumps were exchanged, and Kane smiled at the two teenagers not privy to the comms traffic. "We're gonna be all right. The fighter jets have been shot down and the navy ships are turning around. It looks like they're gonna let us go."

Ray exhaled loudly, giving his sister a shake around the shoulders. "If that's letting us go, I'd hate to see what putting up a fight would be like."

Kane laughed, giving the kid a fist bump. "I like you." He jerked his chin toward the young man's sister. "You two take care of each other and things will be just fine."

Tara nodded but stared at him. "But what about our mother?"

Sepah Command Center

Tehran, Iran

Yazdani slammed his fist against the console, startling everyone in the room, the Americans now in international waters with fighter back up. There was no getting them back now, and there was no shooting them down. He had failed, and failure wasn't tolerated in Iran.

Though he could get revenge.

He had beaten one woman to death today. What was one more? The American woman was a witness to what had happened, but she was also a weapon that could be used against her husband and those responsible for what had just happened. Her death, sent to them on video, would haunt them for the rest of their lives, and perhaps make them think twice before they went up against the Iranian government again.

The doors burst open and he spun to see General Salami enter the room with half a dozen of his staff and another half-dozen heavily armed men. The general stared down the room, anger on his face, when he spotted Yazdani.

"Just what the hell is going on here?"

Yazdani stammered for words but couldn't find them, and was just thankful he didn't have a full bladder to empty, because in less than an hour, whatever remained of his life, would be the most painful thing he had ever experienced.

His life was over.

He just hoped he had done enough to earn his way into Jannah, though he feared with this failure, he might be heading somewhere a little warmer where he faced an eternity of torment by those he had tortured.

Kane/Lee Residence, Fairfax Towers

Falls Church, Virginia

Kane held Fang tight as they watched live coverage on CNN of the Farzan family reuniting at JFK. The extraction had been successful. They had reached Uzbekistan, where the kids were checked over, cleaned up, fed, then put on a plane that eventually got them back to America and their father.

Bravo Team had been directly redeployed to another urgent crisis, but he had headed home with the rescued teens. What would happen to Farzan hadn't yet been decided. Morrison, during the debrief, had indicated the man was definitely losing his job and permanently losing his security clearance, which meant his ability to work for the federal government was finished. Whether he would face prison time was uncertain. The powers that be were still determining that.

But for the moment, the man was with his children, hugging his wife, whom the Iranians had put on a flight the same day, claiming it was a rogue operation shut down the moment they realized it was happening. Apparently, the man responsible, along with those he had worked with, including Farzan's mother and relatives, were all awaiting trial.

And Farzan's father was receiving treatment, his wife indeed poisoning him, zeal for pleasing the regime outweighing her love for her husband.

A piece of work.

Feelers were still out for Shadmani. He had still been out searching when the arrest had been made of the man responsible. He was now in hiding, his family since released. Langley was attempting an extraction.

And a fat stack of cash had been delivered to a helpful taxi driver, who Kane had last seen on TV, relating his harrowing ordeal at the hands of an American Devil.

A zoomed in image of poor Kiana Farzan's face had them both grimacing.

"That poor woman. My God. What she must have gone through."

Kane agreed and his chest ached with the knowledge the woman he loved had been through something similar, several times that he was aware of. "It's over now. She's with her family."

Fang rested her head on his shoulder. "It's never over."

He kissed the top of her head, concerned. "Do you want to talk about it?"

"No." She twisted around and looked up at him, her eyes glistening as she cupped one side of his face with her hand. "But one day, when I'm ready, you'll be the one I want to talk to."

He smiled at her then gave her a peck. "When you're ready." He drew a deep breath. "And now I have a question for you."

She held up a finger. "No, now's not the time."

He regarded her. "What do you mean?"

"You got my father's permission, which I love, but we both agreed. No marriage until you're retired."

Her words hurt, though she was right. They had both agreed to that, and she had no idea he would ask her father's permission for her hand in marriage. It was an opportunity he never thought he would have, so when it had presented itself, he took it. Yet she was right. Asking now would be unfair to both of them. Instead, he covered up his disappointment with a puzzled expression.

"What are you talking about, hon? I just wanted to ask what you wanted for dinner."

She stared into his eyes, her love obvious, and she smacked him gently on the cheek. "I love you so much. I can't wait to be Mrs. Fang Kane." She frowned. "I'm not sure I like the sound of that. Maybe Kane Fang."

He shrugged. "Whatever you want, babe."

She smiled. "Mr. Dylan Lee."

He tossed his head back and laughed, then gripped her gently by both sides of the face. "Whatever we call ourselves, I just know we'll be deliriously happy."

THE END

ACKNOWLEDGMENTS

This one was a mix of emotions for me while writing. I love these characters, and they are always a blast to revisit. Moving Kane and Fang's relationship forward was fun, her loss painful.

The abuse scenes with Tara, and the torture scenes with her mother, were brutal. As a writer, I picture things like a movie, so I visualize everything, making these things emotionally draining.

So, I throw in some fart jokes and turn that frown upside down.

This book dealt with serious issues, and these things are actually happening. *Not Without My Daughter* is a worthwhile watch.

As usual, there are people to thank. Isabelle Laprise-Enright for some Comic-Con ideas, Brent Richards for some weapons info, my dad for all the research, and, as always, my late mother who will always be an angel on my shoulder as I write, as well as my family and friends for their continued support, and my fantastic proofreading team!

To those who have not already done so, please visit my website at www.jrobertkennedy.com, then sign up for the Insider's Club to be notified of new book releases. Your email address will never be shared or sold.

Thank you once again for reading.

Made in the USA
Monee, IL
10 August 2024